This book should be returned/renewed by the
latest date shown above. Overdue items incur
charges which prevent self-service renewals.
Please contact the library.

Wandsworth Libraries
24 hour Renewal Hotline
01159 293388
www.wandsworth.gov.uk

Wandsworth

THE DUST

OF

PROMISES

BY THE SAME AUTHOR

Non-fiction
The Art of Forgetting

Fiction
The Bridges of Constantine
Chaos of the Senses

THE DUST

OF

PROMISES

AHLEM MOSTEGHANEMI

Translated from the Arabic
by
Nancy Roberts

BLOOMSBURY

LONDON · OXFORD · NEW YORK · NEW DELHI · SYDNEY

Bloomsbury Publishing
An imprint of Bloomsbury Publishing Plc

50 Bedford Square
London
WC1B 3DP
UK

1385 Broadway
New York
NY 10018
USA

www.bloomsbury.com

First published in 2009 in Lebanon as *Abrir Sarir* by Dar al-Adab, Beirut
First published in Great Britain 2016

British Library Cataloguing-in-Publication Data
A catalogue record for this book is available from the British Library.

Library of Congress Cataloguing-in-Publication data has been applied for.

HB: 978 1 4088 6626 9
ePub: 978 1 4088 6628 3

2 4 6 8 10 9 7 5 3 1

Typeset by Integra Software Services Pvt. Ltd.
Printed and bound in Great Britain by CPI Group (UK) Ltd, Croydon CR0 4YY

FSC
www.fsc.org

MIX
Paper from
responsible sources
FSC® C020471

To find out more about our authors and books visit www.bloomsbury.com.
Here you will find extracts, author interviews, details of forthcoming
events and the option to sign up for our newsletters.

'The truth is a wayfarer, in whose way nothing can stand'

Émile Zola

Translator's Introduction

THE DUST OF PROMISES is the third part of a trilogy consisting of *The Bridges of Constantine* (London: Bloomsbury, 2014), and *Chaos of the Senses* (London: Bloomsbury, 2015). As each of the novels, interspersed with wry commentaries on Algerian history, society and politics and the inanity of sectarian violence, is narrated by a different main character, they serve together to give us three different perspectives on the trilogy's central themes and events.

The Bridges of Constantine is narrated by Khaled Ben Toubal, who fought on the side of Algeria in the Algerian war of liberation and who has been in self-exile in Paris for two decades, alienated by the corruption that now riddles the country he once fought for. Despite losing an arm in battle he has become a renowned painter, and at the opening of one of his exhibitions Hayat, the daughter of his revered revolutionary commander, Taher Abd al-Mawla, unexpectedly re-enters his life. Hayat had been just a child when he last saw her, but she is now an alluring young novelist. Khaled falls passionately in love with Hayat, who comes to embody his motherland and the city of Constantine, whose bridges he depicts over and over again in his paintings.

However, Hayat proves to be elusive and unattainable. She chooses a path that takes her away from Khaled and, through a traditionally arranged marriage, into a morally dubious alliance with Algeria's modern-day regime.

Set in Algeria in the early 1990s as the country's political conflicts escalate into civil war, *Chaos of the Senses* is narrated by Hayat who, finding herself in a lifeless marriage to a high-ranking officer in the Algerian military, falls in love with a mysterious, unnamed journalist whose identity overlaps somehow both with a character in a short story Hayat has written and with Khaled Ben Toubal, whom the journalist learned of from reading *The Bridges of Constantine*, and whose name he has adopted as a pseudonym to protect himself from government hit men and Islamic extremists.

Although Hayat seems quite autonomous, one soon sees that she is torn between five male figures in her life: her deceased father, who was a great hero and martyr of the Algerian liberation struggle; her husband, who embodies the corruption and cruelty into which the ideals of the Algerian revolution have sunk; her brother Nasser, named after the late Egyptian president and a symbol of Arab nationalism, who has joined the Islamists being targeted by her husband's forces; her lover who, as a journalist, could be killed by either side; and her former sweetheart Khaled, with whom she broke without explanation and who embodied her truest ideals on some deep level even though she seems unable or unwilling to pursue them. Hayat, after all, is shown to be a symbol of Algeria, the motherland that abuses her children, the fickle seductress who misuses those who desire her.

Narrated by the elusive journalist who becomes Hayat's lover in the second novel, *The Dust of Promises* brings us back to France, where the journalist has come to receive a prize for 'Best Press Photograph of the Year'. The stage is set in the opening pages for a reunion with Hayat, whom he hasn't seen for two years. While visiting an art exhibition one day, the narrator finds himself intrigued by an artist whose work is on display and feels impelled to learn more about him. Through a series of chance encounters, he begins to suspect that the artist in question is actually the individual named Khaled Ben Toubal in Hayat's novel, *The Bridges of Constantine*. A subsequent web of circumstances then brings Hayat herself to Paris, where Fate and happenstance conspire once more in the lives of the separated lovers...

In closing, a word might be said about the figure of Nedjma, who is mentioned numerous times in the latter part of *The Dust of Promises*. *Nedjma* is a novel written by Algerian novelist and playwright Kateb Yacine (1929–1989), who wrote in both French and the Algerian Arabic dialect, and who was known for his nationalism and his advocacy of the Berber cause. Published in 1956, the novel tells the story of four young men – Mustapha, Lakhdar, Rachid and Mourad – who fall in love with Nedjma, the daughter of an Algerian man and a French woman, during the French colonisation of Algeria. The central events of the novel take place during the tumultuous period following the ill-fated nationalist demonstrations of 8 May 1945. The character of Nedjma is based on a real person (an unhappily married cousin of Kateb Yacine's with whom he had a relationship). However, she herself rarely speaks in the novel and her character remains undeveloped, facts which contribute to the mystique of her persona and lend support to some critics' symbolic identification of her with Algeria itself.

Chapter One

O N OUR FIRST EVENING together after years of longing, we were lovers being fêted by the rain, lovers for whom happenstance had arranged a rendezvous far from the Arab metropolises of fear.

We forgot for an evening to be on our guard, thinking that Paris made it its business to keep lovers safe.

A love that has lived at the mercy of murderers is bound to seek cover behind the first barricade of delight it can find. So, then, were we practising on joy's dance floor, believing that happiness was an act of resistance? Or is a bit of sadness something lovers can't do without?

After two years of absence, love feels like a time-bomb, and after this first evening of passion tinged with sorrow you worry about how to defuse it without being splintered apart by the force of your confession.

With the ferocity of an embrace after a time apart, you wish you had said, 'I love you, Hayat!' and 'I'm still sick over you.'

Like emotions too proud to allow themselves to be put into words, or an illness that eludes diagnosis, the words you want to speak can't be uttered.

You wish you could weep, not because you're in his house, not because the two of you are together, not because she's come at last, not because you're miserable, and not because you're happy but, rather, because of the sheer beauty of weeping in the face of something so enchanting that it could never happen again by mere coincidence.

Nine fifteen in the evening, and cigarette butts.

You had a smoke. Then you heard her sultry laugh, which put a damper on your sorrow. Before smoking the cigarette, you'd been planning to ask her how her mouth had come of age in your absence.

And just after a kiss that didn't happen, you were going to ask what she'd done with her lips while you were apart...who her eyes had seen...to whom her voice had bared itself...to whom she had said things that were meant for you.

This woman who, to the rhythm of Constantinian tambou-rines, danced for you as though she were weeping – what had tuned her footsteps to trigger this cosmic disturbance all around you?

All that rain...As you chanted prayers for rain at her feet, you felt as though you belonged to all kinds of clouds, to all ways of weeping, to all the tears that have ever poured down on women's account.

She was here. And what were you to do with all that grief – you, the man who doesn't cry, but only tears up, who doesn't dance, but only taps his feet, who doesn't sing, but is only moved by the pathos of the tune?

In the face of all that emotional charge, all you could think about were the details, constantly on the lookout for a storyline.

Do you look for security in writing? What stupidity!

Is it because you're here with neither homeland nor house that you decided to take up residence in a novel, going out to write the way some go out to dance, the way some go out to meet a woman, the way fools go out to meet their deaths?

Are you wrestling with death in a book? Or are you hiding from it behind a pen?

We were face to face in the living room, a subterfuge away from the bedroom, unable to defuse jealousy's bomb under a bed that didn't belong to us.

For this rendezvous of ours to have gone as planned, we would have needed special demilitarized zones – zones stripped of their associations with the past, free of objects' conspiracies against us, and far removed from memory's ambushes. So why, if you were afraid sadness would seep into her feet, did you bring her to this house, of all places?

It was a new experience of love. Never before had I developed a passion for a woman's feet.

She wasn't accustomed to taking off her laughter's high heels when she went walking over a man's grief. Even so, she leaned down with a womanly leisureliness the way a lily bows its head. Then, without removing her silence, she removed her shoes covered in blood – my blood – and went on dancing barefoot.

Did she realise what a loss I felt when I saw her bend down so gracefully, and what an allure her feet possessed as she put on a man's heart, or took it off?

Something about her reminded me of a scene where, back in a lovely cinematic era of yesteryear, Rita Hayworth took off a pair of long satin gloves, one finger at a time, with such deliberate

3

slowness that she probably had all the men in the world swooning without removing another stitch of her clothing.

Is this where artists get their passion for the seemingly trivial aspects of women's beings? Is this why Pushkin died in a senseless duel defending the honour of a wife who didn't even read what he wrote?

In her presence, grief seemed pleasant. So pleasant, in fact, that I wanted to keep its details ablaze in my memory. So I looked all the more intently at this woman as, devoid of mercy, she danced to the strains of desire like someone at a victory celebration. And I lay my head at her feet, contemplating all the losses I'd suffered in my lifetime.

Here she was at last, having come the way life does: full of surprises, shattering all expectations. She seemed to approach every new love with unshod, wet feet, as though she were always either just emerging from the pool of transgression or heading towards it.

I'd missed her! How I'd missed her! Yet, because I didn't know any more how to define my relationship with her, I'd started relating to nothing but her feet.

Here she was, and I was afraid – afraid that if I looked too long at the perspiration glistening on her bare back, her womanhood's current might strike me down like lightning.

She was more tantalizing this way – as a woman with her back turned, who gives you the chance to envision her from behind, and leaves you ablaze with her elusiveness.

I'm a man who likes to go running after a fleeting fragrance, the kind of fragrance that walks by without a passing glance. I like a woman who kills me as my illusions embrace her from behind.

This is why I bought her a certain black muslin dress with a yawning, dazzling opening in the back that froze me in my tracks. Or maybe I bought it because of the veiled disdain I detected in the way I was addressed by the sales attendant, who clearly couldn't quite believe that an Arab who didn't reek of petroleum could belong to the world of obscene acquisition.

I'd been walking around town one day on my way home from the opera when my feet happened to lead me into Faubourg Saint-Honoré. I hadn't counted on going down a street flanked by fancy cars waiting for ladies laden with bags brimming with elegance. Nor did I know enough to beware of shops that put only one or two dresses in their display windows. I knew nothing about the neighbourhood at first.

It was only later that I found out what the neighbourhood was called, when the sales attendant handed me a card on which she'd written the deposit I'd made on the dress.

With a pride tainted with madness, with that Algerian logic of 'excess', you bought an evening dress that cost the equivalent of several months' salary back in Algeria. You, who begrudge yourself even the bare minimum, what were you thinking? Did you do it because you wanted to squander that prize money of yours, as if to free yourself from a curse? Or to prove to love that you're more generous than it is?

Why would you have bought an evening dress for a woman you never expected to see again, and whose measurements time might have done all sorts of things to in your absence? Were you trying to bribe fate? Or play games with memory? You yourself know that the muslin dress you based a whole story on never even existed.

It's just that the colour black serves as a nice excuse for all sorts of things, which is why it's the basic hue of every subterfuge.

I remember the day I happened to see her at a café more than two years ago. The only way I could think of to approach her was to make up a story. So I asked her if she was the woman I'd seen wearing a long black muslin dress at a wedding I'd attended once.

She got flustered. I think she was going to say, 'No,' but instead she said, 'Maybe,' since it would have been too embarrassing to say yes.

As a matter of fact, we'd never met before, but when I encounter a woman, I like to invent memories from a past that never was. I love memories that have no logic to them.

So from that moment on, we started creating a story tailor-made to fit a dress that had never hung in her closet.

Then, when that dress caught my eye a couple of months ago in a shop window, I felt as though I recognised it. It had a sentimental flow to it that I loved, as though it demanded to be worn by her body in particular, or as though she actually had worn it at some party, and had then hung it on some other woman's body the way you hang something on a clothes rack until you're ready to put it on again.

When I walked into the shop, I felt awkward. Lost in a jungle of women's apparel, I gave stupid answers to the obvious questions I was being asked by the sales attendant, who was as fashionable as she was suspicious of my intentions.

'What size are you looking for, sir?' she asked.

How was I supposed to know the dress size of a woman whose body I'd never measured with anything but the lips of longing? Her shudders I'd gauged on the Richter scale of desire, and I knew her longings down to their deepest layers. I knew in which age her cravings had deposited their sediments, in which geological period her earthquake belt had rotated, and at what depth to find her groundwater. All that, I knew. But now that two years had passed, I didn't know her dress size any more!

The sales attendant wasn't terribly surprised by my ignorance, nor by the fact that I didn't have enough money with me to pay for the dress. There was nothing in my appearance to suggest that I was well-versed in women's affairs, or that I would be able to afford to pay such a sum.

However, she was surprised by the sophistication I exhibited when I made a point of telling her that I was less impressed by the name of the person who'd designed the dress than by the humility he'd displayed in choosing the colour black. In fact, it almost seemed that he'd let this colour sign the dress on his behalf, and that for the price of a dress I was actually buying the light that would be given off by a bare back.

'You have good taste,' she said, seeming to have had a change of heart towards me.

I didn't take her compliment seriously, since I was sure that for people of her ilk, a person's 'taste' or lack thereof was determined by how full or empty his pocketbook happened to be.

'It isn't a question of taste,' I told her. 'It's a question of light. What matters isn't the object, but the way light falls on it. Salvador Dalí fell in love with Gala and decided to take her away from her husband, poet Paul Éluard, when he saw her bare back at the seashore in the summer of 1929.'

'Are you an artist?' asked the sales attendant, surprised, since her usual customers, for whom the purchase of this type of dress would hardly have made a dent in their budgets, would never have engaged her in such a conversation.

'No, I'm a lover,' I nearly replied. But instead I said, 'No, I'm a photographer.'

I could have added that I was a 'big name' photographer, since the reason I was in Paris was that I'd won a prize for 'Best Press Photograph of the Year'. There wasn't anything in the photo, which I'd more or less plucked from the jaws of death, that would have been of much interest to a woman like her. Nor would she have understood the fact that this black dress was simply an emotional investment I'd decided to spend part of my prize money on.

After all, who could have known that the Fates would bring her all the way to Paris and that I'd get to see it wearing her?

And now she was wearing it, blossoming inside it like a fiery rose. She was all the more alluring as she danced, in my presence, with another man, a man who was vividly present between us despite his absence.

If Borges had seen this woman as she danced for the two of us, for me and for him, he would have realised that the *zandali* performed by the women of Constantine was as close to Argentinian dance as the tango itself. She was a sorrowful thought dancing to the rhythm of jealousy to break up lovers' quarrels.

For a moment she ceased to be a woman and became a Greek goddess dancing barefoot as she was being spirited away.

After that I was to discover that in reality, she was a goddess who loved the smell of roasting human flesh and who, dancing around lovers' burnt sacrifices, refused to accept anything but their own bodies as offerings.

She was Constantine, which, whenever anything stirred within her, brought about some sort of geological disturbance that would make the bridges around her wobble, and who could dance only on top of her men's dead bodies. At least, when I tried later to understand her Magian caprices, this is the thought that kept coming to mind.

What had turned this woman into a novelist who, in a book, went on dancing with the characters she'd killed off? Was it a fire that, one loss after another, ignited her pen with flames that refused to be extinguished? Or was it her desire to provoke the wind by setting fire to the gangster-plundered warehouses of history?

As a matter of fact, I loved the courage she displayed when she battled history's tyrants and highway robbers. I loved her willingness to risk smuggling such a huge quantity of gunpowder disguised as a book. But by the same token, I couldn't understand her cowardice in real life when it came to confronting her husband.

I didn't know how to reconcile the brilliance she exhibited in novels with the stupidity she revealed in the world beyond literature. She was so stupid, in fact, that despite her apparent expertise in psychology, she couldn't tell the difference between someone who was willing to die for her and someone who was willing to give his life in order to kill her. It's the blindness of the creative genius who lives in a state of endless childhood.

Perhaps the explanation lay in the fact that she was nothing but a little girl amusing herself with a book, who neither saw herself as a literary figure nor took writing seriously. The only thing that mattered to her was fire.

So one day I said to her, 'I'm not going to take the matches away from you. Go on playing with fire for the sake of the infernos to come.'

This was because, for her, a novel was simply a way to communicate dangerous ideas under innocent-sounding appellations.

9

She enjoyed outsmarting Arab customs officials and finding ways around checkpoints. But what was she hiding in those heavy bags and thick books of hers?

Her luggage was stylish-looking, always black, with lots of secret compartments. As such, it was reminiscent of a novel, which, like the handbag of a woman who wants to convince you she isn't hiding anything, is arranged with the intent to mislead. Even so, like the luggage of miserable exiles, it was easy to open.

Is every writer away from home bound to be betrayed by a faulty lock on her travel-weary suitcase, never knowing when, or at which station of life, its contents will come spilling out in front of strangers, who will rush to help her gather up her things just so that they can spy on her more easily? Of course, when they do, they'll often find their own things hidden among hers.

The novelist is a thief par excellence, albeit a respectable thief, as no one could ever prove that she'd stolen the details of their lives or their secret dreams. This is why people are so curious about her writings, just as we are about strangers' luggage as it passes by us on the airport conveyor belt.

I remember the first time this woman's suitcase fell open in my presence. I was sick in the hospital when it occurred to Abdelhaq, my coworker at the newspaper, to give me a book she'd written.

I was healing from a couple of bullet wounds I'd received in my left arm while trying to photograph demonstrators during the disturbances of October 1988. They were the first popular demonstrations the country had witnessed since Algeria's independence in 1962. It was the first time people's anger had come spilling onto the streets, and when it did it brought with it gunfire, destruction and chaos.

At the time I didn't know whether the two shots, which had been fired at me from the top of a government building, had been intentional or not. Did the army think I was holding a weapon and aiming at them? Or did they know that all I had in my hands was my camera? If the latter, then did they shoot me with the intent of assassinating a potential witness for the prosecution?

I'll never know the answer to these questions. Nor will I ever know whether it was by coincidence or by design that Abdelhaq brought me that book. Was the book Fate's gift, or its other bullet? Was it another event, or another accident, in my life? Maybe it was both.

When I first read the book, I didn't like it. I wasn't impressed by it. Rather, I was terrified by it. It's been said that, 'Beauty is nothing but the beginning of an almost unbearable terror.' I was terrified by staggering, unexpected visions, by a deafening collision with the Other.

Anything of beauty is, ultimately, a catastrophe. So how could I not have feared a state of beauty that I would have needed a lifetime of ugliness to achieve?

As I opened the book, I was simultaneously entering the orbits of love and fear. From the very first page, this woman's things came spilling out onto my sickbed.

She was the type of woman who would arrange her closets in your presence, empty her suitcase and hang up her clothes in front of you, garment by garment, while listening to the music of Mikis Theodorakis, or humming songs by Demis Roussos.

How can you resist the temptation to spy on a woman who, so busy is she putting her memory in order, seems not to be aware that you're in the same room with her?

When you cough to alert her to your presence, she invites you to sit down on the corner of her bed. Then she starts telling you secrets that are, in reality, your own secrets, and before you know it, you discover that the things she's been taking out of her bag are your clothes, your pyjamas, your shaving equipment, your cologne, your socks, and even the two bullets that went through your arm.

At that point, you close the book for fear of meeting the fate of a certain protagonist whom you've come to resemble even in his physical handicap, and your first concern becomes: how to get to know a woman with whom you've experienced the greatest inward adventure of your life. Like a submarine volcano, everything has happened below the surface, and all you want is to see her so that you can ask her how she managed to fill her suitcase with you.

There are books you should read with caution. Once inside them, you might find her revolver hidden among her intimate apparel and her short, oblique statements.

It's as though she'd been writing in order to shoot someone dead, that 'someone' being known to her alone. However, when she fired, she missed her intended victim and hit you instead. She had the rare ability to plan a crime of ink between one sentence and the next, and to bury a reader who, thanks to his curiosity, had ended up at someone else's funeral.

I saw her shrouding a loved one's corpse in a novel with the care and attention of a mother swaddling an infant after its first bath.

When a barren woman says, 'In a writer's life, books reproduce,' she must mean to say that 'corpses reproduce'. I wanted her to conceive by me. I wanted to take up residence deep inside her. I feared that, otherwise, I might end up a dead body in a book.

With every experience of ecstasy, I would be drenched with language the way one might be drenched with sweat, shouting, 'Conceive! It's time to create new life!'

My lips would lick away the tears of barrenness that were streaming down her cheeks as if in apology.

These were feelings I'd never experienced with my wife, whom I'd forced to take birth control pills for years. I was obsessed with the fear that I might be murdered and that my child would have to endure the same tragedy I had. So, following Abdelhaq's assassination, I would wake up in terror, thinking I had heard a baby crying.

With Hayat, though, I discovered that fatherhood is an act of love, and I'd never dreamed of becoming a father with anyone else. I'd always had a kind of 'false pregnancy' with her.

But to fail to reproduce through a 'false pregnancy' is to miscarry. In fact, a miscarriage is simply the outcome of a conception that occurred outside the womb of logic, and novels only come into existence because we need a cemetery in which to lay our dreams that have been buried alive.

If I sit down to write today, it's because she's died.

After killing her, I'll go back and record the details of the crime in a book.

Like a photographer who hesitates over which angle to take a picture from, I don't know where to start writing this story, whose pictures I've taken at such close range.

By the logic of the image itself, which the camera captures upside down, and which only 'rights itself' after the film has been developed, I have to accept the idea that everything is born upside down, and that the people we see upside down really *are* upside down, because we've met them before life has had a chance to turn them right side up in its 'dark room'.

They're nothing but rolls of film that have been ruined by exposure to the tragedy of light, and there's no point in trying to keep them, since they were born dead.

On the other hand, the only truly dead people are those we bury in the cemetery of memory. By forgetting, we can put to death whichever of the living we choose, then wake up some morning and decide they no longer exist. We can contrive a death for them in a book. We can concoct some sudden departure from life with the stroke of a pen as unexpected as a car accident, as tragic as a drowning. After this it doesn't matter to us whether they go on living. It isn't that we want them to die. Rather, what we want is the corpse of their memory, so that we can weep over it the way we weep over the dead. We need to get rid of their things, their gifts to us, their letters, and our memory's whole entanglement with them. We need to mourn for a while, and then forget.

In order to recover from being in love, what you need are love's remains, not a statue of the beloved that you go on polishing after you've parted, insisting on achieving the same lustre that stole your heart away once upon a time. In order to bury the person that was closest to you, you need a grave, some marble, and a lot of courage.

You're looking at a dead love's rotting corpse. Don't keep it in memory's cold storage. Instead, write. That's what novels are for.

A number of authors were asked once why they write. One of them quipped, 'To make conversation with the living dead.'

Another said, 'To make fun of cemeteries.' And a third said, 'To make a date.'

Where else but in a book could you schedule a date for a woman whose death you had previously staged, intent on inserting her corpse into the procession of the living even though you know they'll make a miserable match?

Doesn't this irony make mockery of graves which, beneath their marble headstones, hold the living, leaving the dead free to roam the streets of our lives?

I'd read somewhere that when the Gauls, France's original inhabitants, wanted to commemorate their dead, they would throw letters to them into a fire. The funeral ceremony would continue for several days, during which time mourners would cast the deceased's belongings, along with messages conveying their greetings, longings and grief, into the flames.

Fire alone serves as a trustworthy postman. Fire alone can rescue the conflagration. Do we really need all these ashes, ashes that were once fire, to make a good book? As you write, your conflagrations die out. So gather up their ashes, one page at a time, and send them to your dead by registered mail, since there's no surer way than a book to communicate with those you've lost.

Learn to spend years producing a handful of word-ashes for the pleasure of throwing a book into the sea, the way you strew roses over the corpses of those who have drowned. Take the ashes of those you loved and scatter them over the sea, and do it in celebration. Don't worry about the fact that the sea can't be trusted with a letter any more than a reader can be trusted with a book.

Graham Greene once likened the act of writing a novel to putting a letter in a bottle and casting it into the sea, after which it might fall into the hands of friends or unsuspecting enemies. In so saying, Greene forgot to add that, in all likelihood, our bottle will bump up against the dead bodies of ex-lovers lying at the bottom of the ocean of oblivion, bound to the rock of their cruelty and selfishness, and that we have to busy our hands writing a novel to keep ourselves from reaching out to save them, since if we did save them they might brag about having the remains of a love of theirs embalmed in a book.

A love that we write about is a love that doesn't exist any more, while a book that we publish thousands of copies of is nothing but the ashes of a deceased passion that we scatter among bookshops.

To the people we love, we give a manuscript, not a book. We give them a fire, not ashes. We give them what will reserve them a place in our hearts that no one else could even approach.

After corresponding for eighteen years with an aristocratic woman by the name of Lady Eveline Hańska, Balzac married her, only to die six months later. When, after their wedding, they were travelling from Russia back to Paris over snow-covered terrain in a horse-drawn wagon, Balzac said to her, 'In every city we stop in, I'll buy you jewellery or a dress. And when I can't do that any more, I'll tell you a story that I don't intend to publish.'

Because he'd spent all his money simply to reach her, and because it was a long way home, Balzac is sure to have told Lady Eveline many a tale! So his best stories are most likely the ones no one has ever read and only one has heard.

Maybe this is why I'm writing this book for the one person who's no longer able to read it, a person of whom the only part left is a watch for which I am the wrist, and a story for which I am the pen.

It's a watch I never noticed when it belonged to him and which, now that it's mine, seems to be the only thing I do notice. It was from him that I learned that the scattered remains of things cause more pain than the lifeless bodies of the people they belonged to.

He was someone who had mastered the art of loving, although he should have mastered the art of dying. He once said, 'I don't want to make peace with death on a bed. I've always gone to bed to do battle with love, as a way of glorifying life.' Nevertheless, it was on a bed that he died, leaving to me, as to others, a love incomplete, and objects I don't know what to do with.

His watch lies before me on the table where I write. For days now I've been busy bartering my life for it. I'm giving him a hypothetical life, enough additional time to write a book. Lost in the space where our destinies intersect, I have nothing but the compass of his voice to guide me, to help me understand by what sort of coincidence love led us both to the same woman.

I listen tirelessly to our conversations, now preserved for prosperity on tape. I listen to the silent derision between statements, to the 'blank space' that existed between us even when we resorted to talking. O God of the cosmos, how could You have taken him and left his voice? It's as though some part of him hasn't died. That laugh of his!

How do you ward off the harm Fate might do you when two tragedies coincide? Can you say you've fully recovered from a love lost without either laughing or crying?

Speaking of which, crying isn't just a woman's thing. Men need to reclaim their own right to cry. Either that, or sorrow needs to reclaim its right to make fun.

You've got to make your choice: Either you weep the bitter tears of manhood, or, in your capacity as writer, you compose a text that's irreverent and sarcastic. Like love, death is too absurd to be taken seriously. It's repeated itself so often that there are times when you lose track of your tragedies, not knowing which came before the other. So you start relying on death's calendar as a guide to the twists and turns in your life, with the meaning of a given event depending on the order of your friends' deaths. What you have to do now is rein in your tendency to be gloomy, just as you've managed, as you've grown older, to rein in your tendency to lose your temper. You've got to develop the habit of laughing and scoffing rather than, as you have in the past, crying over a woman, a cause, or a friend's betrayal.

Once again death hovers about you, more determined than ever to do you in. It's mean-spirited, like a mine that doesn't explode under you but rather right next to you. It misses you, only to strike you in a place you can't see, and at a time you aren't expecting it. It's playing the Nero game with you – Nero used to charge at one of his friends with a dagger and, after just missing him, snicker and say he'd just been teasing.

Laugh, man! As long as death misses you every time only to strike someone else, it's just joking around with you!

Chapter Two

IN MARCH 1942, JEAN GENET, at the time a penniless vagabond and not yet the famed man of letters he would later become, was imprisoned for stealing a rare copy of one of Paul Verlaine's poetry collections. When, during his interrogation, he was asked, 'Do you know the price of the book you stole?' he replied, 'No, but I do know its worth.'

When I was informed that I'd won the prize for 'Best Press Photograph of the Year' in France's Visa Pour l'Image competition, I remembered this incident from Genet's life, perhaps because I'd stolen the picture out of death's arms. I didn't know at the time what a price it would fetch on the illustrated tragedies market, but I did know how much it was worth. I know how costly a photograph can be, since, ten years ago, a photo cost me the use of my left arm.

In 'war photographs'-turned-'photograph wars', there are some who get rich off a picture, and others who pay with their lives for one.

Only the photograph of a ruler, who never tires of seeing his own picture, will give you peace of mind, that is, if you have the honour of chasing him around every day to catch shots of him in his comings and goings. Nevertheless, you're implicated in a tragedy, and in a history known for calling upon photographers, as happened in Yemen in the 1950s, to capture insurgents' executions on film, and to immortalise the sight of swords sending heads flying in public squares. In those days, cutting off someone's head was the most important accomplishment one could achieve, and the theme with which the country's chief and sole photographer was expected to commence his career.

Then one day, the picture descends on you like a bolt of lightning, and you become a photographer in a time of meaningless death.

There's a risk involved in taking photos of ugly death. It's as though you risk your own inner destruction, and once that occurs, nothing can rebuild your personal ruins, not even the thrill of winning a prize.

Renowned war photographers who have preceded you to this blood-spattered glory assure you that you won't emerge unscathed from this profession. That much you know already. However, you make still another discovery, namely, that when dealing with severed heads, or focusing your lens whilst standing in a pool of blood, you can't remain neutral.

You're implicated in feeding a world that's hungry for dead bodies, enamoured of victims and grotesque death in all its forms, while the macabre, voyeuristic dictatorship under which you live presents you, against your will, with more and more maimed corpses.

They want pictures with warm blood. So you're constantly worried lest your pictures cool off, lest the blood that stains them coagulate and harden before you send them off to the spigot from which images of human annihilation spew forth to news agencies everywhere.

In the meantime, the dead can either go to cemeteries or wait in cold storage. In either case, death has brought them to a halt, and you'll never know whether, by capturing their images, now frozen eternally on your lens, you've immortalised them, or killed them all over again.

The only thing that mitigates your guilt is the fact that, situated as you are behind the camera, you're also photographing the possibility of your own death. Still, you aren't absolved of suspicion. In fact, everyone suspects you: 'Who are you working for?' 'Are you here to glorify the murderers' achievements and whitewash them in the media? Or, by publicizing their crimes, are you trying to pass others off as innocent and justify their claim to remain in power?' 'Which party of the victims do you belong to?' 'Which of the murderers are you helping by sending your pictures to the enemy?'

You'll spend your time apologizing for sins you didn't commit, for a prize you didn't try to win, for the fact that you have a decent house to live in while other journalists have none, for a friend of yours who was killed, and for another who, last 13 June, murdered his wife and then committed suicide after failing to become a picture broker.

I've always believed that a good shot, like love, is something that comes your way when you least expect it. Like all rarities, it's the gift of happenstance.

Happenstance is what led me to a certain village one morning while, against the advice of some, I was driving with a colleague from Constantine to the capital. Our attention was arrested by a village that hadn't awakened from its nightmare yet. It was still in shock over its losses.

We personally didn't have any reason to be afraid, since death had retreated with its booty and its virgin captives into the thick forests nearby and would only reappear to launch night raids on some other village. The criminals had chosen primitive instruments of death with the declared intention of mutilating their victims, since a so-called Islamic legal ruling had been issued to the effect that the 'freedom fighters' would win a greater heavenly reward if they used rusty axes, swords and cleavers to cut off heads, slit bellies, and slice newborns to pieces. Only rarely did they come to the same place twice, since only rarely did they leave behind any sign of life. Even a village's farm animals would be found inert next to their owners, having died a death that at last placed them on a par with human beings.

Algerian villages seemed to invite me to photograph them, perhaps because of the nostalgic pull they'd exerted on me since my visits to them in the 1970s. University students would come in bus caravans to celebrate the inauguration of this or that village, an event that was usually attended by the head of state as part of the One Thousand Socialist Villages programme being carried out at the time.

I'd always felt as though I knew each villager individually, and this made it especially painful to photograph them in their wretched deaths, their corpses heaped around me in plastic bags. These were people who had treated us to veritable banquets out of the little they had. And now I had the unhappy task of serving as a witness, through photography, of 'banquets' that consisted of their severed heads.

During a time of visible obsession with massacres and heinous, premeditated deaths, who could be expected to trust in the good intentions of a photographer whose profession entitled him to hunt down the corpses of the slain? Governed not by the ethics of chivalry but those of the professional picture-taker, a photographer might prefer to immortalise your tragedy rather than save your life.

In an attempt to capture death in its most photogenic moment, the photographer-sniper can go on shooting his flashes at dead bodies in search of 'the winning picture'. He knows that death, like other things, can be divided into various classes, and that people may enjoy privileges dead that they didn't alive. So, you have first-class corpses that belong on magazine covers. Then you have second-class corpses that belong on the inside pages, and still others that wouldn't catch anybody's eye and whose picture nobody would want to buy. These are the pictures whose subjects' misfortune goes on haunting you.

Death lies spread out before you as far as the eye can see. So rise, O photographer, and photograph!

Then I saw him.

What was he doing there, this little boy sitting dazed by the roadside?

Everyone else was too busy burying the dead to pay him any mind. There were forty-five bodies – more than a village cemetery could hold – so they took some of them to be buried in a neighbouring town.

After the Bentalha massacre, they had needed three village cemeteries in order to bury the more than three hundred bodies. So had death been kinder this time? Had it been so sated that it had let some souls escape from its clutches?

The little boy went on sitting there in a daze. Someone told me he'd been found under the narrow metal-frame bed that his father used to sleep on. He had stolen away from the spot on the floor that he shared with his mother and two brothers and slid under the bed to hide. Or maybe his mother had pushed him under the bed to save him from being massacred. It was a trick that didn't always fool the killers. A mother in a neighbouring village had hidden her daughters under a bed, but the attackers had discovered their hiding place, since the bed took up fully half of the tiny room. The intruders pulled the girls out by their feet and dragged them into the outer courtyard, where they killed them and mutilated their bodies.

What might that little boy have seen, to be too sad to cry?

Silence had clapped its hand over his mouth, and the only language he had left consisted in blank stares at something he alone could see. He hadn't even noticed his dog, which the criminals had poisoned to ensure that it didn't bark. Its carcass lay nearby, waiting for people to finish burying their human dead before doing the same for their animals.

He sat hugging his little knees to his chest, perhaps out of fear, perhaps out of shame, since he had wet himself as he lay under the bed, the effects being visible on his tattered trousers.

He was leaning against a wall on which someone had written, in his family's warm blood, slogans that he would have been too young to decipher. And because he hadn't ventured out of his hiding place, he would never know in which of his family members' blood the murderers had signed their crimes. The words had been scrawled across the wall in poor handwriting, some of their letters still dripping. Was it the blood of his mother? His father? One of his brothers?

He would never know a thing. He didn't even know by what miracle he had escaped death's clutches, only to fall into the clutches of life. I myself don't know by what force, or for what reason, I left death somewhere nearby and, post-mortem, began taking photos of objects' stillness, the noiseless din of destruction, and the tears of survivors forever struck dumb.

I wasn't photographing what I saw myself but, rather, what I imagined the child to have seen before losing his ability to speak.

As I took that little boy's picture, I thought of something an American photographer had once said in a similar situation: 'How do you expect us to focus our cameras when we've got tears in our eyes?' I had yet to realise that in order to take your most 'successful' picture, what you need isn't a high-resolution camera but, rather, a scene that makes you cry so hard that you can't focus the lens.

You don't need advanced techniques for getting your colours just right. All you need is some black-and-white film. After all, you're here to document not objects but feelings.

When I found out I'd won an international prize for 'Best Press Photograph of the Year', the first thought that came to me was to go back and look for that little boy. The idea of seeing him again pressed itself upon me with increasing urgency as the days went by. Sometimes it took on a humanitarian dimension, and at other times it took the form of photographic projects that involved taking pictures of the village as it came back to life.

Even before receiving the prize money, I'd decided to devote half of it to helping that little boy overcome the shock of being orphaned, and to sponsor him to the best of my ability for as long as I lived.

I didn't know what had caused me to sympathise so deeply with this particular little boy. Was it our shared orphanhood? Or the fact that he'd become my camera's adopted son?

And why had I been in such a hurry to dissociate myself from money that smelled suspiciously of a crime when my only part in it had been to document the atrocities of others? Maybe I'd wanted to whitewash it, to purge it of the blood that clung to it, by sharing it with the victim.

Of course, I thought about the story of my colleague Hocine who, four years earlier, had won the 'Best Press Photograph of the Year' award for his picture of a weeping woman. With her headscarf slipping down around her shoulders as she cried out in pain, she appeared at once beautiful, proudly defiant, and defenceless in the face of death. Like Michelangelo's Pietà, the sight of her was enough to make you weep.

When he reached the village of Bentalha, Hocine was faced with more than three hundred corpses laid out in their shrouds. He headed for the Ben Mousa Hospital, where he took a picture of a woman who suddenly broke into sobs, and who was described to him as having lost her seven children in the massacre.

Later, after the picture had gained worldwide circulation, Hocine discovered that the woman hadn't been the children's mother, but their maternal aunt.

He had taken a picture of death at the height of its deceptive-ness. All the absurdity of war was summed up in the photograph of a woman who had ended up by chance in front of a photog-rapher's lens, and children who had ended up by chance in the clutches of Death.

Death, like love, entails a lot of meaningless details. And both are masterful ruses born of happenstance.

This woman took no legal action against the butchers who had slaughtered her seven young relatives, nor did she demand that the government prosecute them. However, when she discovered that pictures enjoy rights in the West that even their subjects lack in the Arab world, she allowed herself to be persuaded to press charges against the photographer who'd become rich and famous by exploiting her tragedy. Certain organisations came forward to sue the international magazines that had published the photograph, purportedly in defence of the dignity of an Algerian citizen whose privacy had been violated as she wept in death's shadow. The hardest thing in the world for some Algerians is to see one of their countrymen succeed. For people like this, succeeding is the worst crime you could possibly commit against them. They might forgive a murderer for his crimes, but they would never forgive you for your successes.

The closer you are to such people – whether professionally or geographically – the more reasons they have to hold a grudge against you, since they can't understand how you, who seem to be like them in every way, could have succeeded where they've failed. Take, for example, the neighbour you grew up with and played with as a child. If he saw you drowning, he'd risk his life to save you. However, you graduated from high school while he dropped out. You're going to university, while he slouches against the wall of failure. And one of these days, out of his revolver will come the bullet that leaves you dead, shrouded in your successes.

The news of my having won the award appeared at the bottom of the front page of the country's most widely circulating newspaper under the title 'Algerian Dog's Carcass Wins

Prize for Best Photo in France'. When this was followed the next day by an article in a French-language newspaper entitled, 'France Prefers to Honour Algeria's Dogs,' I realised that some sort of plot was being hatched, and that it went beyond a mere agreement on points of view. In short, the curse of success had descended upon me.

However, some time had to pass before I realised that behind all this bitter animosity lay, of all things, the efforts of a 'friend'. I had put in a good word for a neighbour of mine in Constantine so that he could come work in the capital at the same newspaper I worked for. With friends like that, who needs enemies? Now that I'd done somebody enough favours to make an enemy out of him, I could see more loyalty in that poor dog's carcass than I could in a world full of so-called 'friends'.

However, the issue came up for me again in the form of a question: Had they awarded me the prize for a photo of a little boy, or for a photo of a dead dog?

Now that we'd exported our massacres for so many years, inuring people to the sight of our slain, what if the body of a dead dog had come to arouse more feeling in them than the sight of our own dead bodies? What if, given its relative rarity, the sight of a lifeless animal had become more heartrending than the sight of a lifeless human being?

Wouldn't it be a tragedy if modern-day people's consciences were stirred to life by the sight of a dead dog that reminded them of their own pet, while remaining unmoved by the dead body of a fellow human being in whom they saw no resemblance to themselves, since he was from a world they viewed as different, backward, a world of dead bodies at war with one another?

Questions like these disturbed me so much that I decided in the end to go back to that village in search of answers.

One morning I headed for the village with a colleague of mine. We prepared ourselves, of course, for unpleasant surprises by not taking any professional identification with us in the event that we came to a sham security checkpoint. The murderers had taken to setting up bogus checkpoints as a way of hunting down people who had no choice but to travel certain roads. In particular, they targeted individuals who worked for the 'infidel state' – in other words, anyone who carried a card that bore an official stamp, even if he happened to be a rubbish collector who worked for the municipality. In fact, if they didn't like somebody's looks and they had no need for him, they would slit his throat. If, on the other hand, he was someone whose services they could make use of, they might take him back to their lair.

Fake checkpoints were now rampant, and the terrorists who set them up had mastered the art of looking exactly like the security officials whose military uniforms and weapons they had stolen. The situation was causing major confusion. If people showed their real IDs at a given checkpoint, they might find out after it was too late that it was fake, and be killed. One day a certain elderly man approached a checkpoint that he felt sure was official. 'So,' he said jovially, 'I see the bastards aren't here today!'

In reply, one of the people manning the checkpoint shot him, saying, 'We're the bastards!'

If, on the other hand, people hadn't brought identification with them for fear of meeting a bogus checkpoint which then turned out to be real, they were accused of being terrorists and treated as such, since terrorists also went around without identification papers, claiming to be government employees or military recruits. Even so, weighing up the two dangers, people had started going from place to place without any identification whatsoever in their possession – no ID card in their pocket, no professional ID, and no calendar that might reveal their appointments and the names of their associates.

My safe arrival in the village after an uneventful journey was, in and of itself, an accomplishment that I took as a good omen. Once there, however, I found nothing I'd been looking for. People's hearts were shut up tight, just like the houses of their dead. I felt lost, blown to and fro by questions, and I wondered how I'd find the house I was looking for when every dwelling looked as miserable as every other.

How would I recognise the wall that little boy had been leaning against now that, in an attempt to purge the village's memory of its people's blood, all the walls had been washed down for fear of what secrets they might tell?

Who would I ask about the boy? And what was the use of asking when the answers I got, for all their brevity, were so contradictory? Somebody said he'd been taken under the care of a charity for orphans. Someone else said a relative had come and taken him to another village. Others swore the child had disappeared in a fright after he'd seen people take away the dog's body to bury it in an outlying field. One person said he'd never heard of the boy. Or maybe he just didn't want to deal with me, and had no time for my curiosity.

Shock always causes us to lose something, and the loss plunges us into silence. No one there did any chattering. Even the walls, which had once ranted deliriously about the murderers, had been struck dumb since being painted over with lime.

It saddened me to see that the villagers who had once welcomed strangers were now afraid of them. The same people who, in the 1970s, had gathered gregariously around visitors now just stood gaping at them as if they'd come from another planet. You didn't even know what to say to them, as though you no longer had a language in common. And, in fact, theirs was a new language, a language invented for them by subjugation, poverty and mistrust. It was the language of those who feel helpless and at a loss since discovering what Fate has dealt them.

It's the lay of the land that determines your fate when, at a time when human beings are more beastly than humane, geography places you at the foot of a mountain or at the edge of a forest or jungle. Once that happens, you're just a destiny's throw away from your demise.

In their isolation from the rest of the world, the inhabitants of these remote villages had come to have a single set of features, a single language, and a single fate that could well land them in a single cemetery, where they would be buried on the same day after a night raid wiped them out to the last man, woman and child.

It was a death which, in its absurdity, was a carbon copy of the monotonous lives these people had led: a life in which everyone in the family had eaten one meal a day out of the same pot, frequented a single café where young and old alike smoked the same bad, locally made juniper cigarettes, and when they got sick, went to the clinic in Dashrah, where a single doctor prescribed a single medicine for whatever ailed them.

Every Friday they would gather in the only mosque they had to pray in and make supplication to the one God – that is, until the murderers came and killed them in the name of some other deity.

It's as though for generations on end they'd been repeating the same lifetime over and over, dying, war after war, on others' behalf for the simple reason that, as they always had been, they were in the same wrong place. It's as if they had fought against France and paid the heftiest possible tax – martyrdom itself – simply in order to have a municipality that sported a sign saying, 'From the people, to the people,' with an Algerian flag waving overhead, and that provided graves for the dead bodies mutilated at the hands of other Algerians.

These people to whom I bore so little resemblance had no pictures of ancestors on the walls of their huts as I had on the walls of my house, since they were descended from the line of the soil. I wished I could hold the scent of their sweat close to my heart. I wished I could approach them warmly and shake their rough, cracked hands. However, they extended no hand to me. Instead, Death lolled its tongue at me wherever I turned.

So I left them behind, patiently enduring until the next death, in their miserable stone hovels with their scrawny farm animals.

As I left the village, an unbounded grief came over me. I caught a sudden, painful glimpse of what had once been a forest on the outskirts of the town. Some time since my last visit there, the authorities had burned the forest to the ground on the pretext of protecting the villagers from the murderers who had been hiding there.

In every war, as one generation of human beings settles scores with another, an entire generation of trees loses its life in battles whose logic defies the trees' understanding.

'Who's killing who?' they ask, bewildered. But no one has time to answer a mountain that's gone bald, once because France set fire to its trees in order to rob freedom fighters of their hideouts, and once because the Algerian government launched sweeping air strikes on them for the same purpose.

So not even trees get to die standing up any more! What recourse do they have against a country that sets fire to anyone who calls it home?

So we cry, and the sea laughs bitterly, saying, 'Enemies don't approach us in barges any more. They're born among us in the jungles of hatred!'

I don't know why, but the sight of those burned trees spreading out towards the horizon hit me with the kind of despondency you feel when you're kissing your dreams goodbye. It was as if, with the assassination of those trees, part of me had died, too. Their charred remains took me back to a happy time when thousands of young people around my age had completed their military service by building what we called the Green Dam. We spent two years of our lives planting trees to protect Algeria from desertification. The slogan you heard everywhere you went back then was, 'Algerians advance, the desert retreats!'

So had that all been just a joke?

That was when oil had just been discovered, and we were fired up with enthusiasm. But the golden sands we had dreamed of ended up slipping through our fingers into the pockets of people who were swallowing up the country, and who were advancing more quickly than the encroaching desert.

What a mirage slogans are! They do about as much good as leading people into dunes of quicksand, where there's no place to drive a tent peg, and no oasis on the horizon!

The Arabian Peninsula may have an Empty Quarter, but now we're in the Empty Half! So how did we get here? Or rather, how did the sand get inside us, infiltrating our every cell? We're no longer on the desert's edge. We *are* the desert. (This must be what they call emotional desertification.)

It started in December 1978, when Boumédiène flashed us that mysterious smile of his on the television screen, and then left. His features were less stern than usual, and his penetrating glance less sharp, while the hand with which he usually stroked his moustache as he delivered a speech was motionless, weary from its repeated attempts to help Algeria rise above the vicissitudes of history.

He said nothing, since he had nothing to say that day. During his stay in Moscow, where he'd gone to be treated for a rare disease, he'd been told that his death was inevitable and imminent. So, like a wounded race horse, he'd come home to die. He'd come back to test our love for him, having been received coolly in the beginning by a people who still preferred Ben Bella's eloquence and spontaneous kindness.

Boumédiène's rustic origins had bequeathed to him a sense of decorum, while his life of struggle had smoothed down his self-important rough edges. Accordingly, he'd insisted on treating death with the reverence it deserved, and he died a great man. He died a death suited to his mysterious, private, complex character.

On December 27 1978, as the world was celebrating the Christmas season, we were bidding farewell to the man who had personally attended the birth of Algeria's institutions and grandest dreams. He was a man of such integrity that he hadn't owned so much as a house. We knew virtually nothing about his family or relatives. However, he had left us the political and financial institutions that had grown up under his wing and which, following his death, would undertake to suppress our dreams, plunge us into penury, and hold our future in escrow for several generations to come. He took leave of us amid streams of tears which, unbeknownst to him, would turn after his death into rivers of blood.

People mourned his loss as a tragedy that concealed a conspiracy. It was as though his death were a mere rumour, and his illness an evil plot. After all, Algerians had learned from Boumédiène's rule itself to believe that there was no such thing as a death from natural causes, at least when it had to do with politicians. Consequently, like all the men of Algeria for whom transcontinental deaths, fabricated suicides, and retaliatory murders had been masterminded, Boumédiène died shrouded in questions.

Actually, there were two things no Algerian believed in any more: death of natural causes, and wealth through legitimate gain. Having witnessed the wonders of one-party rule, Algerians had arrived at the conclusion that whoever died had been murdered, and that whoever became wealthy was a thief. Thanks to this collective skepticism, the 'green dam' of confidence had collapsed, and we'd been swallowed up by the dunes of disillusionment.

Sometimes I feel nostalgic for the Algeria of the 1970s. I was twenty years old, and I'd never been beyond the boundaries of my own neighbourhood. Even so, I was sure Algeria must be the envy of the rest of the world. After all, we were exporting revolutions and dreams to people who were still in awe of a defenceless people who had brought France to its knees.

The world was brought to us by a black-and-white television set that we gathered around every evening, incredulous at the miracles this extraordinary contraption could perform. Because we were the first family in the neighbourhood to get one, the neighbour ladies would send their children over to our house in the late afternoon with plates of cookies and other sweets in the hope that we'd let them watch it with us.

The joy and excitement we shared over our independence brought us together in a new way, causing our lives to intertwine and overlap to an unprecedented degree. We learned to live together, though without necessarily feeling tranquil, in a building that, until just a few years earlier, had been the sole province of high-ranking French employees. Some enjoyed it as the 'spoils of independence', whereas my father, in his foolish integrity, denied himself this pleasure. In his capacity as an official charged with distributing the vacant real estate that had been abandoned by the French after Algeria's independence, he insisted on living in an apartment for rent. Little did he know that he would stay there until, thirty years later, he left it for his grave. In the meantime, his health deteriorated as fast as the building did. After Algeria's first few years of independence, the wheel of fortune broke down, and he spent his later years trudging breathlessly up and down the building's five flights of stairs.

During those early days of independence, while the neighbours were busy watching television – or us – I was waiting with the patience of an adolescent for the window of a certain Polish lady to open. Her husband was one of the hundreds of technical engineers who had come from Socialist countries to promote Algeria's 'industrial revolution', but who had no inkling of the other, small-scale revolutions they were sparking in the lives of young men and women.

Algeria, which had just emerged from a time of war, was a teenage girl who fell all too easily in love with the glamorous foreign visitors who arrived to compliment her and to manage her affairs. This paved the way for her to experience her first trans-continental, transnational, trans-linguistic romances. Thousands of love stories were born between her and Palestinians, Iraqis, Egyptians and Lebanese who came to work as professors, teachers, engineers and consultants, and who had fallen under the spell of her name. They had come to share in some of the distinction and nobility of her history, and to share with her some of the Arabness she had lost.

For me, love came in a Polish wrapping. It happened this way by virtue of the geography that had placed a certain fair-skinned woman within my range of vision. The building she lived in overlooked our apartment, though at a distance that demon-strated due respect for the elegance of the street on which it was located, and which the French had designed with a stateliness that befit the government buildings nearby.

One morning I saw her drying her hair in front of the mirror. She was wearing a white bathrobe, and nothing private was showing, maybe because she knew somebody was spying on her. Even so, she looked delectable with her wet hair and her unin-tentionally seductive movements. As time went on, her image was transformed in my youthful memory into a symbol of female magnetism, one in which a woman was never actually naked, but only potentially so.

Like all female 'comrades' of the Socialist Bloc, she was ablaze with the causes that were being spewed forth all over the world by the volcanoes of the 1970s. And I, being at the age of first discoveries, was ablaze with her, and with global causes that were far too big to be shouldered by a human ant like me.

When I married several years later, I found myself living in a bedroom that looked out on the one that had once been hers. I often reflected on that apartment which, for two years of my life, had been my first laboratory, fertile ground for my madness. Fate had placed that room directly across from what would later become the site of my highly prudent, and frigid, conjugal life.

There's always a first woman to whom you come as a timid boy and at whose hands you learn to be a man. Then, some years later, there's another. You dazzle her with what you learned from the first, and with her you test out your manly powers. It's only with your wife that your body has to be both dull and stupid. If you gained your sexual experience before her, you have to avoid showing it off out of modesty. If, on the other hand, you've acquired it since you married her, you have to avoid showing it off out of shrewdness. Consequently, passion's elixir slowly seeps away, and your bodies fall into the torpor of platonic affection.

Olga was the first 'womanhole' I fell into. I don't recall who it was that said, 'A man will fall into the first "womanhole" he comes to. In fact, the story of a man's life is nothing but a record of the holes he's fallen into.'

I laugh when I remember something my grandmother said about my father, who had a habit of squandering his money on women because of the 'traps' they were so good at setting for him. What she said was, 'Take hold of a cow's tail and it'll throw you into a hole!'

Before Olga, I hadn't been as interested in women as I was in animals and objects. However, it isn't lust that makes a young man fling himself into the first womanhole he comes to but, rather, a feeling of orphanhood. He's looking for a womb to hold him in the hope that it might give birth to him all over again.

38

The one person who, for me, embodies all the women of the world is my paternal grandmother. It was she who embraced me from the time I was taken from my mother's bed as an infant. It was her bed that I slept in for several years of my childhood. And it was on the pallet on the floor that she and I shared that I began my journey as a wayfarer who would be received by many a bed.

There's some event in your childhood which, without your being aware of it, becomes the pivot around which everything else in your life revolves. If you've never called any woman 'Mother', it does harm not only to your relationship with language but to your relationships with everything around you. I could sum up my entire life in a statement similar to one that Rousseau makes in his autobiographical *Confessions*: 'I cost my mother her life, and my birth was the first of my misfortunes.'

From the time I was orphaned at such a young age, I established mother–son relationships with everything around me. During each successive phase of my life I would choose something or someone to be my 'mother', until reality caught up with me and reminded me that I wasn't their child.

I discovered motherhood the way Archimedes discovered the principle of buoyancy: in the bathtub. This big white vessel, which held me in a watery space like an unborn child, gave me the strange feeling that it was my mother. I would spend all my time there, refusing to get out for any reason, for fear that the water would empty out of it the way I imagined the blood emptying out of my mother's body as she gave birth to me.

Sometimes motherhood causes me pain even when it has nothing directly to do with me. When I was a little boy, I had a cat that I fed and doted on. I would let her sit on my lap while I did my homework. Then suddenly she turned bad-tempered, and refused to let me pick her up or even stroke her fur. One day after she'd left scratches on my hand, my grandmother scolded me roundly and ordered me to leave the cat alone, since she was pregnant and didn't like anyone to come near her. I cried, since I realised that the day was coming when she would have children of her own, and would abandon me. Once she'd had her litter, I saw her nursing and grooming her kittens and checking on them one by one. Even though it was a large litter, she didn't neglect a single one, and if any of them wandered off, she went looking for it and brought it back, clutching its tiny neck between her teeth.

Orphanhood, like barrenness, will make you jealous even of an animal – so jealous that you cry out to God, demanding the right to be treated as well as your fellow creatures.

My existential questions began with that cat: How can a mother cat carry her young between her teeth without hurting them? Does she really hide them from their father, who might eat them if he gets hungry? Are all fathers cruel and uncaring? Are there cats that are more motherly than women, whose breasts produce milk but who withhold mercy and compassion?

Later, when I'd grown up and experienced the loss of a homeland, my 'cat questions' got bigger and more painful. I wondered: Is it possible for a country to inflict harm on its people that an animal wouldn't inflict on its young? Are revolutions more brutal than father cats that devour their offspring? After all, don't they devour their advocates without even being hungry? How is it that a mother cat, no matter how many kittens she has, won't let any of them stray from her, and won't rest until she has them gathered around her, whereas a homeland will cast its sons and daughters into exile and diaspora, indifferent to their fates? And isn't a cat, by burying its wastes in the dirt, more civilised than men who shamelessly display bellies bloated with stolen wealth?

But I haven't looked for answers to these questions. After all, answers are blind. Only questions see.

Chapter Three

ONCE UPON A SEPTEMBER in Paris...
It was autumn, but it felt more like winter.

I decided to start squandering life with the indolence of someone who, having stopped running for the first time, finds the troubles of a lifetime catching up with him.

I was forty, and I couldn't help but think about all that had gone to waste, the brokenness and the losses, the friendships that hadn't been friendships, the victories that hadn't been victories, and those lustful passions that had cooked over the low fire of patience.

Wishing I could experience what it was like to exercise the indiscretion of a complete outsider, I'd dream in the late mornings of women whose names I didn't know. Passing strangers of a passing tedium, they would invite me wordlessly to take them by storm. But how can you revel in the realms of pleasure when the terror you're running from has robbed you of your manhood, and when you have to live with the guilt of harbouring unfulfilled cravings?

Wherever I went, I'd pack my bags for a make-believe journey into her arms. Restless with grief, I had gone in search of a woman whose grief would offer me a womb in which I could nestle.

Even though I was happy to be making the trip, the grief around me sabotaged everything that, to others, appeared to be cause for rejoicing. I realised, for example, that I'd have to endure weeks of demeaning red tape in order to be able to travel to Paris to receive a prize for a picture that could reach the entire world over the Internet in a single moment. The Visa Pour l'Image had granted a visa to the photograph, not to the person who had taken it. It turns out that the free movement of photographs doesn't extend to people!

I didn't stop to ask myself, 'Which is more important, then – you, or a picture you took?'

I was busy, but there was a city of clamouring desires waiting for me. Metal staircases grabbed me and flung me towards Metro cars, where I mixed with people on the move, people in a hurry, people without homes. Amidst the waves of humanity, I happened to collide with my native land – not the one that sweeps the streets of alienation, not the hopeless loiterer who invites caution and suspicion, but, rather, another native land that had once been my pride and joy, and whose dreams had been dealt the death blow by hired assassins.

Later I would realise that Algeria had arrived in Paris before I did, and that the bullet which those thugs put through her head had sent her blood gushing all the way to France in the form of writers, cinematographers, painters, playwrights, doctors and researchers. I also came to know that the newest wave of Algerians in diaspora had established several organisations to support the intellectuals who were still in Algeria, living in the grip of death and terror.

A few days after my arrival, I headed for the Algerian community centre in Paris in the hope of scouting out news from home and acquainting myself with the Algerian press, some of whose titles didn't reach France.

Beautiful though it was, the building was desolate, like a mausoleum that had been constructed in opulent commemoration of culture on the pretext of celebrating its ongoing life. Or maybe it had just been built to give people whose merchandise was selling badly back home a chance to make a living in hard currency.

It was so cold, I didn't feel inclined to linger long enough to leaf through the pages of the country's troubles, and the only thing that distracted me from the chill was some flyers announcing various cultural activities in Paris. I got out my notebook and jotted down the date of a theatrical performance, and the address of the gallery where a joint exhibition was being held for some Algerian artists.

Never would I have imagined that forty-eight hours later, when I went to the exhibition on its opening day, all the bizarre Fates in the universe would start joining forces and, using this exhibition as their springboard, turn my life upside down.

The exhibition hall was invitingly warm. It made me think of standing in the cold on a Paris street in front of carts of roasted chestnuts. It was a warmth that had a smell, a colour, and even words. The words bore a message from the artists themselves, who put me in an emotional tight spot by interspersing their paintings with pictures of innovative figures who had been assassinated, by placing a small Algerian flag next to the gold leaf guest book, and by appending a statement to the exhibition guide book pleading with visitors not to assassinate such people all over again by forgetting them and neglecting the orphans and bereaved loved ones they had left behind.

It made me feel like crying, and I almost regretted visiting the exhibit. I thought to myself: Did you come all this way just to find all these photos waiting for you?

Some of the exhibition goers were engaged in a heated discussion over who had been killing whom in Algeria. It was as though they'd been waiting to meet only to disagree. I didn't feel up to joining the debate. But even though I wasn't in the mood to take on any more grief, I could feel the intense provocation being hurled back and forth between statements, so I left early.

I remember several days going by. Then, one early afternoon, I found myself at a Metro station not far from the gallery and decided to go back.

Everything there seemed calm and peaceful this time. Nothing remained of the hubbub of opening day apart from the silent racket being made by the paintings themselves as they conspired against me.

As I wandered around the exhibition, my eye was drawn to several groups of three or four paintings. Each group depicted the same bridge at different hours of the day, with each depiction so similar to every other that, taken together, they were charged with an unsettling magnetism.

There was the Bab El Kantara ('Gate of the Arch') Bridge, the oldest bridge in Constantine, the Sidi Rached Bridge set atop towering stone arches of varying widths and heights, and Jisr El Shallalat ('Bridge of the Falls'), nestled among the valleys like a sleeping child. The one bridge that was set apart from the others was the Sidi M'Cid Bridge, Constantine's highest, to which the artist had devoted a single, unique painting of a hanging bridge suspended between steel ropes at such a dizzying height that it resembled a swing dangling from the sky.

I stood for a long time in front of those paintings. I felt as though I'd seen them at some previous time, or as though I'd shared with the artist in painting them. Simple though they were, they had an emotional charge to them that brought me back to myself, as though they'd penetrated me or split me in two.

As I stood there gazing at the paintings, I thought about how there are some bridges that we cross, and other bridges that cross us, just as, as Khaled Ben Toubal comments in *The Bridges of Constantine*, there are some cities that we live in, and others that live in us.

I don't know what got me to thinking about that creature of ink whose name I'd borrowed as a journalist for several years. There was a time when I had signed my newspaper articles with his name, seeking protection in it from the murderers who lay in wait for anyone who had the temerity to be a writer, and confident that, as the writer of that novel claimed, this man had never existed in real life.

The idea of taking on his identity had come to me because I was so enamoured of his personality, and because of all the similarities we shared. In fact, we were identical in every respect with two exceptions: first, he was a generation older than I was, and second, he'd become a painter after losing his left arm in a battle for Algeria's liberation, whereas I, although I hadn't lost my left arm, had lost the use of it on the day I was shot while photographing those demonstrations.

I thought ironically about how someone else might have read that novel, and then taken to stealing the man's canvases and painting the bridges that Khaled Ben Toubal had been so fond of based on the book's descriptions of them. The paintings didn't appear to be a mere exercise in drawing. Rather, they appeared to be an attempt to heal a wound, with the painter touching the locus of the pain over and over with his brush as though he wanted to show you where it is.

He must be one of those devoted 'children of the rock' – the rock on which Constantine was built – who are haunted by her sufferings.

The paintings aroused in me a sudden, urgent curiosity. I went over to the woman overseeing the exhibition and started up a conversation with her, hoping she might supply me with information about the artist. Pointing to a shapely woman who looked to be around forty years old and whose auburn hair cascaded wavelike over her shoulders, she said, 'That's the lady assigned to the paintings you're interested in. She can give you the information you need.'

The woman introduced herself cordially, with the peculiar warmth that the French exhibit towards each other at gatherings occasioned by human solidarity.

'Hello! I'm Françoise. What can I . . . for you?'

Not knowing yet 'what she could . . . for me', I replied, 'I'm interested in these paintings. I'd like to know something about the person who did them.'

'They were done by Zayyan,' she responded enthusiastically. 'He's a leading Algerian painter.'

'I've heard the name,' I said apologetically, 'but unfortunately I've never seen any of his works before.'

'That's understandable,' she replied. 'He rarely exhibits his work, and he doesn't paint a great deal, so his paintings run out quickly. As you can see, most of them have been sold.'

Standing before the collection of paintings, I said, 'Strange, the effect the use of colours here has on one's psyche. The gradation of light between one painting and the next makes you feel as though you're accompanying the bridge through the course of its day. But the colours don't change. They're the same in every painting.'

She said, 'He learned the art of chromatic reductionism during a time of destitution. At the start of his artistic career he didn't have any money, so he economized on materials. He could just barely afford three or four colours, and with the colours he had on hand, he painted a bridge.'

'All artists have had rough beginnings,' she continued. 'When he first emigrated to France, Picasso did paintings dominated by the colour blue. Critics could see only one reason to explain this 'blue period' of Picasso's, namely, that being an impoverished new immigrant prevented him from buying other colours, and determined his choice. Van Gogh did more than one painting of wheat fields for the simple reason that yellow was almost the only colour he had at the time.'

I would have expressed my admiration for this woman's cultural knowledge if it weren't for the fact that my mind was so taken up with the artist himself. I'd begun to sympathise with the man and, as I tended to do in such situations, I began trying to think of some way to help him.

'I don't understand,' I said to her. 'Wouldn't somebody have thought of helping a gifted artist like this who couldn't afford to buy the paints he needed?'

With a laugh she said, 'That isn't exactly the way things were. I've been talking to you about his early beginnings. Zayyan did this painting forty years ago, when he was being treated in Tunisia during Algeria's war of independence.' As she spoke, she pointed to a painting entitled, 'The Hanging Bridge'.

I took a close look at the painting. At the bottom of it was written: Tunis, 1956.

Something was beginning to confuse me. A crazy thought passed through my mind, but I dismissed it for fear that it might cause me to doubt my sanity.

'I thought he was a young man,' I said. 'How old is he, then?'

'He's around sixty.'

'And what led him to paint these bridges?'

'His obsession with Constantine, of course! He did most of these paintings ten years ago. He went through a period during which bridges were the only thing he painted. This collection is part of what remains of that madness, but most of the paintings from that period have been sold.'

I was afraid that if I went on asking questions, I would make a frightening discovery. As if to run away from a surprise whose consequences I couldn't predict, I asked her, 'What has he put on display other than these paintings of bridges?'

Pointing to a painting of fishing nets filled with old-looking shoes of various sizes and shapes that were dripping wet and bloated, she said, 'This painting is one of my favourites. I'm amazed it hasn't sold yet.'

Seeing that I was unimpressed by this painting that I didn't understand, she explained, 'This is a painting Zayyan did in memory of the victims of the 17 October 1961 demonstrations. A number of Algerians had taken to the streets of Paris with their families in a peaceful demonstration to demand an end to the curfew that had been imposed on them, and the French police threw dozens of them into the River Seine with their arms and legs bound. Many of them drowned, and their bodies and some of their shoes floated for several days on the river's surface.'

'I know,' I broke in, not wanting to appear less knowledgeable of my own history than she was. 'Since Papon, Paris's chief of police at the time, couldn't send them off to gas chambers the way the Germans had done to the Jews before them, he dispatched twenty thousand of his men to throw the demonstrators into the Seine. A police officer would ask a demonstrator, "Muhammad, do you know how to swim?" to which the unfortunate being interrogated would generally reply, "No," as though he were denying an accusation. Once the police officer had gotten his answer, he would push the demonstrator off the bridge, since the only reason for the question was to save himself the trouble of tying up his victim's arms and legs with his necktie!'

Continuing her narrative in a more lighthearted tone, the woman added, 'A certain anti-racism group was inspired by this painting to memorialise the crime in a new way. During the last commemoration of the 17 October massacre, they loaded fishing nets with as many pairs of tattered shoes as the estimated number of those killed in the massacre, and lowered them into the River Seine. Once the shoes were saturated with water, they pulled them out and displayed them on the river bank for people to see as a reminder of those who had drowned.'

I suddenly lost my voice in the face of this painting, which had ceased to be a mere display of conflicting colours, and had become, instead, an articulation of conflicting histories.

I felt an urge to embrace this woman, who was half Françoise, and half France. I wanted to kiss one part of her, and to slap another. I wanted to cause her pain, to make her cry, and then go back to my miserable hotel to cry alone.

So, was that the moment when I began to want her?

Interrupting my train of thought, Françoise surprised me by telling me apologetically that she had an appointment to keep. Then she left me standing in front of the painting, my thoughts scattered as I watched her exit the exhibition hall.

That evening I felt an insistent, growing curiosity about this artist, and I couldn't rid my mind of the sight of that painting, which had given rise to some strange thoughts and ruined the cordial relationship I'd established with the Seine.

The artist must have made a point of painting what the dead leave behind, since our torment lies not in a loved one's lifeless body, but in the objects that bring him or her to mind.

He had deliberately presented his viewers with shoes even more miserable than their owners had been: shoes as neglected as our fates, shoes weighed down by life's filth, shoes that decompose in the water the way a corpse does. Here was the life story of objects which, through their tattered remains, told the life stories of the people they'd belonged to.

I spent the evening pondering the fates of those demonstrators and their shoes. They'd put them on one day not knowing they were putting them on for their final journey. They hadn't expected their shoes to let them down at the moment they drowned. They weren't life boats, of course. Even so, they had clung to them as though they were: a pair of shoes here, a single shoe there, shoes that had walked distances whose ending point no one knew, only to breathe their last when they parted with their owners' feet. There had been 30,000 demonstrators (60,000 shoes), of whom 12,000 were led away to detention centres and sports stadiums. As for how many of them drowned that day, the River Seine, which has always had a bad memory, couldn't say exactly.

I began picturing the river banks on the morning after all those miserable creatures had drowned, leaving passersby to interrogate their shoes. One shoe had lime on it, another mud, and a third... What do you suppose their owners did for a living? Were they painters? Construction workers? Rubbish collectors? Assembly line workers in a Peugeot factory? These, after all, were the only professions an Algerian could have practised in France in those days.

Each two shoes had belonged to someone with simple dreams that had evaporated with the loss of one of the pair. A single shoe, no longer a pair, embodies a hope emptied of all hope. It's like a hollow shell cast onto the beach, since oysters only become lifeless seashells when they've been split in two and scattered in pieces along the shore.

What I finally arrived at, after a sleepless night that took my thoughts in all directions, was a decision to go back to the gallery the next day to buy the shoe painting. It would be a way of winning Françoise's friendship, and of contributing to the charitable exhibition by buying a painting I'd fallen in love with.

This, at least, was my stated intention. As for my other intention, it was to meet Françoise again and to get her to talk more about the artist who had so captured my fascination.

Thinking that Françoise worked at the gallery, I went there the next day at noon expecting to find her. However, the gallery supervisor informed me that she worked at the Institute of Fine Arts, and that she wouldn't be at the gallery until four in the afternoon.

So I decided to take care of some personal concerns and come back later.

When I returned, I found her. She was wearing a black winter coat as though she had just arrived. She seemed happy to see me again. In fact, she seemed to have been waiting for me, or at least anticipating my visit. She welcomed me warmly, apologizing for having had to rush off the day before.

'That's all right,' I reassured her. 'I looked around the gallery for a while after you left. By the way, I've decided to buy the shoe painting. I know it won't be easy to find a place to hang it given its subject matter. But that doesn't matter.'

'My God!' she replied, 'If only you'd told me yesterday! This morning I got a call from the anti-racism organisation I told you about, and they've reserved it.'

'So be it,' I said. 'Maybe it should go to them instead of me. As a matter of fact, I've been wishing I'd bought the "Hanging Bridge" that you told me Zayyan had painted forty years ago. But I suppose it's been sold, too.'

'Unfortunately, it has,' she replied.

'Which painting would you advise me to buy, then?'

'Let your own taste be your guide,' she replied. 'The important thing is to hang whatever you buy on the walls of your heart before you drive a nail into a wall in your house.'

'Are you a painter yourself? Or a professor of fine arts?'

'Why do you ask?' she replied, laughing. 'Is it because I talk like an artist? I'm a subject for painters, but not a painter! I work as a model at the Institute of Fine Arts.'

Her words hit me like a thunderbolt, and for a few moments I was in shock. I felt as though life had begun taunting me, or trying to drive me mad by placing me in scenes fresh out of a novel.

'You work as a model at the Institute of Fine Arts?' I asked, repeating what she'd just said.

'Is there something wrong with that?'

She'd apparently misunderstood my reaction.

'Not at all,' I assured her. 'I was thinking about something else.'

Then, sensing that I was about to lose her goodwill, I added in explanation, 'Actually, I was thinking about how lucky you are. It's a profession that gives you a chance to have lovely encounters with lots of different artists.'

'True,' she said, taking the bait. 'I met most of my friends at the Institute. In fact, I met Zayyan there ten years ago during a painting session.'

I nearly shouted, 'So you're Katherine, aren't you? I read about you in that novel!'

I was bowled over by the succession of little discoveries I'd been making. I was waiting to see how far life would go in its attempts to play tricks on me, in a crazy situation where a novel's protagonists bear the names of people in real life while real-life people like me take on the names of their favourite characters in novels.

I was still chuckling at this idea when she said, 'Pardon me, but you haven't introduced yourself.'

Wanting to take the absurdity of the situation to its logical conclusion, I decided to test out a certain name on her to see if it might turn out to be this artist's real name.

'My name is Khaled Ben Toubal,' I told her. 'I work as a photojournalist.'

The name didn't appear to mean anything to her. What I failed to realise at the time was that, from then on, I'd have to go on using this name as if it were my own, even when the Fates placed me, at a later time, in the presence of Zayyan himself, since nothing mattered more to me now than to unravel this man's mystery.

When I voiced my desire to meet him, Françoise told me he was currently undergoing treatment in a hospital in Paris. However, she added, he was expected to be leaving the hospital in time to attend his solo exhibition, which was scheduled to be held in ten days' time. Then she continued, 'The exhibition calendar is set a year in advance, and sometimes two years. So when Zayyan agreed to this date for his art showing, he hadn't been expecting to get sick. He also didn't realise it would be so soon after this joint exhibition, which was put together at the last minute to bring in funds to help the families of artists who'd been the victims of terrorism.'

'What does he suffer from?' I asked, finding myself concerned about his health.

'Cancer,' she said. 'Only he doesn't know. The doctor thought it best to keep it from him for fear of bringing his morale down. There's no point in him knowing.'

What Françoise had just told me ruined the excitement I'd felt about the possibility of meeting him. From now on, I'd antici-pate the encounter with him as a joy to be followed by tragedy, as if I'd come into his life at the wrong time.

Thus it was that, in the space of a mere twenty-four hours, I found myself enmeshed in this man's life – from his wretched beginnings to the infirmities of old age, from his obsession with bridges and his ability to get shoes to talk, to Françoise, the bridge that had linked him to me.

The next day I invited Françoise to dinner. It made me happy to think of finally having dinner with somebody after having eaten by myself for so long. Having dinner alone is even more difficult for me than going to bed alone. After all, while you're asleep you forget you're by yourself, whereas when you have dinner by yourself, you're constantly aware of the bleakness of the bed that awaits you.

Françoise was kindhearted, helpful, and cultured within the bounds of her world, which revolved entirely around painting. There was something sensual about her that began gradually announcing itself. My appetite for her also developed gradually, since I was wary of the ennui that follows passions that are quickly ignited, and pleasures that end quickly in regret.

At the same time, I needed her, not to take me in and support me as women were wont to do for drifters but, rather, to distract me from other things, the things that become more serious depending on what phase of life you're going through and the vicissitudes of Fate. But most of all, I needed her to bring me together with this man.

It was a rainy evening. However, I did my best during dinner to resist the mood generated by the time of day, which could easily have kindled our desires.

In my buccaneer days I'd loved the women I'd met at port calls, the kind of women in whose arms sailors cry before going back out to sea. However, this sailor had stopped crying from the time when, taking it as a new adventure, he'd boarded the ship of fidelity. And I was pleased with my accomplishment. I'd held out in the face of temptations, though not so much out of fidelity to someone as out of the satisfaction of resisting the sirens' call.

After dinner, Françoise drove me back to the hotel and bade me farewell at the entrance on the understanding that we would meet the following day.

When I got back to my room, I found a voice message from my friend Murad telling me he was back in Paris and would be expecting a call from me.

Little did I know that Fate would use his coincidental arrival to give me the strangest experience of my life. Murad had decided that, beginning the following day, he would relocate his raging pandemonium, his grumbling and complaining, and his countless projects, into my life. When he proposed that I move into the apartment he'd just rented, the only thing that spared me having to accept his offer was that I'd paid for my hotel room in advance.

Actually, I loved Murad. But, given our radically divergent inclinations, I found it difficult to share a house with him. It was hard for me to live with his edginess and the sudden mood swings I'd seen in him when we were together in Mazafran.

Even so, I was happy to have him in Paris after his two months in Germany, where he'd been hosted by an organisation that supports freedoms across the world.

As for what had brought him back to France, that's another story, the stuff of a good novel or movie. A lot of Western newspapers had even carried his story, since he'd become a symbol of the absurdity of what was happening in Algeria, and an example of the fate that awaits the Algerian intellectual. Certain people in mosques had issued fatwas declaring him fair game to whoever wanted to kill him for being a leftist, while government authorities had sentenced him to prison in absentia on charges of belonging to Islamist organisations!

Murad was a prominent intellectual in Constantine who was known for his leftist sympathies and his fiery pronouncements against crooks in high places. In addition to running a publishing house, he took part in most of the city's cultural activities and sometimes wrote for the local press.

Then one time he redirected his weapon, and began firing the bullets of his wrath at a certain general who was steadily swallowing up everything in his path. Murad couldn't bear to see people being turned into human shields to protect those who cut off both people's livelihoods and their heads, and who spend their time pelting each other with the lives of the innocent.

What Murad hadn't realised was that his pen might spell his doom, because a mafia of fearsome spiders decorated with medals and stars had wrapped him tight in a web of enough accusations to have him condemned to death.

And in fact, Murad nearly lost his head in a prearranged death. If he had lost it, it would have served as booty for the winning side of the battle, and as a lesson for other intellectuals. However, not long after surviving the assassination attempt, he fled to Europe.

Within a week of the first time he was interviewed by a well-known French magazine, his sister was assassinated. Despite the fact that she'd been a teacher and that many teachers had been assassinated, Murad discerned a clear message in her death.

But rather than being silenced by fear, the lava of his rage went spewing forth onto the pages of newspapers, exposing the practices of 'Mr...', the general who, with the multiple stars on his shoulders and sleeves, decided whether Constantine's sky would be clear or overcast, its weather calm or stormy. 'Mr...', in fact, was none other than the husband of that writer who, just as her spouse made it his profession to mastermind assassinations, amused herself by killing off the characters in her novels.

Herein lay the secret behind my affection for Murad and my patience with his shortcomings: the two of us shared a love for the same city, and a hatred for the same man. Unlike me, however, Murad was unaware of the missing link between the city and the man. He knew nothing of the existence of the woman with whom I'd fallen so devastatingly in love, and my passion for whom I guarded through silence and deft concealment.

Like a photograph that's taken in the light but is only born in the darkness, my love for her needed to be concealed. From those tiny dark rooms where film is developed, I'd realised the need for darkness in everything.

Murad and I had lots of shared memories. However, I hadn't expected the coincidences of life abroad in Paris to reunite us so that we could practise in concert for the experience of freedom after having lived together through the days of terror in the 'safe house' in Mazafran. Following a wave of assassinations that had plucked the lives of seventy journalists, the government had reserved a hotel on the shore of Sidi Faraj to serve as a refuge for the surviving members of our now endangered species.

There were some who lived there as vagabonds for as long as four years, and some who never left it to go anywhere but the hospital following a twelve-day hunger strike in protest against being asked to vacate the premises. As for me, I spent a year and a half there.

I didn't go there so much out of a fear of dying as out of an urge to experience a kind of death-like separation from things after what I had gone through with that woman after Abdelhaq's assassination. Going there would also give me a justification for another separation from my wife, who I was sure would prefer to stay with my family in the capital.

I spent a year and a half cut off from the world, sleeping 'securely' in a vagrant's bed. I was taken by private bus to a barracks that had been turned for security reasons into a press headquarters that housed all Algerian publications in both Arabic and French, and I never left it except to go to my new residence.

It was hard to know what to call the place where I lived. It wasn't a home. It wasn't a hostel. It wasn't a prison cell. It was a newly invented type of lodging called a 'safe house' located on a beach that had once been a tourist resort, and which was now shared by the government's charges and security guards. It was a place where you sought protection from fear by submitting to humiliation. After all, what we wanted wasn't just a bed to sleep in and a door to protect us from hired gunmen, but our dignity.

During the summer of Mazafran – the days of fear, injustice and daily terror – I knew she was staying nearby in her summer house on the beach adjacent to where I lived. She was in the other half of the world – the half that was the polar opposite of my misery – on the Nadi al Snobar Beach where there was an exclusive, four-star and five-star 'preserve' whose villas were reserved for the country's leaders.

This awareness caused me a torment for which I hadn't been prepared. I'd chosen this place of exile not so much to protect myself from hired hit men as to protect myself from her love, and what should I find but that the first thing I lost was my emotional security!

So is this what had led me to hate her and rebel against her? To have her so close to me, yet always on the other side of the world, the side diametrically opposed to mine, with nothing to connect me to her, was the ultimate torment. In reality, however, nothing separated her from me – neither rain, nor sun, nor sand, nor sea, nor terror.

Sometimes I would go out to the balcony and wait for her with the cheerlessness of a lighthouse on a rainy night, hoping the boats of winter longing might bring her my way. I would dream of the lovely gasp of surprise, her tremulous, agonised longing when we would meet, her look of surprise, our first embrace. In the words of 'Umar Ibn Abi Rabi'a, I would think, 'I scan the heavens with my gaze in hopes that, when she looks up, my gaze might meet hers.' Then I'd go to sleep hoping for a rain that would baptise the two of us into the religion of love while death and its servants slept.

Murad, who shared a room with me at the safe house before he went from being protected by the government to being its intended prey, found it strange that I would stand for so long on the balcony and would call me inside to have a drink with him and indulge in some merriment.

I was neither addicted to drink nor given to hilarity, and Murad often became irritated when I declined his invitations. He also tended to misunderstand my excuses. He'd come out to the balcony and pull me inside, saying grumpily, though not without a touch of his customary charm, 'What's wrong with you, man? Damn it all. What are you thinking about? Look, I don't even care what people think of me. They can all go to hell as far as I'm concerned!'

Murad represented the Algerian's disastrous relationship with the sea. He saw a sea with which he didn't know how to establish a healthy bond. Between him and the sea there was an apprehension, a suspicion, a historic misunderstanding. So we were living in a beautiful coastal city that had its back turned to the sea, while the sea reciprocated the indifference.

It was there that I realised why Borges had likened the loneliness of the sea to that of a blind man. Or maybe it was there that I realised that I was the sea!

When I called Murad the next morning, he scolded me, since he'd had such a hard time locating my phone number in Paris. Then he started teasing me with that endearing Algerian sarcasm of his. He said I'd forgotten him after winning a prize for a picture of a dog's cadaver instead of photographing his handsome face, which had dizzied so many European women that an ambulance had started following him around to pick up the damsels who'd swooned at the sight of him.

'The ambulance was behind me, brother. I was walking along, and it was so loaded down with girls, it started weaving back and forth across the street. Now tell me, please, what was I supposed to do!'

Murad robbed death of the chance to claim him by making light of it. He may have owed his survival to his unfailing joviality, while he owed the beauty that radiated from him to the way he made light of beauty. This was how he coped with his complex. Speaking of which, he used to remind me that even my reasonably good looks would never outshine his homeliness. He liked to quote a saying by French singer Serge Gainsbourg to the effect that ugliness is more powerful than beauty, since it lasts longer! And in fact, despite his unattractiveness, Gainsbourg won the affection of dazzling beauties that were out of others' reach. It's as though, when ugliness overflows its banks, it becomes – in its extraordinary superfluity – a form of enticing beauty.

There was a logic to it that defied my understanding. However, it might be explained by Proust's comment to the effect that beautiful women should be left to men that lack imagination. In keeping with Proust's counsel, Murad always banked on women's imagination, overcoming the timidity of breathless bachelorettes and sober-minded women alike with his unexpected, scandalous quips.

Some weeks later, I arranged for him to come to the gallery with me. As we were making the rounds of the paintings, most of which depicted bridges and old, partly open doors, we were joined by Françoise, to whom I'd already introduced him. She asked him cordially what he thought of the exhibition. After a serious exchange in which he displayed the breadth of his artistic knowledge, he added suddenly, 'As an Algerian I can relate to Zayyan's pain, and I know the tragedy his paintings convey. But as an ordinary recipient, I see these bridges and half-open doors as a feminine symbol. So if I could choose a title for this exhibition, it would be "Women".'

Then, to our wonderment, he proceeded to expound his idea. He said, 'The door ajar is the membrane behind which femininity crouches, bound by the chains of expectation. The door's open aspect is the eternal invitation to enter. As for its closed aspect, it represents seduction's blatant game of "hard to get". This is why I've never known a woman whose door was impossible to open. It's just a matter of time, so you've got to be patient.'

A sudden silence descended on Françoise and me, and I sensed an awkwardness on her part as a woman, whose doors seemed to have begun opening for this man in whom she'd showed no interest at first.

I didn't know where Murad had gotten this Freudian analysis, although he had a tendency to bring sex into everything. One time, during an impassioned defence of democracy, he'd tried to convince us that, like other Arabs, Algerians had failed to achieve any victories. All they'd done, he claimed, was come up with some grammatically masculine catch words. They'd lost millions of lives trying to prove the virility of 'independence' whilst belittling grammatically feminine terms the way they belittled their women. Consequently, Murad had developed an obsession with the idea that the Arabic words for 'democracy', 'freedom' and the like should be made grammatically masculine, since if they were, male chauvinist Arabs might actually translate them into reality!

When I objected to his idea, arguing that Zayyan belonged to a generation that didn't see things this way, he said, 'Creativity is born of feelings and unconscious motives. So no matter how hard you try, you'll never know what an artist or writer meant by a particular painting, poem or whatever else.'

I countered, 'If you know something about an artist's life, you'll realise what he wanted to communicate to you. His life is the key to his works.'

As the debate heated up, he said mockingly, 'For God's sake, how do you expect to be able to wage war on the people who deprive you of freedom of speech when you refuse to let me disagree with you over how to interpret a painting? After all, whatever is "true" in the world of art, its opposite is also "true".'

More important than whether I was convinced of Murad's opinion was my conviction of the need to get him away from Françoise, since I was afraid he might ruin the plan I'd been laying over the course of the previous month. This need became all the more urgent when, as we sat together in a café one day, he launched into a semi-jocular, semi-serious discourse on what he considered to be points of similarity between types of doors and types of women. He saw European women, for example, as being similar to the glass doors in modern-day shops that open the moment you approach them, whereas Arab women, by contrast, brandish their staid propriety in your face like thick wooden doors to give you the illusion that they're impregnable fortresses. There are women who, lest you think them 'easy', take things slowly, like the rotating glass doors in hotels that take you around in a circle in order for you to cross a threshold that you could have crossed in a single step. Others hide behind a modern armoured door with all sorts of locks and latches, but they leave you the key under the doormat, hoping you'll think it was unintentional.

As far as Murad was concerned, gaining entry was just a matter of patience. However, he hated the humiliation of having to wait behind a closed door. Consequently, he appealed to his insight into human nature and his knowledge of physiognomy to determine what kind of woman he was dealing with, and to his burglar's expertise to discover what kind of door he would have to weasel his way through.

So, even though I was happy to have him with me and needed the energy he brought into my life, I decided to keep our meetings as infrequent as I could so as to avoid his macho advances on Françoise.

The following morning I headed for the gallery in search of Françoise. I wanted to make sure she was still attracted to me. I'd never been given to fleeting romances, and I didn't take to sleeping under the sheets of happenstance. However, Françoise had become of interest to me for a reason, and now she was of interest to me for two reasons.

At a time of emotional instability, I may have become attached to her on account of a man to whom she had unique access. But now I wanted her on account of still another man, whom I'd decided not to let take her away from me just because he happened to have an audacity that wasn't in my nature.

I had some reasonable excuses for not feeling guilty in the event that I succumbed to her oblique advances. I couldn't help but notice the malicious intentions that lurked behind certain innocent questions being posed to me by a woman who held out – or, at least appeared to hold out – the possibility of breathtaking pleasure.

With a single statement Françoise could open the floodgates of infernal lusts and leave me in a daze, not knowing whether to try to resist the flood of molten lava or give in to it. Whichever choice I made, the possibility of regret remained.

Sometimes, in order to escape from your questions, you have to play dumb in relation to sex. That way, you don't notice that you're going for pleasure because you need something slightly painful to distract you from a greater pain, and a small disappointment to take your mind off bigger disappointments.

In order to indulge guiltlessly in stolen whims and fantasies, you need the body's lies, its stupidity, its depravity, its ability to feign oblivion. You need to surrender to the pleasure that will prepare you for pain, and to the delicious, numbing pain that will prepare you for death.

The Marquis de Sade once said something to the effect that the best way to know death is to bind it to a lascivious imagination. I was sure to need that kind of imagination in order to awaken the rowdy cacophony of male senses that had been suppressed for so long that they'd gotten used to lying low. I was haunted by the thought of people who go every morning to their death, prepared to face it sometimes with prayer and sometimes with a few final trespasses. But I needed to set fire to desires that were being endlessly deferred.

I tried to do just that. However, my acceptance of Françoise's invitation to have 'a fun time' brought a delight that was vitiated by a terror I'd never known before. It was the fear that my manly prowess would give out on me when we came together. I recalled hearing a certain opera singer say in a television interview once that the night before every concert she was to perform, she would have a nightmare in which she saw herself standing on stage having lost her voice. She would wake up in a fright, sit up in bed and start singing at the top of her lungs. Once she'd reassured herself that her voice was all it should be, she'd go back to sleep.

So, I wondered: Have I gotten to the age when I have to be worried about my manly competence, the age when I suffer a pathological fear of suddenly losing my potency at the moment when I need it most, and with the person I most want to impress? Is every man a terror-stricken opera singer whose body is so silent that he doesn't know how to test out the voice of his manhood?

Françoise found something seductive in my reserve and lack of haste to be alone with her, something that aroused a kind of unspoken womanly defiance, as well as something that commanded respect. This was especially the case after I declined her offer – which I suspect arose from her naturally hospitable disposition – to put me up in her apartment for a while in order to save me the expense of living in a hotel.

In confirmation of her good intentions, she said, 'I have an extra room where friends passing through Paris sometimes stay. Most of them are acquaintances of Zayyan's. The last person to occupy it was the wife of the director of Algeria's Institute of Fine Arts. Both her husband and her son had been assassinated at the institute. The idea behind the exhibition was to provide financial support for the families of artists who had been victims of terrorism, and it had been organised on this woman's initiative. So, given her need for psychological support after the ordeal she'd been through, I thought it would be a good thing to receive her in my home.'

Little did Françoise know that she had uttered the magic words, words that would have been enough to convince me to agree to anything she happened to propose from that day onward.

'So does Zayyan live in your apartment?' I asked, dumbfounded.

'Yes,' she replied with a laugh. 'Or, rather, I'm the one living in his apartment. When he went back to Algeria, he left the place to me for a long time. Later I offered to share the rent with him. It was a perfect arrangement for me: He would pay half the rent in return for staying in the apartment when he visited Paris. I'm really lucky, since it's such a lovely house. You couldn't find an apartment like this, one that overlooks the River Seine, for a reasonable rent any more!'

Incredulous, I asked her, 'And does the apartment overlook Pont Mirabeau?'

'Have you visited it?' she asked, amazed.

She would have thought I was crazy if I'd told her that I'd visited it in a novel. So with feigned calm I replied, 'No. It's just that I love that bridge, and I was hoping it might be true.'

'Well,' she said, 'it is true, and you can come over whenever you have the urge to see it.'

Then suddenly, swallowing my pride, I asked her, 'Does your offer to put me up in your home for a while still stand?'

'Of course.'

Then she added, 'Oh my God, you remind me so much of Zayyan! This is crazy. And all of this on account of a bridge!'

She was mistaken, of course. It hadn't all been 'on account of a bridge'. On the other hand, maybe she was right to see something in me that reminded her of Zayyan.

After all, this bridge wasn't just a bridge to either of us.

'By the way,' she added, 'his exhibition will be opening two days from now. I hope to see you there.'

Thinking about all the surprises that still awaited me, I replied, 'Absolutely. I'll be there.'

Chapter Four

IATTENDED THE OPENING of Zayyan's solo exhibition even though I knew he wouldn't be there. For some reason I felt like using up the reserve of sadness that I keep for such occasions.

I don't think it was his illness that deprived me of my first chance to meet him. It was simply that he was reserving his right as an artist not to keep an appointment, even if it happened to be his own paintings' wedding celebration.

Françoise told me that he didn't like attending the openings of his exhibitions because, with its bustle and bright lights, opening day was a day for strangers. Zayyan didn't have the patience any more to indulge people who were more concerned about attending an exhibition's opening festivities than they were about reflecting on works of art, some of which had taken years of the painter's life to produce. In fact, before one of his exhibitions he had asked Françoise not only to manage the gallery but to hang his paintings wherever she thought they should go, since this would allow him to come visit the exhibition later as a 'stranger'.

The perpetual fugitive, his only refuge was blank space.

So he'd gotten what he wanted. But had he feigned illness in order to give himself an excuse to withdraw gracefully, his dignity intact, only to fall into the clutches of actual illness?

In the painter's absence, everything reverts to its primary colour, and the gaiety of those who make a profession of attending opening rituals is extinguished.

I felt as though I'd lost something that hadn't yet been mine. I was overcome with grief over a man I'd never see, while his presence-in-absence – his terrible, wonderful absence – concealed him from me.

He was a man who, as I would realise later, hated for his presence to be misunderstood, for his words to be misinterpreted. After all, painters haven't mastered the art of speech. Rather, they're perpetually silent musicians.

Like a grand piano with its cover down, he was there: closed in on his own silence in a hall that thundered with his paintings, that was filled to overflowing with his raucous absence. He was there: scattered, dispersed, flowing onto the walls, the clouds of his soul pouring down rain on the visitors.

I couldn't help but sympathise with him as he confronted losses with a paintbrush. As he practised the art of strewing grief over the bridges and doors that called out from his paintings, I could see that this was simply a way of reclaiming exquisite losses.

As I left the exhibition, a certain quest was fixing itself more and more firmly in my mind: to pursue this man's phantom all the way to Françoise's house so that I could go on gathering up his secret, one piece at a time – the secret of someone who had also mastered the art of strewing absence along the path.

As though I were a character in a novel, I left the small hotel where I'd been staying for nearly a month and packed my bag for an unexpected journey to a house I'd thought existed only in a book.

I'd become interlinked with bridges, with cities bisected by bridges, and with women who, wherever I alighted, were prepared to cross.

On a lover's pretext, I rode away on the gaunt steeds of suspicion towards a house that belonged to him and constructed an illegal settlement atop others' memory, where this artist was certain to have rendezvoused with a certain writer.

How do you monitor the vibrations of a house you enter as though it were an internment camp for sweet melancholy?

Surprised by the familiarity of the various places in the house, I resumed a life I'd begun in a book, as though I existed to pick up the lives of others where they'd left off.

I entered it as a character in a novel. I opened it the way I would have opened a book written in Braille, running my fingers over things to make sure they were real, or rather, to make sure I was experiencing a real moment, and that I wasn't there just to go on identifying with a fictitious hero in a book where I seemed to know things that I really didn't, and where I imagined I'd experienced moments that I really hadn't.

I'd thought that life was entangling me in a book, only to find that a book was entangling me in a life. So which of the two people inside me was more unhappy: the reader who'd fallen for a trick played by a novel, or the lover who'd fallen for a trick played by the novel's author?

And why was I happy, then? With a peculiar sort of delight, I would do the most painful things: cohabiting with the corpse of a love now deceased, copulating with the cadavers of scandalous things, searching in trivial, neglected details for something that might expose the betrayal of the one I loved. Was this an attempt to pull a prank on memory, to outsmart literature? Was it my need to be jealous, and to sleep in beds whose sheets still smelled of the men who had occupied them before me? Was it my need for light blankets due to the panting of a woman who'd caught her breath on someone else's chest? Or my need to cry on a pillow that cradled my head alone, but that had once cradled two heads together?

There's nothing worse than an impotent jealousy, a jealousy that's too late for you to do anything about.

At some point – I don't know when, exactly – I was afflicted with the melancholy of the deceived, and after having tried countless times, after the manner of Sherlock Holmes, to decipher the book's code by comparing its details with the contents of the house, I decided to call off the search for whatever it was I'd been looking for.

For a long time I'd looked for things' 'lips' so that I could interrogate them in search of the possibilities of a tryst, a disagreement, or pleasures stolen in this place or that.

Like an investigator who's found the black box of a crashed aircraft, I wanted to know the last word the lovers had uttered before disaster struck, from what elevation their love had fallen, exactly where it had landed, in which room the lovers' body parts had been strewn, and whether anything but that book had survived this romantic catastrophe.

With no little fanfare, Françoise put me in the room next to hers, explaining that it was the room Zayyan had used as a studio.

Then she added jokingly, 'You're lucky. You can actually spread out your things in here now! A couple of months ago there were paintings everywhere. Even the bed was unusable!'

Amazed, I asked her, 'And what did the two of you do with them all?'

'Zayyan showed some of them in the joint charitable exhibition, and he's showing what's left of his paintings in the solo exhibition he's putting on currently, half of whose proceeds will go to the same charity. I tried to convince him to keep some of them. But he's always the extremist. For years he refused to sell a single one, and this time he refuses to keep a single one! Imagine... The only paintings left are the ones hanging on these walls. If he hadn't given them to me, he would have put them up for sale as well. Maybe it's the illness. I think he wants to get rid of them while he's still alive, and these two exhibitions serve as a nice excuse to sell them. There's nothing he hates more than to sell a painting to somebody who only cares about hanging it up on the wall of his pride, so to speak. He used to like to quote another painter who said once, "You don't lose a painting when you sell it. You lose it when it's acquired by someone who won't hang it on the wall of his heart, but only on the wall of his house to be seen by others."

'Maybe what motivated him to put all his paintings up for sale was his fear that they might fall into the hands of people like this – the ones who only hang them on the walls of their houses. He knows that the people who'll buy his paintings or those of these other Algerian artists, whether they're known painters or still new, are sure to be people with big hearts, even though some of them might have limited means.'

In her bedroom Françoise kept a painting Zayyan had done of her in 1987, when he first met her as a model at the

Institute of Fine Arts. Despite its nudity, the painting wasn't without a touch of modesty – thanks not to this woman who made it her profession to take off all her clothes, but to Zayyan's brush.

Françoise struck me as a woman who didn't belong to any particular artist but who was, rather, a female meant for every paintbrush. She had covered her bedroom walls with paintings bearing the signatures of other artists. Her persona came across so differently from one painting to the next, I felt, when I was with her, as though I was giving myself over to a whole tribe of women.

Nothing here held any allure for me, and I had no desire to enter into a challenge with the men who had known her before. As intense as my bodily cravings were, I was selective not only about how, when, and with whom I indulged in pleasure, but, also, about what pleasures I chose to deprive myself of. I, who was infatuated with a robe slipping off an imaginary body, failed to find any fascination in this woman's unclothed frame.

I wanted a woman like Venus, with her robe sliding off one shoulder. I could clothe half of her and denude her other half as I liked. I wanted a woman who was half pure and half dissolute, one of whose halves I could reform while I corrupted the other, measuring my manhood in a different way by each of her halves.

As for Françoise, she was a bad test of manhood. She was a woman composed of two seasons living side by side: the spring of her auburn hair, and the autumn of her wan lips. My first problem was her mouth: How was I supposed to have sex with a woman whose thin lips didn't tempt me to kiss her?

75

I got up the courage to engage with her lips by thinking about Zayyan, who had undoubtedly done so before me. I would picture him, like me, having relations with Françoise while conjuring images of Hayat. So had he discovered before me that a counterfeit kiss is more miserable than counterfeit sex?

During that first rendezvous, our bed was of necessity teeming with the ghosts of those who had lain in it before me. But only I was aware of this fact, and I tried to get its memory to talk. Beds that hold an accumulation of sins, I would expect to violate the rule of secrecy. But did I really want this bedchamber steeped in deception to break the law of silence, and speak? After all, beds' silence is one of God's blessings, since all of us, wherever we alight, are 'bedfarers' in the end.

I know the awkwardness of two bodies that come together for the first time before having invented a shared language. In our case, however, it was obvious that we didn't even have the same alphabet to work with.

I don't like women who scream at the moment love reaches its peak. A scream involves a wiliness that conceals certain deceitful intentions. In my experience, there are only two forms a woman's pleasure can take: she'll either cry, or faint. There's no pleasure without reaching a consciousness of unconsciousness. Like a bird in flight with its wings spread, and not a flutter to be heard, pleasure is a state of breathtaking, silent stupefaction.

However, Françoise knew nothing of the silence of two entities at the moment of union. She meowed like a cat, jumped like a fish, writhed like an adder, and, like a lioness, put on a show of fierce resistance. She was the female of every species, and I was a man who didn't know how to bridle his headstrong filly.

Lovemaking with Françoise had the taste of dried fruit, and sometimes, careworn man that I was, I'd suddenly feel the need to be alone and have a smoke in the courtyard. Love had come to an end, and I would find myself naked and trembling like a leafless tree.

There's nothing more dismal than an act of love from which love is absent. Afterwards you feel a desperate urge to cry. It was my first infidelity to a woman who may have been unfaithful to me repeatedly since our last time together. I wasn't sad for her sake, but for mine. After enjoyment like this, you feel empty all of a sudden, as though you're missing something, though you don't know what it is.

I used to think that, with that first fling of mine, I'd erase the effects of the pain that still clung to me. Instead, it was like passing a sponge over a chalkboard, only to find that it's messier than it was before.

Once, while talking about having relations with her husband against her will, Hayat had said, 'Bedrooms should have signs saying, "No contamination" like the "No smoking" signs you see in some places, since we're always being contaminated by people we don't love.'

Why had I made love, then? Why had I been in such a hurry? Was it because, after living with my own body for so long, contenting myself with its clandestine enjoyment, I'd lost the ability to relate to the body of someone else?

After spending sixteen years in an Arab prison on charges of belonging to a banned political party, a friend of mine got married a few years ago to a lawyer who had loved him enough to wait for him all that time. They'd spent years wishing they could have just one special, intimate time together with no guard to listen in on their whispers of ecstasy. Then one day the man was suddenly released, just like that. After deciding one holiday to give him his freedom, prison officials tossed him out on the pavement with a satchel containing his meagre possessions.

But when at last, with the anguished passion of a former prisoner, he embraced the woman he had dreamed of for so long, he discovered that he'd lost the male potency of his youth. It had happened in the dank underground cells where he had languished, and the effect had been permanent. As he ran his hands lovingly over freedom's body, he'd come up against the impotence engendered by his slavery, and discovered that the dreams he'd cherished bore no relation to his body.

Life had failed to repair the damage done by Arab prisons, and I hear they've separated.

If you fritter your lifetime away being faithful, you should expect your body to betray you, and its members to treat you badly. After all, your fidelity to someone else's body is a betrayal of your own.

Sunset on the last day of the heart's autumn ushers you into a long emotional hibernation. Your body feeds off the richness of memories and the store of hope that, like animals of the northern arctic regions, you'd laid up in anticipation of the icy seasons of desolation. But one of these icy winters, it won't do you any good to go on hiding under the thick fur of hopes. Little by little, your heart, no longer occupied with the business of love, will start to weaken, while your manly potency, no longer engaged in giving and receiving pleasure, will shrink down to nothing. And before you know it, every member you've stopped using will have wasted away.

You know that you're indebted to love alone for your manly feats of the past. But the days of passion are over. Your past disappointments have taught you to be wary of a love that establishes itself on the word 'forever'. As one love has given way to another, your illusion of a love as strong as death – a love till death do us part – has breathed its last.

All your tragedies now revolve around this disillusionment.

The next day I went to the market for groceries so that I could stock the refrigerator. I couldn't stay in a house without helping to pay its expenses.

I was walking around looking at the weekend 'makeup' on the face of a shivering Paris when my attention was drawn to a butcher shop whose owner had decorated its iron meat hooks with rose-coloured pigs' heads, each of which held a red carnation between its teeth.

I stood pondering them for a moment, wondering whether it was an insult to carnations to be inserted into pigs' mouths, or for the mouths of living creatures to be turned into flowerpots in a butcher shop.

The scene took me back to the 1970s. Our Eastern European neighbours always used to make enthusiastic plans for the weekends, when they would go out in droves to hunt wild boars in the forests on the outskirts of the capital.

Today no one would dare go on a hunting trip. Instead, murderers go out bristling with butcher knives and axes to hunt down unarmed villagers, after which they leave the boars the job of destroying survivors' livelihoods by ruining their crops. It used to take hunters more time and effort to chase down a wild pig in the forest than it takes today to behead an entire family of villagers, since the murderers know the exact locations of their huts, and can butcher them like sheep with the greatest of ease. How easily, with other people's lives, do they buy the paper-thin notoriety of a front page story that's carried by all the news agencies.

Those European hunters used to be filled with pride over a single boar's head. As for those who hunt human prey, they need a lot more than one head to guarantee a front page. Thus was born the phenomenon of displaying some human heads as a statement or as an investment, and others as a public spectacle or as a lesson. Once, when the princes of death had some time on their hands, they decorated the trees of a certain village with their victims' heads. Then they booby-trapped them so that they were set to blow up the first person who tried to 'pick' a relative's skull.

In the midst of the war of the 'big heads' which, when they fall, thrust an entire homeland into the problematics of history, the 'little heads', a huge number of which are required to make the headlines, and the 'nobodies' heads', whose harvesting nobody will even hear about, I couldn't help but run my hands over my own head, even though I was standing in front of a butcher's display window in the heart of Paris. As I stood there, I grieved for the carnations that used to bloom in my childhood home. They used to make bouquets of little carnations that exuded a perfume you don't find in flowers any more, and whose lives have been bombarded in honour of the butchers of the civilised world.

In the city where Henry Miller had once wandered, hungry and horny, through the Tuileries Garden, seeing nothing but female bodies of marble that might leave their stony naked-ness behind and accompany him to some vagabond hotel, all I could see were heads hanging everywhere, anywhere, and for any reason.

Pigalle Street was rife with prostitutes, who populated the pavements of the night in a state of undress whose allure no man could have withstood. Even so, as I walked down their street I couldn't muster the least bit of curiosity about their fur coat-clad naked bodies. They reminded me of another scene, details of which had been carried by the world press, of the prostitutes of Arab misery. It was a sight that, if Zorba had seen it, would have caused him to burst into agonised dance for the women whose heads had been hung on the doors of their desolate abodes in an Arab city endlessly at war. As the next generation of martyrs was growing up, the houses were being emptied of their men, their furnishings, and their daily bread, to be inhabited by the widows and orphans of armed conflict.

But don't worry, Zorba, friend of widows, and don't grieve. The pretty young ones weren't widowed. Instead they decorate the mansions of Arab warlords. It's only the older wretches who died to cleanse the honour of the homeland the way their husbands had died to redeem it, and whose fifty heads, which were cut off with the blessing of certain esteemed, virtuous individuals representing the Women's Union, who were allowed to go on hanging on the doors for an entire day in affirmation of the purity of the hands that severed them, and as a lesson to the poor souls who had risked submitting to the humiliation of 'pleasure for food', daring to hope for something in this world other than having their skulls added to the decorations on top of the leader's birthday cake.

Mistaken are they who believe that when we enter a new city we leave our memory elsewhere. Someone who comes to live in a new place does so laden with another. She resides with others in

81

an unfamiliar city without necessarily sharing it with them. Instead, she wanders about in a ruin that she alone sees.

A certain poet once said, 'If you've destroyed your home in this little corner of the world, destruction will follow you wherever you go.' However, you hadn't heard this line before, nor did you know that your suitcase was packed with skulls. If you had, you wouldn't have travelled anywhere.

So write, then. You still don't know whether writing is an act of concealment, or of exposure, an act of murder, or of resurrection. You wish you could shoot all the tyrants dead with a sentence. But remember, O writer, that all the rivals you battle with a pen are seated on thrones of skulls.

Before putting pen to paper, you should have chosen your words carefully the way a boxer chooses his punches, and aimed your blows at the murderers with the least possible risk. You should have developed the ability to write inane books that keep their writer safe and protect him from suspicion without his having to worry about the damage a bad novel can do, or about being the sort of cowardly author that no reader would entrust his life to or commission with the charge of avenging his blood.

Who are you to try to avenge all the Arab blood ever spilled with a book? Ink alone is a basis for suspicion, O you who sit upon a mound of suspicions. So write as a way of cleaning a lifetime's accumulation of scrap metal out of your garage, the way a warrior cleans an old weapon.

The murderers still have some measure of prestige left, whereas the only thing you have left is a deceased man's watch, which ticks on your wrist and gives your hand the strength to write. Even so, you may not find the courage to tell him what happened to that painting!

Two days after moving into Françoise's apartment, I phoned Murad. I didn't want him to have to go looking all over Paris for me because I'd left the hotel without informing him. I suggested that we meet the following day, though of course I avoided giving him any details about my new place of residence.

It was then that he dropped a bombshell on me. 'I won't be able to meet you tomorrow,' he said apologetically. 'I'll be tied up waiting for Nasser Abd al-Mawla. He's coming from Germany to stay with me for a while. But if you'd like, all of us can get together day after tomorrow.'

'Nasser who?' I asked, incredulous.

'Nasser, son of the martyr Taher Abd al-Mawla. As you know, he's been living in Germany for the past couple of years. He was granted political asylum there after being accused of belonging to an armed Islamist group. He can't go back to Algeria, of course, so he's coming to Paris to visit his mother, whom he hasn't seen for the past two years. I spent a lot of time with him in Germany, and we agreed that he'd come to Paris after I'd rented an apartment so that he could stay with me. For security reasons, he prefers not to stay in a hotel.'

In this way, Murad had conveyed two pieces of news: the news of Nasser's coming, and, by implication, the news that his sister would be coming, too, since it was unreasonable to assume that her mother would travel to Paris alone.

The surprise descended on me like a thunderbolt, leaving me in a stupor.

Was it really true that this woman, with whom I had no more appointments in life's date book, would be coming?

She *would* be coming, after I'd waited so long that I'd finally stopped expecting her to come.

We'd been separated for two years, in the course of which Time's corpse had lain between us, while next to it lay something resembling my own dead body. I'd fallen in love with her in a moment of passionate vertigo like someone jumping into a void without opening his parachute. Then... just as I'd loved her, I'd left her, the way someone who's lost all hope flings himself off a bridge without looking down. Wasn't I a native of Constantine, where bridges are a way of life, of death, and of love?

The woman no man had ever abandoned, I had abandoned for fear that she would abandon me first. It was as if I were saying, 'Many an abandonment has occurred for fear of abandonment, and many a silent farewell has been endured for fear of uttering farewell.'

Unlike lovers who defend their emotional gains to the death, when I'm jealous I withdraw, since I want to allow the one I love the opportunity to choose me all over again.

I was the man of self-chosen losses par excellence. At the same time, I couldn't accept the idea of a woman leaving me for another man or of someone else having been with her before me. So how was I to have confidence in a woman who, with every word she spoke, planted fields of suspicion inside of me?

I remember the first time she asked me if I loved her.

'I don't know,' I said. 'What I do know is that I'm afraid of you.'

As a matter of fact, I was afraid of the trackless desert I was sure to end up in, since, once a man's loved a woman like her, he can't love again without her becoming his punishment.

I thought the only way I could cope with my fear was to deal her the death blow by leaving her. There was also another possibility: to adopt her method of euthanasia inside a beautiful book.

She'd given me some things that tempted me to write – things she'd chosen with the care of a mother buying school supplies for her child's first day at school.

Two weeks after Abdelhaq's death, I ran into her at a stationery shop in Constantine, where she was buying envelopes and postage stamps so that she could send a letter to Nasser in Germany. She was holding a black notebook in her hand, and she told me jokingly that she'd bought it because it had picked a fight with her. Then suddenly she asked me, 'If I give it to you, will you write something nice in it?'

'I don't think so,' I said. 'You'll be needing it more than I will.'

Ignoring my response, she went over to the sales attendant and asked for several fountain pens of a particular kind. Handing them to me, she said, 'I want a book from you.' She said it the way she might have said, 'I want a child by you.' So had she been trying to keep me around by means of a book, the way some women keep a husband by having his baby? Or was she preparing me for the long separation?

'What's the occasion?' I asked her, suspecting some sort of prank.

'We can invent an occasion whenever we want to,' she said playfully. 'So I'll assume that today is your birthday. After all, I can give birth to you as many times as I like.'

Motherhood was her lovely ruse, like our jokes about my being her father. Handing me the notebook, she said, 'Bon anniversaire!'

Unless she switched to formal Arabic, French was the only language she had for making such a wish. In colloquial Algerian there's no expression or formula for wishing someone a happy birthday, whereas this same dialect is full of terms for expressing one's condolences!

I laughed at the idea. It seemed like a good enough launch pad for a book some Algerian might start writing on his birthday. But for a long time I didn't write anything in the notebook she'd given me. In fact, I forgot all about it when I went to live in Mazafran, and it wasn't until recently that I came across it, or, rather, that I went looking for it.

If you're going to write, it isn't enough for someone to give you pens and a notebook. Rather, somebody has to hurt you to the point where writing is the only choice you have left. I wouldn't have been able to write this book if she hadn't supplied me with the bitterness and resentment I needed to fuel the project. We don't write books for people, but against them.

I had her notebook in front of me, his watch on my wrist, and an abundance of time shrouded in blank paper. So I started writing about her with the same ferocity with which I'd once made clandestine love to her. Because I rejected her during my waking hours, my desire for her would erupt violently in my dreams. When the dream-time depravity had come to an end, I would cry out her name, and my body would burst secretly into tears. Then I would be stricken with grief, and hate my hand for hours. I hated all the parts of my body that had done her bidding.

I wrote with the same hand I'd used to do what I hated myself for and I conjured her on paper with the same violent passion with which I'd made love to her, since I needed a surge of virility to confront the nakedness of the blank page. Whoever doesn't succeed in approaching a female will never know how to approach a piece of paper. We write the way we make love. Some people take writing by force, while others believe that writing, like a she-camel that will only yield her milk in response to gentle coaxing, only gives itself to you if you win it over quietly. As a consequence, they spend years wooing their muse to produce a single book.

But how are you supposed to win over a blank page and humour a reader when you're writing, to the rhythm of death, to a person who isn't around any more, but that you insist on telling what has happened? And what's the use of knowledge that would only make the dead sadder than they already are?

My life with Françoise had started out peacefully and pleasantly, but without enthusiasm or passion. It proceeded against the backdrop of the silence that follows the body's loud clamour – an unspoken disappointment, a regret concealed beneath a veneer of words.

Every morning this bitter-sweet regret would take a bath, smoke a cigarette, and plant a kiss on wan lips. It was a regret which, although it knew that being alone is better than sharing a bed with the wrong partner, was amusing itself by trying out a new bed as if to give itself the lie. Regret has a habit of chattering a lot both before and after lovemaking, as if it wants to persuade itself that it feels no remorse over what isn't really love.

When I woke up the next morning, I didn't find Françoise. Concluding that she must have left early for the Institute, I decided to have my morning coffee with Venus, the only female left in the house. Standing, life-size, in a corner of the living room, she looked like a woman awakening from a pleasant slumber and prepared to flower: awaiting your hands' fervent touch or a command from your eyes that would cause her wrap to fall to the floor, and her marble frame to turn into a woman.

Like the other things in the house, she concealed half the truth, draped in flowing lines that tempted me to go searching for what lay beneath her robe of stone.

The only thing I could know about her was that he had acquired her because she was 'his female' – the woman he could live with without complexes or complications. She was more damaged than he was. However, this hadn't prevented her from being the most famous, most alluring female of all.

I could understand why Rodin said that Venus has the ability to ignite the senses because she represents the joy of life. She's constantly smiling, and she wakes up in a good mood every morning because, despite being the goddess of love and beauty, she's never been polluted by a man. She's a woman with lusts too lofty to be indulged!

She is definitely happier than women who spend their lives like some rubber plant that decorates the living room, waiting for the owner of the house to do it the honour of watering it once a week.

I spent a long time – I don't know how long – in a kind of bodily tangle with her, surveying the geography of her desires, and pondering the beauty of a femininity that shrouded every part of her in mystery.

In the life of a photographer there's an abundance of silent time, neglected hours, and that distinctive blank space that precedes a picture. He enjoys a kind of alert, focused monotony that creates time for dreaming, which is why he can spend an hour meditating on a tree, the movement of the wind as it plays with the curtains in a window, or the reflection of a lighthouse – like the one I used to stare at for hours during my nights in Mazafran – on the surface of the sea.

Yet Venus alone gave me the sense that beauty – like love, and joy, and the graceful flow of her stone robe – was something I might find at my feet if I'd just stop running long enough to reflect on life. Consequently, the morning time I'd spent with her was nicer than the night time I'd spent with someone else.

I didn't try to get her to speak after that. Like all the silently gloating objects in that house, she had no intention of saying any more than she'd already said, so what was the use of extracting misleading confessions from her?

Being as unfamiliar to her as I was proximate, I myself wasn't going to see anything. My suspicion alone could see.

During my first time alone with things, I lost my ability to see them. I lost even the intuitive understanding that, as I interrogated them, I'd become part of their memory. They had objectified me – turned me into a thing like themselves – and what should I find but that I, like other human beings, was a mere transient, while they were the abiding, stable entities that bore witness to my short-lived appearance.

After an hour of helpless stupefaction in Venus's presence, I left her and went out to the balcony to look at the scenery and to say good morning to Pont Mirabeau. Based on the account given by a certain writer – who only tells the truth in novels – I could be confident, at least, that once upon a rainy day the two of them had stood here and that, after reciting part of a poem by Badr Shakir al-Sayyab, he'd given her a long kiss as the bridge looked on.

Pont Mirabeau may still remember a kiss shared by a couple of Algerians who had left their love in its safekeeping. Yet, beneath its everlasting feet there flows a river that couldn't be trusted with Algerians' lives in October 1961, when dozens of their dead bodies floated along its surface after being cast into the water with their arms and legs bound.

If the River Seine had a memory, grief would have changed its course.

Sports stadiums and prisons were filled to overflowing with 12,000 detainees, while 600 others either went missing or were drowned, their lives having come to a halt atop bridges that didn't cast even a passing glance at their corpses as they passed beneath them.

I could understand Khaled's inability to establish a friendly relationship with the lovely sight I now found before me.

I don't condemn the River Seine, nor am I at odds with it. The waters that, down the ages, have been laden with the corpses of people of all nationalities and races, can't distinguish between the French citizens who were cast into this river in the name of the revolution in 1789, and the Algerians who, on charges of fomenting a revolution, were cast into it two centuries later. All of them without distinction were washed downstream towards the river's mouth.

I'm confident of rivers' innocence. As for bridges, however, I suspect their intentions. I'm also suspicious of revolutions' grandiose slogans. When the French Revolution named a bridge after one of its spokesmen, it involved an element of deception. When Mirabeau stood up in the French Parliament to utter his famed declaration, 'We are here by the will of the people, and we shall depart only at gunpoint,' did he know that two centuries later he would be witness to a war against the will of another people?

I closed the window, not knowing where to go with the train carriage of my life, packed as it was with others' sorrows.

Wherever I went, my balcony overlooked some new tragedy. Even in Paris, I was like someone who's so hungry he doesn't know how to sit at life's table of abundance. At times I manufacture my misery out of the memory of loss, and at other times, out of the memory of deprivation.

I took a bath and went down to explore the neighbourhood where Khaled had lived for a number of years. From the time I'd moved into Zayyan's house, he had recovered his original name. Like Paul Sartre's protagonists, who are always picking something up off the streets, I was constantly sniffing out his news, tracking him, gathering up his dust in the streets, investigating, and questioning every place that might have meant something to him. And all the while I was making use of that novel as though it were a guidebook to the tourist attractions he'd visited before me.

I was experiencing what it's like to be infatuated with a character in a novel, trying by stealth to capture his charm and identifying with him wherever I passed.

But was I shadowing a man, or nosing about for the scent of love?

The distances between the two of us seemed insignificant, and sometimes I would experience situations as though I were him. Following his tracks in beds, streets, exhibitions and coffee shops, I would lie with his woman in a bed that had once been his, make appointments in the coffee shop he used to frequent, gaze at Pont Mirabeau from his balcony, sip coffee I'd prepared in his kitchen, sit with his favourite marble lady and, at night, go to sleep in a bed on which he'd left a trace of his scent, and a load of insomnia. Not only that, but I'd spend hours thinking about the very woman who had robbed him of sleep years before. Now isn't that bizarre?

For reasons unbeknownst to me, I was still anxiously awaiting an encounter that I despaired of ever taking place.

The very woman I'd been trying to track down on the pretext of looking for someone else – today I would be putting my finger on the place where her secret lay hidden. Life's painful coincidences had arranged a meeting for me with a man who was a patient at the Ville Juive hospital in Paris and who, or so she had claimed, existed nowhere but in her book.

I was aware that I'd have to prepare for the encounter with a considerable degree of caution, since I didn't want to spoil it after having spent a whole month working to convince Françoise to let me meet him, if even on his sick bed. My appointment with Zayyan, whatever the nature of the relationship that might develop between us thereafter or the outcomes it might yield, would be a major event in my life.

Chapter Five

I BOUGHT A BOUQUET of flowers and headed over to see him.
I avoided white, since it wouldn't have been fitting for an artist who had devoted his life to cancelling out this very colour. I also avoided anything so elegant that it would have made me seem insensitive to his illness, or that would have aroused the jealousy of someone who hadn't discovered love until middle age – the age of uncertainty.

I hadn't forgotten to bring him some of my articles so that he'd believe my excuse for visiting him, especially since they bore the signature of Khaled Ben Toubal.

Even though his room didn't bear the number '8', something about it was reminiscent of Amal Donqol's last poetry collection, *Papers in Room No. 8*, since all patients' rooms are a number in the realm of whiteness. He wrote,

> The doctors' masks were white
> The colour of their coats was white
> The wise women's crown was white
> As were the nuns' habits,
> The sheets,

The beds,
The gauze bandages and the cotton,
The sleeping pills,
The tube of serum,
The glass of milk.

He was as welcoming as empty white space, but with a swarthy smile and a countenance as bright as the colours of a rainbow after an afternoon downpour.

He rose and greeted me cordially, placing a bit of colour between us.

'Hello, Khaled! Come in.'

Not knowing how to address him in returning the greeting, I just embraced him, saying, 'Hello! I'm so glad you're all right.' I wondered what Françoise might have told him for him to give me such a warm welcome.

He sat down across from me. So, here he was at last.

He wore the cares of a lifetime with elegance.

He had the kind of Constantinian good looks that had been smuggled into Algeria centuries earlier through the genes of the Andalusians. He had thickish eyebrows, hair that, despite some flecks of grey, was still mostly black, and a smile which – as I would realise later – bespoke a silent derision whose effects had been left in the form of a time-chiseled dimple to the right of his mouth.

He had profoundly alluring eyes, and the weary look of a man women had loved for his disdain for life.

How old was he? It didn't matter. The autumn of his life was speeding to a close, and he was awaited by winter's chill. It was the superb midpoint of despair, the first half of death, which was why he had a smile on his face. He seemed at the peak of his magnetism, the magnetism of someone who knew a great deal because, as I would come to understand later, he had lost a great deal.

On the chair across from his high bed, I felt small, but I was learning how to be content with lowly questions.

How could I knock gently on the door to this man's memory? How could I extract answers from him when I couldn't even bring myself to ask the questions that were my reason for coming?

How do you open the window of words in a sick man's room without coming across as either stupid or selfish, like some opportunist who's vying with death for the chance to steal his secrets?

Apologetically I said, 'I've wanted to meet you for a long time, but I'm sorry it had to happen in a hospital! I hope your health is improving.'

'Don't worry,' he said lightheartedly. 'I'm incurably patient!'

'First of all, I love your art, and I feel as though I share a kind of secret understanding with many of your paintings. So when I found out unexpectedly that you were in Paris, I asked Françoise to put me in touch with you. In commemoration of the November Revolution, I'm conducting a number of extended interviews with Algerian figures who contributed to the War of Independence, and I suspect our interview will be a good one.'

'I suspect the same,' he said, smiling. 'From what I've heard, the two of us have the same interests, and we have a shared love for a lot of the same things.'

I didn't know enough about him at the time to realise that, long before, he had acquired an ability to intuit the truth, that he'd trained himself in the art of acting dumb, and that by 'things' he may well have meant...women.

I asked his permission to turn on the tape recorder as a way of lending a more official tone to the encounter.

'Your memories are important to me,' I said. 'You fought in Algeria's war of liberation, you lived through its battles, and you witnessed its acts of heroism. So what do you remember of the leaders and heroes of that period?'

'The memory you're running after is a deceptive one!' he retorted jokingly. 'There's no such thing as great acts of heroism. They're nothing but myths that we invent after the fact. Your greatest battles are the ones you fight with the courage of conscience, not with a weapon or with muscular strength. These are the battles fought by ordinary, nameless people who manu-facture the myth of the great victory. Nobody will mention them, and no journalist will come to interview them on their deathbeds.'

I was surprised by the reverse perspective with which our conver-sation had started out. Even so, I tried to go along with the direction he'd established.

'But,' I said, 'do you agree with those who say that revolutions are planned by sly old dogs, carried out by heroes, and profited from by cowards?'

He smiled and shifted position on the bed as though the conversation had just now begun to interest him. After a short silence, he replied, 'If I were to sum up my experience of this revolution, which I lived through from beginning to end, it would be by correcting the saying you just quoted, since it's subject to revision by every new generation. From where I stand today, I'd say that revolutions are planned by the Fates, carried out by idiots, and profited from by thieves. This is the way things have happened throughout history. There's no justice in revolutions, whose spoils are divided up by the Fates over the dead bodies of the freedom fighters who held out until the final hour, and the martyrs who died in the final quarter of an hour. Imagine the absurdity of two warring parties embracing in the presence of the final battle's final martyr. It's over the last martyr's corpse that the first deal is struck.'

I remained silent. His answers were so categorical that I couldn't think of anything to add. Even so, I kept looking for some way into his personal life, something that would tell me whether he had a past that matched that of Khaled Ben Toubal in the novel I'd read.

So I decided to approach the matter in a roundabout way.

'And you,' I said, 'what were those beginnings like for you personally? What was your past like?'

Like an aged warrior who's begun making light of his victories, he said sarcastically, 'In honour of old, unfulfilled dreams, I like to talk about the past in the first person plural. In the past, when people were gullible and it was considered improper to say "I", I forgot to be an "I". And now, it's only natural that even thieves and gang leaders would have the audacity to talk about themselves in the plural!'

As he uttered his last sentence, he laughed.

He possessed the beauty of a quiet sorrow. It was a sorrow that had imbued him with the eloquence of silence, the expressiveness of an unspoken cynicism, so that if he laughed, you realised he was inviting you to cry with him.

Hoping to get him to talk about himself again, I said, 'But your reputation as a leading Algerian artist gives you the right to be an individual, to be unique.'

'Well,' he rejoined sardonically, 'That's a right you win not by virtue of your talent, but by virtue of old age and illness. When you reach this final bed, you go back to being what you were in the beginning: defenceless and alone. You become an "I" again, since everyone has scattered from around you.

'You have to train yourself to speak in the singular, to think in the singular after having spent a lifetime speaking in the plural, not because of your importance, or the importance of some seat you occupied, but rather, because the "I" simply didn't exist in your generation. It was the generation of collective dreams, and of death for the sake of a single communal aim.

'It's not that we weren't selfish sometimes, or concerned about "getting ahead" at others' expense. We didn't lack the ability to be treacherous, or even to murder our comrades. Rather, what we lacked was a sense of irony. Therein lies the tragedy of a life of struggle that was doomed to be ruled by discipline and seriousness, and that viewed discernment and clemency as a kind of subversion. For a long time I've suffered from a deficiency in "laughing cells", which is why I ended up here!'

Not knowing what to add, I commented, 'That's life. We all cope with it the best we can.'

'What you mean is: We all give up our convictions wherever we can. You get off the steam engine of refusal. Then you see your comrades doing the same, stealthily, one after another. That's when you realise that you're actually still standing on the train, and that you'll be the last to get off. But what can you do if you weren't born in the days of fast trains?'

The conversation was taking us wherever his words led.

'And life in a foreign country,' I asked him, 'which station in your journey does that represent?'

'Life in a foreign country isn't a station,' he said. 'It's a train that I ride to the very end. The punishment inflicted by life abroad lies in the fact that it takes from you the very thing you'd come to take from it. You find yourself living in a country which, whenever it takes you in its arms, intensifies the chill inside you because, in everything it gives you, it brings you back to your initial deprivation. You go to live in a foreign land in order to discover something, to expose something, only to find that you yourself are exposed by your foreignness.'

'And what about you has been exposed?'

'My handicap. Not the one you see, but something that's in my limbs, and that you can't see.'

Suddenly he stopped talking, but in a way that suggested he was continuing a silent conversation with himself about things he didn't wish to reveal.

I didn't interrupt his silence. I saw him looking thoughtfully at my left arm as if he'd sensed my invisible handicap. Did he have the sixth sense with which so many of the disabled are endowed? Or had he already been told about my handicap?

'But you wouldn't understand this,' he went on. 'It's something that can only be understood by people who've lost a limb. They experience the phenomenon of "phantom limb" – the feeling that a missing limb is still there. In fact, sometimes the feeling spreads to the whole body. It might hurt, or itch. Or they might have the urge to trim their fingernails on a hand that isn't there any more!

'It's the same with objects we've lost, homelands we've left, and people who've been taken away from us. Their absence doesn't mean they've disappeared. They move in the nerves at the tips of our amputated limbs. They live in us: like a home-land, like a woman, like a departed friend. Only we see them, and as we go about our lives in a foreign land they inhabit us, though without actually sharing our lives. So the chill in our limbs goes deeper, and because of their presence inside us we're compromised by the cold!'

His words sent a chill through my body. Yet he'd uttered them calmly, like someone who casually shoots himself, only to wound the person across from him!

He'd been summing up his life for me through the autobiography of an arm that, in its orphanhood, had become a 'memory in the flesh'. Yes, even a person's limbs can be orphaned. But how could he have thought that I wouldn't understand?

I felt like crying, or like kissing the stub of his missing arm, where our shared losses had begun.

Oh, my God. It really was Khaled!

I fell in love with that man. I fell in love with his language, with the proud way he had of rising above his pain, with the music he chose to express that pain, and with the gracefulness that effortlessly created its own beauty with every passing moment until it radiated from within him. Now I knew why Hayat had loved him so much. He was made to be a character in a novel.

He was always attuned to the ring of his own words, and to the value of the silences that interspersed them. When you asked him a question, he would take it from you and rephrase it as another question that usually started with, 'Do you mean…?'

In those Socratic reformulations lay his answers to your questions. He would correct you, but always in pencil, and in a softer tone than your own. He had no red pen. After all, he wasn't a teacher. He was just a man, like Borges, who was making fun, who possessed a droll sense of humour that made spending time with him a pleasure I'd never experienced before.

'You know?' he said, as he leafed through my articles, 'I envy people who write. Writing is like rowing with one hand. Yet even though I'm missing a hand, I can't seem to do it. I've lost the urge to sail. Maybe it's because, in order to sail, you have to have a port to sail to. But I've got no direction. I haven't even painted for the past couple of years.'

This confession gave me a sense of his emotional state. I remembered Picasso saying something to the effect that to go back to painting is to go back to loving. Every phase of his career as a painter was associated with the entrance of a new woman into his life. But maybe writing is just the opposite. Over the course of the two years I spent with Hayat, whenever I asked her why she wasn't writing she would say, 'Writing comes with an estrangement from love. It's a kind of remedy that helps you heal from it. I'll start writing again when we separate.'

'It's really unfortunate that you haven't painted for all this time,' I said.

'Like writing, painting is weak people's way of warding off impending harm. I don't need it any more, since my losses have made me stronger. The strongest people are those who don't have anything to lose. So don't be fooled by my appearance. I'm a happy man. Never in my life have I been so lighthearted, so able to thumb my nose at things I used to think were important.

'In the evening of your life, you have to take off life's burdens the way you take off the suit you've been wearing all day long, or the prosthesis you've been carrying around. You've got to hang your fear on a peg and stop dreaming. All the people I've ever loved died as punishment for their dreams!'

Suddenly I realised that the secret behind his special allure lay in the fact that he'd become free. He no longer had anything to lose or worry about.

Unlike the way he'd lived before, he realised his beauty by acting on his own inclinations rather than on what other people might say. He was bankrupt and travelling light, and you couldn't help but envy him. His lightness was something he'd acquired when he finally saw through the hypocrisy people had burdened themselves with, and he could now say things he hadn't dared say before.

He could say what he really thought of the ungifted artist whose work he'd always praised so disingenuously, the neighbour he used to humour by wearing a beard for fear of his disapproval, the friend whose embezzlements he'd been too timid to expose, and the hypocritical enemy in whose presence he'd played dumb.

I asked him, 'Aren't you afraid of ending up without any friends?'

He chuckled. 'I didn't have any friends to lose. My friends all fell off the train some time ago. Leaving your homeland is like turning your back on a tree that had been a friend, and on a friend that had been an enemy. Success, like failure, serves as a good test of those around you: of the person who tries to get close to you in order to steal the limelight, of the one who turns against you because your light has exposed his faults, and of the one who, when he fails, devotes his life to proving the illegitimacy of your success.

'People always envy you for something that isn't worth being envied for, since they get their kicks out of seeing you lose what you have. They even envy you for being a stranger in a strange land, as though homelessness were a benefit that you should have to pay for, if not in cash, then by enduring other people's hatred and resentment. I'm a man who likes to pay in order to lose a friend. I'm keen to test people and find out how much I'm worth on their emotional slave trade market. One person's friendship might seem to be valuable until you find out that he'd be willing to ditch you in return for 500 francs – the fee he'll earn for writing an insulting article about you. Somebody else might borrow money from you not because he needs it, but because he gets a kick out of depriving you of it. And somebody else might even become your enemy because of all the good you've done for him. To some people's way of thinking, there are services so great that the only way to respond to them is by being an ingrate! So you've got to excuse people who shut you out for no good reason. After all, what are you going to do to change human nature?'

'And how do you live without friends?'

'I have no need of them. What I'm looking for now are power-ful enemies so that I can get that much stronger. The frogs that croak under your window, challenging you to a duel in a bog, are too small to be proper enemies. They just cause static, roil the waters, and keep you from working. It's a despicable time we're living in. Enemies have even shrunk in stature, which is a tragedy in itself for a man like me, who spent three years in the moun-tains, fighting against the armies of France. How do you expect me to duel enemies who are such runts? My sword wouldn't lower itself to fight them!'

'So you're living alone?'

'Not at all,' he said with a smile. 'I'm always there for anybody who needs me. I may have no friends, but I'm a friend to all. The last friend I lost was a Palestinian poet who died some years back in Beirut during the Israeli invasion of Lebanon. Once he was gone, I never found anybody who could occupy the lovely space he used to fill inside me. Some part of me died with him. I've never found anybody else who matched my temperament and who could identify with my pain.'

He fell silent for a bit before adding, 'You know? This is the first time I've talked to anybody this way. But you remind me of him. He was around your age, and handsome, like you. He wasn't a well-known poet, but he had an amazing ability to choose just the right words. I still have some of his poems, and when I get out of the hospital, I'll show them to you.'

Then suddenly, as if in apology, he said, 'Maybe I've talked too much. Most of the time I'm pretty tight-lipped! Somebody once described artists as "the children of silence."'

'Not to worry,' I said teasingly. 'Photographers are the children of patience!'

'I like that!' he said, his face lighting up with a smile. 'My God, you even talk like him!'

I nearly replied, 'Of course I do. After all, all that woman's men are alike.' But I held my tongue.

I stood up to bid him farewell. He locked me in a warm embrace and asked me, 'When will you be publishing this interview?'

'It isn't ready to be published yet, since it isn't finished,' I replied fondly. 'If you're open to it, we'll have a number of meetings. I want to do a thorough job, and write something that touches on all aspects of your personality.'

'Don't tell me you're going to write a book about me!' he said jokingly. 'I've never met a writer but that I've tried to persuade him to gather up the pieces of my memory into a book!'

'No,' I replied, sensing that he was serious. 'I'm not a writer, actually. When you write, you're just enshrouding Time in white paper. I'm a photographer. My profession is to preserve Time's corpse, to fix a moment in place the way you mount a butterfly onto a Styrofoam slab.'

As he escorted me to the door, he commented, 'In either case, the only thing you're enshrouding is yourself.'

Then, as if as an afterthought, he said, 'Next time you come, don't forget to bring that prize-winning photograph of yours. Françoise tells me you're a renowned photographer!'

As though I'd begun to resemble him, my only response to his description of me as 'renowned' was to give him a half-sardonic smile.

Leaving him to blank space, I departed the hospital bursting with colour.

When Françoise got home, she found me listening to the recording of our conversation. She asked me if I was transcribing the tape in preparation to write the article. I told her I was filling myself with its contents. In reality, I had no intention of writing an article. Nor had I ever imagined that, like those who had known this man before me, I would aspire to gather up the tattered remains of his memory into a book.

All at once, life had decided to shower me with such an overwhelming abundance of coincidences that I felt terrified – terrified of a happiness so completely unexpected. No sooner had I taken in the reality of my encounter with Zayyan than I found myself, the very next day, getting to know Nasser.

Were these chance encounters, along with the events that followed them, really nothing but happenstance? Someone once defined happenstance as 'the signature God affixes to His will'. And God's will is what we refer to as 'fate'.

The intersection of our respective fates at this particular point in time and space was mind-boggling in its synchrony. However, I'll never know whether it was a gift from Life, or just one of its pranks. All I know is that after I left Algeria I ceased to be the journalist or photographer I'd once been. Instead I'd become a character in a novel, or a movie, who lives in constant expectation of the unexpected, and now I was prepared for something: for some fortuitous joy, or some impending tragedy.

Here we were, those whom Constantine had scattered, coming together in capitals of sorrow, in the suburbs of a fear-ridden Paris.

Even before we met, I'd felt sad for Nasser. I felt sad for someone with a name too illustrious to reside as a mere guest in the suburbs of history. I felt sad for him because his name was all his father had bequeathed to him. I felt sad because some people had turned the homeland into a piece of real estate they could pass down to their children, managing it as though it were a family farm that raises murderers instead of cattle while the country's heroes languished homeless in exile.

Nasser was lovely, just as I'd imagined him to be, and so was my encounter with him. As he embraced me, I embraced both history and love together. He was half Si Taher, and half Hayat.

Murad seemed to be the happiest of us all. He loved bringing old friends together, and he was constantly in search of an occasion to celebrate life.

Simple though it was, his apartment exuded the warmth of someone who had compensated for some loss through beautiful furniture, and who used Constantinian music to drown out an incessant inner lament.

'When did you manage to do all this?' I asked, amazed.

'While you were busy doing art exhibits!'

I got his drift.

'And the Constantinian songs – where did you get them?'

'I bought them here. They've got all the songs you could want on the market, from Cheikh Raymond and Simone Tamar, to Fergani. Jews from Constantine produce most of these tapes in France.'

I asked Nasser how he was, and whether his trip from Germany to Paris had been stressful in any way.

'The questions were longer than the distance from there to here!' he quipped. Then he added, 'I mean, the polite insults you receive at airports in the form of questions.'

'Come on, brother, what are you going to do about it? If a guy's innocent, it'll be obvious. You can tell a sheep by its face.'

'So what could they tell by my face?' Nasser demanded. 'That I was a wolf?'

'Well, even if you aren't a wolf, there are still plenty of wolves around these days, and I don't see why you should be angry. Here, at least, you've got nothing to be afraid of as long as you're innocent and you pose no danger to others. In our country, on the other hand, you can't guarantee your well-being even if you're innocent!'

'All we're doing is comparing one death with another, one humiliation with another,' Nasser grumbled. 'In Algeria they come looking for you to take you out, so your torment only lasts as long as it takes for a bullet to go through you. But in Europe, on the pretext of rescuing you from murderers, they "murder" you with constant exposure and vulnerability. Your agony is prolonged by the fact that exposure and vulnerability don't kill you. You feel as though you'll never be one of the people you live among. You're naked, exposed and suspect because of your name, your religion, the way you look. Even though you're in a free country, you lack all privacy. You love, you work, you travel, and you spend your money under the watchful eyes of surveillance cameras, within earshot of bugging devices, and with your life story stored in intelligence files.'

'The same thing happens to you in your own country,' Murad shot back.

Then, as if to put a stop to the debate, he got up and asked us, 'What would you all like to eat?'

I was happy to hear the question, not because I was hungry, but simply because I was anxious to see an end to a discussion that didn't serve as an auspicious beginning to a social gathering. I laughed to myself at the thought of all the daily debates and squabbles that awaited poor Nasser, knowing that the biggest sacrifice Murad was likely to make in honour of his guest would be to abstain from alcohol when he was around.

Before we'd had a chance to answer his question, he headed for the kitchen, and before long he'd returned with a plate of bread, and another plate of cheese and pickles.

As he set them on the table, he said, 'Get your appetites going before supper!'

I suggested that we order pizza so that we wouldn't turn into guinea pigs in Murad's kitchen-lab.

Indulging himself in the hope of a feast, Nasser said, 'When Ma comes, she'll make us some Constantinian dishes that will get the taste of German hamburger out of my mouth. God, I miss Algerian food!'

'Get off the subject of Algerian cooking, man, or you really *will* turn into a terrorist!' joked Murad. Then he added, 'Did you know that a book that came out recently in the United States shows a connection between criminal tendencies and certain types of food? If government officials in our country read it, they'll conclude that it's their duty to intervene from now on in what Algerians eat, since terrorism has its roots in Algerian cuisine.'

Given the seriousness of his tone, I asked, 'Is that true?'

'Of course. Have you ever seen a people as obsessed as Algerians are with eating roast sheep's heads? Even here in France, if you ask an Algerian what food he likes, he'll ask you to get him some *bouzellouf*. You see Algerians lined up outside halal butcher shops for a couple of roast sheep's heads to take home. And if this delicacy isn't available, they'll settle for green beans with sheep's trotters. I swear to God, if Gandhi himself had followed a modern Algerian diet for a month or so, with *bouzellouf* for lunch and sheep's trotters for dinner, he would have sold his staff and his goats and bought himself a Kalashnikov!'

Murad gave us a lot of good laughs that evening. He's the perfect representative of a people who've been delivered from death by their sense of irony.

Carrying on with his playful argument, I said, 'Maybe it's because we eat so many sheep's trotters that all we think about is running away from Algeria!'

He interrupted me with an Algerian proverb: 'And since we eat so much *bouzellouf*, we've become like a roast sheep's head: There's nothing left of us but the tongue!'

When our order arrived, Nasser said lightheartedly to Murad, 'I hope I don't spend my entire stay with you devouring pizza on the pretext that there's a causal connection between Algerian food and criminal tendencies! After all, pizza was born in the land of the mafia. So, considering its Italian line of descent, it isn't all that innocent, either!'

Even the rare merriment of our gathering couldn't make me forget the topic that was my sole concern. Hoping to get Nasser to share more of his news, I said, 'Your mother should be arriving any day now. It must be hard for somebody who's been raised on home-cooked feasts to settle for a slice of pizza. At the same time, I hate to think of how hard the trip will be on the poor woman at her age.'

Then I continued, 'Will she be staying here with you?'

'No, she'll stay at the hotel with my sister. But she's sure to visit me here. I don't know yet exactly how things will go.'

He'd given me the one piece of information I'd been looking for. The rest was mere detail.

So, she *would* be coming! After all, how could these earthshakingly lavish coincidences have been complete without her coming, and without this sort of a thunderbolt?

I sank into a reverie. My thoughts wandered far afield as I thought about some coincidence that might bring us together or, at least, let her know I was here. How could I find out which hotel she'd be staying at, and whether her husband was coming with her?

I was still trying to think of a way to draw Nasser into a conversation about his brother-in-law in the hope that he might reveal more of her news when, unable to resist the temptation to badmouth the man, Murad said to Nasser, 'So, is that good-for-nothing coming with her?'

'Who are you talking about?' I asked stupidly.

'His brother-in-law. No number of stars can lift a swine out of the mud!'

'I don't think he's coming,' Nasser replied. 'He's afraid that if he visits France, some of his victims' relatives will demand that the French authorities prevent him from going back to Algeria and try him as a war criminal for the torture he's overseen, and the assassinations that have been carried out on his orders. His affairs abroad are all managed by his sons.'

Nervously lighting a cigarette, Murad grumbled, 'War's a good investment. How could they get rich if they didn't have a steady supply of corpses coming in? This way, they can keep others so busy burying their dead that they've got no time to notice what people in high places are doing. Even when the death machine isn't operating on their orders, it's still operating to their benefit. So tell me, for God's sake: who's the bigger terrorist, and who does more to destroy our country – these guys, or the murderers roaming the streets?'

I was afraid the atmosphere of our get-together might be spoiled by differences of perspective which, I suspected, weren't new to either of the two men, and for which the time wasn't right. Be that as it may, it gave me a welcome opportunity to ask Nasser the question that had preoccupied me for so long.

'Pardon me,' I broke in, 'but I can't understand how your sister's been able to live with this man, and why she's never asked for a divorce.'

After a pause, Nasser retorted, 'Because people like him aren't divorced – they're murdered.'

A chill went through me. For a few moments, my mind began reviewing all possible scenarios of premeditated death. My God – could something like that actually happen?

My macabre thoughts reminded me in the end that I needed to get back to Paris. I looked at the clock, and to my surprise it was already a quarter to twelve. I got up, in a hurry to be on my way. I feared the suburb trains and the surprises they might bring by night. Murad advised me to stay overnight, enticing me with a soiree that might be a once-in-a-lifetime experience.

I hesitated to accept his offer. I thought about Françoise. I hadn't told her I wouldn't be coming home that night. Then I thought about how I hadn't brought my toiletries with me, and how there might not be enough room for us all.

However, Murad settled the matter, saying, 'We've got everything you'll need right here, sir!'

I knew the chance to spend the night with Nasser might also be once in a lifetime, and I hadn't forgotten for a moment that he was the brother of the woman I loved.

I asked Murad if I could use his telephone without telling him I'd be calling Françoise. Later, however, he sprang a crafty question on me: 'So, did you tell her you wouldn't be back tonight?'

'Who do you mean?' I asked, pretending not to know what he was getting at.

'That lioness of yours!'

I don't know what prompted him to refer to Françoise as a lioness. Maybe it was her red hair, or maybe some exhilarating ferocity he saw in her.

Changing the subject with a quip, I said, 'Listen, brother, I'm running away from the jungles of the homeland. So please, keep the lions away from me!'

'What are you so afraid of? We'll show them who's boss!'

I don't know who he was intending to show 'who's boss': the terrorists? the army? Françoise?

'You can show whoever you want "who's boss",' I jibed, wanting to settle the dispute. 'I, for one, am a scaredy-cat!'

Nasser came in wearing a house dishdasha after praying the final evening prayer. He looked older than his age. He radiated a purity that I loved, and that had nothing to do with his white garment.

He was still untainted. Life abroad had done nothing to corrupt or pollute him, nor had he been marred the way some expatriates are. However, he was guilt-ridden over being somewhere other than Algeria. He seemed scattered by the freedom he now enjoyed. Yet he hadn't lost his self-composure, and he wasn't prone to making fiery speeches. He defended his convictions in a low voice, and sometimes without a word.

'What are you two talking about?' he asked.

I said, 'I was just telling Murad that I'm a scaredy-cat. Is there something wrong with a person's being afraid?'

He made no reply. I felt as though I'd disappointed him. As if to justify my fear, I went on, 'Believe me – I've lived for so long with an invisible enemy, fear never leaves me any more, especially at night. Whenever I go down the dark staircase in my apartment building to take out the rubbish, I expect somebody to be waiting to attack me. And when I go out, I expect somebody to jump out at me from some dark alley. I think about the movie star Ali Tanaki, who was murdered in my neighbourhood when he was taking out the trash one night. Imagine somebody's memory being associated in your mind with trash, with entire lifetimes that have been stuffed into plastic bags at ten pm to be picked up by Fate's rubbish collector. He'd just finished shooting a movie called *The Butterfly Will Take Wing No More*.'

'If you wouldn't mind,' Murad broke in, 'you can spare us those stories. What time do you think it is?'

We all looked at the clock.

'It's nearly one am. So, man, enough of this talk about burglars and murderers! As the saying goes, "I got a cat to keep me company, but it scared me when its eyes glowed in the dark!" We tell you to stick around and keep us company, and then you go scaring us to death with your horror stories about people being murdered when they take the rubbish out at night!'

Nasser and I burst out laughing in a way we hadn't done in a long time.

Murad had been imitating Inspector Taher, a popular comedy figure who died in the 1970s. A Columbo-like, trench coat-clad detective, Inspector Taher specialised in thefts and murders. He was also known for his distinctive accent: he pronounced the Arabic letter *qaf* as a *kaf* like the residents of the city of Jijel in northeastern Algeria. He pronounced the word *qalb* ('heart') as *kalb* ('dog'), and instead of saying, *qala li* ('He told me'), he would say *kalli*.

Like an elderly person who's afraid he'll have a heart attack if he laughs too hard, Nasser went back to being serious. 'Well,' he said primly, 'I really shouldn't be laughing this way!'

'Now if that doesn't take the cake!' Murad scoffed. 'One's afraid to die, and the other's afraid to laugh! Laugh it up, man — you're going to die in the end anyway!'

This had been Murad's motto during our days in Mazafran. He would lecture us on the importance of happiness as an act of resistance. As he saw it, our problem in Algeria was that people had no time to live. For years they'd thought about nothing but martyrdom. In fact, they were so busy looking for a reason to die a beautiful death that they forgot why they were dying, whereas we were so busy trying to stay alive that we forgot to live. So in the end, they found no happiness in their deaths, and we found none in our lives.

He'd been right, that's for sure. We were so lousy at being happy — since being happy had been a 'banned activity' in

Algeria for years on end – that, as he put it, we needed to form clandestine cells where we could take 'joy pills' behind closed doors. A professor I know has told me how, as he sat one day talking and laughing with a couple of friends at a roadside café near his university, two men dressed in Afghan attire came up to them and asked them in a hostile tone, 'What's so funny?' The only thing that saved them from God knows what sort of a painful fate was the fact that one of the two men recognised someone in the group. Even so, they wouldn't leave until they'd extracted a promise from them not to laugh any more!

When I related this bizarre incident to Murad, he saw it as confirmation of his theory that tyrants always view happiness on the part of their subjects as a violation of the laws of subjugation and a challenge to the institutions of oppression. Consequently, the greatest act of opposition to a dictator is to decide to be happy, since it's in the nature of a dictator to be pained if people rejoice in anything – unless, of course, it happens to be related to his birthday or his accession to power.

Murad headed over to the tape recorder and inserted a tape of Constantinian songs. Before we knew it, we were listening to the strains of a dance song that I seemed never to have forgotten even though I hadn't heard it for ages. It was the type of song that almost seems to give off an aroma and to have a body of its own, like the women you saw in your childhood with their tresses flowing, transported through dance to the point where they were on the verge of fainting, their beautiful dresses embroidered with gold thread.

His cigarette dangling from one side of his mouth, Murad got up and seemed to begin dancing with himself to a *zindali* cadence tinged with an erotic, manly solemnity. His shoulders quivered, their every move seeming to accentuate the rhythm of the defiance that inhabited him, while his waist undulated right and left at a leisurely pace that betrayed the mood of his lusts and his body's secret pulse.

Suddenly he seemed more handsome to me than he really was, more handsome than he ever had been, and I understood why women found him so desirable.

Somehow or other, the sight of Murad's dancing took me back to Hayat's husband, whom I'd seen once on television during a live broadcast of a military ceremony.

Decked out in his military regalia, he looked like someone who makes pretensions to dignity. He was seated in a front row with men who were too important to be moved by a piece of music and who, when the hall was set ablaze by the sound of Fergani's voice as he crooned, 'Beloved leader, parting sears my soul!', contented themselves with some sedate applause in the singer's honour, fearful that if they stood up, the stars affixed to their shoulders with the glue of their sham prestige might go flying!

I pitied him. After all, a man who doesn't spring to his feet in music-induced rapture couldn't possibly be able to tremble with bodily ecstasy.

At the time I'd felt grateful for his frigid presence in her bed.

Murad grew more and more handsome with the beating of the tambourines. It was as if the music were celebrating his manliness and, in its rapture, his body seemed to be making supplication to something that he alone could see.

> In the name of God I begin to speak:
> Constantine is my passion.

In my dreams I remember her
As dearly as my mother and father.

Together with the tambourines, voices responded to the singer at the end of every stanza with an enraptured 'Allah!' as the song proceeded to list by name all Constantine's neighbourhoods and markets:

For Eswika I weep and wail,
O Rahbet Essouf, my heart is wounded!
Where are you, O Bab el-Wad and Elkantara?
O places of beauty, you've been lost!

At the same time, this song – which was leading me somewhere I couldn't yet identify – was weaving a plot against me. Its moving strain was leading me to sorrow, and its rapture to grief. And by reminding me of the weight of my losses, it confronted me with the sudden extinguishment of the pleasures of my youth.

Had Murad really wanted to cheer us up with a song that, despite its upbeat rhythm, was – given our situation at the time – an open invitation to weep? We'd gotten out of the habit of being happy, and weren't fit any longer for membership in the Felicity Party he was inviting us to join whether we wanted to or not!

In vain he tried to get us to dance with him in celebration of our deferred pleasures. But our evening gathering ended the way it had begun, with conflicting feelings that concealed losses we no longer knew what to do with.

I respected the grief Nasser didn't feel at liberty to express. So when, after that, I had to share a makeshift bedroom with him, I gave him the sofa that had been transformed into a double bed and sacked out on the floor. It was only fitting, since he was the one with the dignity and authority of history, whereas I was the man of earthly passions and low-lying grief who'd always slept at Constantine's feet.

Another morning in a cold suburb. I was a bedfarer wherever I slept. My heart, which had awakened as topsy-turvy as the chairs that lay upturned on the tables in Paris's cafes, was waiting for someone to mop up the footprints of those who had tracked mud on my dreams.

Did my mood have something to do with a night I'd spent tossing and turning on the floor? I, who'd been experiencing the strangest coincidences, had now shared a bedroom with the brother of the woman with whom I'd dreamt of spending a night!

How could I have gotten even a wink of oblivion when I'd spent the night on the floor of deprivation, right at my memory's feet?

Where could I get away from a woman who haunted me wherever I went? And how could I climb out of this prison when it had no walls?

Before closing my eyes, I chatted a bit with Nasser in the way women in our part of the world do between two balconies of an apartment building.

As I lay in the darkness waiting for drowsiness to overtake me, and after I thought he'd already dozed off, Nasser suddenly turned to me and asked, 'How was Constantine when you left her?'

I suspected that he'd postponed his most important question for fear that it would expose him, or because he wanted to go to sleep remembering his city the way some people go to sleep remembering a beloved woman.

I wanted to envelop him in something beautiful, but instead I found myself saying, 'She's fine. She's finally taken off the clothes of mourning she wore for so long over the loss of Salah Bey. You hardly ever see malayas in Constantine any more. Whenever an old woman dies, her malaya is her shroud, and with the birth of every girl, a new hijab appears.'

He didn't reply, and I said nothing more to add to his grief. I think he must have fallen asleep holding his mother's malaya, perfumed with her scent, close to his heart.

At the time I'd been thinking of a woman who was the sole heiress to that beautiful bereavement, and slipping beneath the sheets of her absence.

My bed had never been empty of her. After every visit her sweet fragrance was renewed, and I would hide her robe the way, when we were children, we used to hide our new clothes under our pillows the night before Eid. Then I would revisit her scent, and be visited by her nightdress in my solitude.

For two years I'd been faithful to a negligée that had stolen the sweet fragrance of womanhood, aged like wine in the bottle of the body.

Every night I'd want her all over again. And every morning I'd wake up to find the telltale signs of Hayat-tinged dreams on my bed.

So, then, would she be coming – she who had been brought my way by one coincidence and taken from me by another? I, who had never looked behind me, never gone back to a rubbish bin in search of something I'd thrown into it, had been gathering up her pieces in others, reassembling the parts of me that had shattered apart when she was broken. And now at last I'd stumbled upon a ruse to draw her into the trap of coincidence. I gave Nasser a card announcing Zayyan's exhibition, fully confident that he'd tell her about it, especially now that I'd informed him that Zayyan was ill and was looking to sell the last of his paintings.

Moved by the news, Nasser said, 'I'm so sorry to hear he's been ill! What does he suffer from?'

'Cancer. But he doesn't know it.'

'Somebody like him, not know it?' Nasser scoffed. 'You must not know him very well. He's always known more than he's supposed to.'

'How long have you known him?'

'For a long time. It's as if I've always known him. I first met him as a little boy, when he used to visit us in Tunisia after my father died. I lost track of him for a while, but then we met up again in Constantine at Hayat's wedding. To this day I don't understand how he could have agreed to attend it. It was the only time we'd ever disagreed about anything. But, like my father, he's always had a special place in my heart.'

After we'd gotten up, Nasser went to shave and take his morning bath. While we were having our coffee, I asked him jokingly, 'Did you shave off your beard for fear of harassment?'

'I've never had a beard to shave off,' he rejoined, unhurriedly stirring his coffee. 'I like the saying of Imam Ali that "the best asceticism is the kind you hide". Some beards are nothing but disguises, like the ones we used to grow in the 1970s. Men of that generation all know the story of the guy who, when he was young, was wounded in the face with a razor blade in a brothel in Constantine. After that he grew a beard, which covered up his scandalous scar with an appearance of piety.'

Later Nasser asked me for the address of the hospital where Zayyan was being treated. He told me he wished he could go visit him that same day, but that he'd be busy receiving his mother and sister.

So there. I'd set the traps of coincidence everywhere. All that remained now was for me to await her approach with the patience of a hunter, or of a photographer who hangs on for hours to capture a shot. Just as a woman only yields herself to a lover who's willing to squander a lifetime waiting for her, a picture only yields itself to someone who's prepared to wait for as long as it wants him to.

I went back to the house happy. Murad's the type you're happy to see, but he's also the type you're happy to take leave of so that you can retreat again into your own peace and quiet.

But I hadn't retreated into my peace and quiet empty-handed. I'd borrowed two cassette tapes from him – the one containing the song he'd danced to, and another I was intending to cry to. In my experience, every joy tends to be accompanied by sorrow, just the way, in France, every cup of coffee you order comes with a glass of water.

Françoise welcomed me back with a bit of fanfare, and I sensed that she'd missed me.

She asked about Murad, and I told her he was his usual scattered self.

'He's funny!' she said with a laugh.

For this man to be 'funny' and 'nice', as she put it, didn't arouse my suspicions at the time. The fact was, all I could think about was how to set the most airtight traps for coincidence.

Wanting to prepare her for the fact that she'd be seeing a lot more of me in the exhibition hall from then on out, I said, 'Would you mind if I spent more time at the gallery over the next couple of days? I need to see the paintings and meet with the people visiting the exhibition so that I can write about Zayyan in a more lively way.'

'Nice idea. Of course I wouldn't mind. Carole thinks you're sweet. She asked about you yesterday.'

'Really? What was the occasion?'

'I told her I might be going to the south of France this weekend to visit my mother. She asked me whether you'd be coming along, and I told her you probably wouldn't be.'

Even though I wouldn't have gone with her even if she'd invited me, since that would have meant missing a chance to see Hayat, it hurt my feelings for her to convey the news to me in this particular way. Even so, I excused her. I'd only been staying with her for a few days, so I would have had no right to tag along and embarrass her in front of her mother.

Françoise walked over to a corner table in the sitting room that held pictures of various sizes. She came back with a photo of a woman in her sixties. Showing it to me, she said, 'This is Mama, my favourite person in all the world. I've been going to see her often to comfort her since she lost my dad last year.'

I took the picture from her and gazed at it affectionately.

'She's too pretty for you to hem her smile in with this huge silver frame,' I commented.

'But I like it. It's a valuable antique. I bought it a couple of years ago at the flea market.'

'It may be valuable, but it doesn't suit her. The people we love don't need to have their pictures enclosed in expensive frames.

It's an insult to them for us to be so busy looking at the frame that we forget to look at them, and the frame becomes a barrier between us. A photo's value isn't increased by its frame, since it isn't a painting – it's a memento. A frame confuses our emotional relationship with our loved ones and tampers with our memory. It's best for their images to stay the way they were when they were inside us: bare of anything but the transparency of glass.'

Françoise remained silent for a while, taken by what I'd said. Then she remarked, 'Maybe you're right. But this is the kind of logic only a photographer would understand.'

'Or somebody who loves somebody!' I added.

The fact that she'd been persuaded so easily by my arguments gave me the urge to make her a gesture of affection.

'Would you allow me to give you a frameless cover for this picture? If she's the person dearest to you in all the world, then honour her by not adding anything to her picture.'

She wrapped her arms around me. Planting a kiss on my check, she said, 'Do you know that I love you?'

'Do you really?' I asked in feigned amazement.

How do you respond to a woman who wraps you about with a sweet confession in the form of a question – 'Do you know that I love you?' – except with another question – 'Do you really?' Otherwise, you may not be able to avoid other questions that could lead you to bed in broad daylight with a woman who's ever aflame.

'Postpone your questions till evening,' I said flirtatiously. 'Then I'll answer them one by one. But quietly, and if possible, without any screaming!'

'You wicked boy!' she said, giggling. 'I'll try!'

'I'll be visiting Zayyan this afternoon. I haven't checked on him for the past couple of days.'

'All right. A good article's been published on his exhibition, and I'm sure he'd be happy to see it. Take it to him when you go. Tell him also that three of his paintings were sold yesterday. It was a fruitful weekend for the gallery.'

'I don't know any more whether I'm supposed to be happy or sad when one of his paintings is sold. On the one hand, the proceeds go to charitable work, which is good, of course. On the other hand, though, I feel as though he's doing violence to his works by clearing them all out in the course of two exhibitions less than a month apart. It's the most bizarre artistic massacre I ever heard of.'

'I hope he knows what he's doing!' I echoed with a sigh.

It was two in the afternoon when I went to see him. A nurse was on her way out of his room, and as we passed, I asked her about his condition.

'It's improving,' she said.

Then she added, 'If you're one of his relatives, try to convince him not to leave the hospital this week.'

'Why?' I asked. 'Is he insisting on that?'

'Yes. He wants to visit his exhibition and gather up his paintings when it's over. But the doctor is afraid it might cause him a relapse. Is he an artist?'

'Yes, and quite a famous one.'

I showed her the magazine I had in my hand, hoping this might give him a special place in her attentions.

'He certainly seems to be,' she conceded after seeing his picture and the title of the article. 'In that case, he needs more care than he's getting. Artists are hypersensitive.'

When I came in to see him, a look of happy surprise lit his face. He got out of bed and greeted me warmly. Then he sat down across from me on a leather-upholstered chair.

'Where have you been?' he wanted to know. 'I thought you'd forgotten me!'

'Of course not! I just got busy with some things.'

I didn't want to tell him about Nasser's being in Paris, and of course I wasn't going to inform him that Hayat would be arriving with her mother that very day.

'I see you're better today,' I continued. 'Even the nurse says your health is improving.'

'Maybe. But I'd be still better if I could visit the exhibition. I'd like to see the paintings that have been sold one last time, and the others I'd like to gather up personally.'

Handing him the magazine, I said, 'By the way, Françoise asked me to bring you an article on your exhibition that's appeared in *Arts* magazine. I read it on my way over on the Metro. It's good.'

He glanced at the magazine, noting the title of the article. Then he set it aside, saying, 'I'll read it later.'

Trying to think of something else that would make him happy, I said, 'I also brought you the photo I won a prize for, and which you'd asked me to show you.'

With a sudden rush of enthusiasm, he took it from me and stared at it for a while.

'It's quite moving. It shows death right up against life. Or it's as if death is encroaching on what appears to be life, although the only thing representing it is a dog's dead body.'

I interrupted him momentarily to ask his permission to turn on the tape recorder so that I wouldn't miss any of our conversation.

'Go ahead,' he said, slightly startled. After a pause, he continued, 'I can see why they awarded you a prize for this photo. In times of war, the death of an animal becomes as painful and tragic as the death of a human being. Suppose some criminals, in order to break into your house, killed a dog and bashed its head with a rock. That dog's corpse would be a harbinger of your own death.

'There's an image that comes to mind now: during our attempts to cross the Morice Line along the Algerian–Tunisian border during the War of Independence, we would see animals that had been electrocuted, their dead bodies still caught in the barbed wire. Others had been blown apart while passing over a mine. Whenever I saw those animals' bodies, I'd see a possible scenario of my own death or maiming. Then one day my feeling was on the mark: a mine went off and took my arm with it. All living creatures' corpses are alike in some way. The people who are in a hurry to bury a dead dog or cat tend to be the ones who weren't in a hurry to feed it when it was alive. They act this way because, in these animals' corpses, they see their own remains.'

'I'm glad to hear this is what you think. I've been tormented by all the interpretations of this picture, especially by the Algerian press, some of which say that by giving me this prize, France was honouring not Algeria's dead, but its dogs.'

Smiling, he commented, 'This interpretation also has some validity to it. However, some people adopt only the interpretations that will hurt you, since they take pleasure in ruining whatever happiness you might derive from your success. This particular interpretation is based on the fact that Westerners have more compassion for animals than they do for other human beings. This is why, in the West, the homeless go out to beg accompanied by a dog or two. You see them sitting on the pavements with huge dogs sleeping beside them, since they realise that a dog will mediate for them with passersby. One time I heard a homeless person being interviewed on television. He said that people would give donations for his dog's sake, nor for his, since their sympathy was directed not towards him, but towards his dog. He said that before he started bringing his dog out with him, he'd been starving to death.

'So, in countries where people are better to animals than they are to each other, it's only logical that they might honour a picture of a dead dog, not the wretched little boy next to him!'

His arguments made me feel even sadder. At the same time, they made me admire him all the more. I was impressed by the soundness of his analysis.

Then, as though he'd made a new discovery, he said suddenly, 'There is, unfortunately, another possible reason this photograph of yours won the prize: it bears witness to the death of the Algerian revolution, a death that can be seen in the fact that, after seven years of holding the French army at bay and forty years of independence, human beings in Algeria meet the same fate as dogs. Awarding a prize to this photograph sets the French conscience at rest, and slakes an unspoken thirst for revenge.'

Cutting short a heavy silence that had suddenly descended upon us, I said sadly, 'It doesn't matter to me to know any more about this picture. All that matters to me now is to dispose of the prize money in a way that will help victims of terrorism.'

'By the way,' I added as an afterthought, 'three of your paintings were sold yesterday.'

'Wonderful!' he said happily. 'I don't know which ones they were. But that doesn't matter. I suppose all of them will sell in the end.'

After a brief silence I said, 'I don't understand how an artist could give up all his paintings in one fell swoop. This kind of complete, sudden forfeiture seems to presage tragedy. It's as if he wants to lose everything he has.'

'Is that what you think?' he said.

He then fell silent for such a long time that I didn't think he was going to say anything else. At length, however, he started talking again, this time in an extended monologue, and with the mournful monotony of a telephone that rings and rings without anyone to pick up the receiver. He said, 'Tragedy is for things to give you up because you didn't have the courage to give them up. You shouldn't try to avoid your losses, since you'll never be enriched by things unless you've also lost things. As a friend of mine used to say, "My only possessions are my losses. As for my profits, they're nothing but rubbish." I prefer big losses over small gains. I like the kind of glory that one loses all at once. If only you knew all the bizarre things I've been witness to. If you knew, you'd enter deep into the womb of wisdom.'

He was quiet for a bit. Then he continued, 'On 16 November last year, a fire broke out at night in the gallery where Moroccan artist Mehdi Qotbi was showing his works in the city of Lille. I don't know the man. But when I read in the newspapers that this exhibition of his had represented twenty-five years' worth of artistic production, he became my comrade in tragedy.

'He'd spent thirty years in Paris, working assiduously to produce paintings that consumed the best years of his life. During those years he'd deprived himself of everything in order to prepare for an exhibition which, rather than being visited by art lovers, was visited by fire instead.

'In a case like this, you might say: If only thieves had shown up instead of a fire! There might be some consolation in knowing that the paintings still existed, at least. This is the way we're taught to think by the news agencies that report from time to time on thefts of world-famous paintings. But, like fires, thefts are a matter of destiny. They aren't determined by the fate of the paintings but rather by the fate and standing of those who produced them. Consequently, you'll never hear about a fire that consumed the works of Picasso or Van Gogh, just as you'll never hear about a thief stealing my paintings!'

'Strange!' I murmured.

'You think this is strange?' he asked derisively. 'Sometimes paintings give themselves to their enemies and to those who stole them! Listen: I have an Iraqi friend who's lived in Europe for twenty years. The man is as obsessed with Basra as I am with Constantine. His city is the only thing he paints, the only thing he talks about. Well, he was so well regarded that many people had offered to buy his paintings. However, even though he needed the money, he refused their offers, saying, "I'm keeping them until Iraq is liberated from its oppressors. When that day comes, I'll give them to the Basra Museum, which is where they belong."

'Then one day he received a visit from a wealthy Kuwaiti lady known for her passion for art acquisitions and her interest in helping Arab artists in exile. She tried in vain to persuade him to let her buy his paintings. Instead, worried that his works would be scattered after he died and confident of the woman's appreciation for art, he agreed to let her keep them for him until Basra was "liberated", at which time she would donate them personally to the city's museum.

'What happened next is so wild, even a screenwriter couldn't have come up with it. A year after the woman had taken my friend's paintings into her possession, Kuwait was invaded. Soldiers occupying her mansion seized the paintings as war loot and took them to Iraq, where they vanished along with the missing and the kidnapped. For all anybody knew, they'd been executed in place of their creator, who'd been sentenced to death twenty years earlier! Or they might have been used to decorate tyrants' palaces, or sold dirt cheap on the scrap market. That's what the Nazis used to do. Whenever they wanted to humiliate some famous artist, they would confiscate his works and sell them for a pittance – sometimes for as little as thirty marks!

'As you can see, there's a kind of wisdom you only attain when you've reached the height of loneliness and alienation, when you've chalked up enough losses to make you an old, old man. You need big losses in order to realise the value of what you still have, and to see that your little tragedies aren't as big as they seem. That's when you realise that happiness lies in mastering the art of reduction. It's when you learn to sort through your possessions and decide which of them you can do without and which of them you need for the rest of the journey. At that point you discover that most of the things you surround yourself with aren't necessary; in fact, they're a load that weighs you down. It's because I've made this discovery myself that I've decided to sell all my paintings. Even the one that's dearest to my heart. However, I've got a "reserved" sign on it. The fact is, I've reserved it myself for fear that it might be bought by somebody who isn't worthy of it. I need to know who its owner will be, and whether it will be hung on the wall of a house, or on the wall of a heart.

'In the end, when you start to simplify, you discover that your entire lifetime might be reducible to a single achievement, which is painful. But what's even more painful is to leave your lifetime achievement to a relative who doesn't appreciate its value, and who will inherit it from you not by virtue of artistic ties but by virtue of blood ties alone. Would it be acceptable for me to leave my work to my terrorist nephew, who for all I know might be responsible for the deaths of artists and writers? Somebody who kills other human beings can't be entrusted with anything.'

Suddenly he fell silent, and the silence that fell was the type that has a greater impact on you than any words could.

My thoughts carried me somewhere far away for a few moments before I mustered the courage to say, 'I'd like to buy that painting from you. Would you sell it to me?'

My question took him by surprise. With the shrewdness of someone who's just discovered a way out of a predicament, he said, 'But you don't know which one it is! How can I be sure of your love for a painting you don't recognise?'

'I love all your paintings,' I told him, 'but I love this one the most. I stood looking at it for a long time, wondering how you could have sold it!'

He shifted position. Then, in a tone of amazement he asked, 'You know it, then? How could you? There are seventeen paintings in the exhibition with red "sold" tags on them!'

With a pleasant sort of stubbornness I replied, 'Doesn't the fact that I recognised it out of a total of seventeen paintings say anything for me?'

Seeing that he was cornered, he said resignedly, 'If you can actually identify it for me, it's yours!'

He paused. Then, as if to show himself a good loser, he added, 'I mean...it's yours free of charge!'

'Rather, it will be mine in return for all the prize money I have left.'

In a further attempt to persuade him to accept my offer, I continued, 'It would be a good deal: I have money I want to give away in charity, and you have a painting that you don't know who to leave to. So, by selling it to me you'll bring happiness to three parties: to me, to yourself, and to the people who'll benefit from its proceeds.'

Then, in response to a crazy idea that flashed through my mind at that moment, I blurted out, 'And you might just bring happiness to a fourth party as well.'

'Who's that?'

'The woman I might give it to!'

Then, fearing that this might prompt him to change his mind, I added quickly, 'But don't worry about your painting. Like all Constantine's women, the one I'm thinking of is a bridge lady!'

It was as though I'd told him everything at once. Or at least, I'd said more than I should have in a single session. For a moment he seemed grief-stricken, like a warrior who's just learned that his wife has abandoned him while he was on the front.

Nevertheless, he handled the situation with aplomb: with the required astuteness, and with the appropriate degree of feigned stupidity. At the same time, he was such a cynic that he seemed able to fend off grief with sarcasm.

In a voice as dim as a lighthouse on a rainy night, he said, 'Beware of loving a woman who loves bridges. You don't want to build a house next to a bridge, and it won't put a roof over your head. To build a house at one end of a bridge is to let down your defences against the abyss!'

He was so steeped in cynical wisdom that it was aggravating his suffering. He had the perspicacity of someone who, afflicted with his final infirmity, has been given the chance to think, and who's begun noticing things he never saw before. Was it because illness turns a person back into a child, restoring to him the ability of the innocent to intuit who loves them and who doesn't, who tells them the truth, and who feeds them lies?

I was sure he had loved me from the first time we met. But what did this man know about me – this man who had welcomed me as a relative or friend as though he'd been awaiting my arrival, and who, as far as I could tell, wasn't receiving any other visitors? He was certain not to have believed the excuses I'd made about wanting to meet with him for journalistic purposes. Even so, there were times when he spoke to me as if he were addressing a journalist. At other times he would speak to me as a friend, yet never failing to discern in me the rival he feared.

Almost apologetically I said, 'If it bothers you to think of my giving the painting to someone else, then I'll keep it for myself.'

He gave a sardonic laugh. Then he made a statement the truth of which I would discern only later. 'Don't worry,' he said. 'Even if you keep the painting for yourself, you aren't the one that determines its fate. In the course of an object's lifetime it changes hands repeatedly, and you're nothing but one of those hands. Everything changes hands at some point, and some things exchange their owner's hand for that of his enemy. Like it or not, your wife, your job, your house, your possessions, and everything you have will pass on to someone else. The important thing is for you not to know about it. Even so, you have to train yourself from early on to accept treason.'

He paused briefly. Then, pointing to his stub with his left shoulder, he said, 'When you've been abandoned by the members of your body, your own flesh and blood, you won't be surprised to find yourself being abandoned by a sweetheart, a relative, or a homeland. How much less surprising would it be, then, to be abandoned by a painting?'

I felt as though, as he spoke, grief had made me as old as he was. I'd aged within moments, and gone bankrupt as I watched him display his losses.

'I envy you,' I said. 'I've never met such a wise man before.'

Coming back with his usual searing cynicism, he said, 'There's a Bible verse I like that says, "Even the wise die; the fool and the stupid alike must perish and leave their wealth to others."'

I was about to take my leave of him when, calling me by name for the first time, he said, 'Khaled…'

Then, like someone who cares less about how you'll reply than he does about whether you'll belittle his intelligence, he continued, 'Is your name still Khaled?'

'Sometimes.'

'And other times?'

Evading his question, I admitted, 'Most of the time my name is Khaled Ben Toubal, since it's the most like me. I got it from a novel, actually.'

As if to spare me the effort of looking for an excuse, he broke in, 'Do you know why Khaled Ben Toubal commits suicide in Malek Haddad's novel, *Le Quai aux Fleurs ne répond plus*?'

'Actually,' I said apologetically, 'I read the novel a long time ago, but I've forgotten what happens in it.'

'It's a short novel, just a hundred pages long. Practically nothing happens in it apart from the fact that its main character commits suicide at the end. During a stay in Paris, he reads in the newspaper that his wife Warida has run away with a French paratrooper, and that their affair was exposed when they died together in an accident. He'd loved her passionately and, anxious to get back to Constantine to see her, he'd resisted the advances of a certain Monique. When he learns of the matter, Khaled jumps off a moving train. Somebody else might have thought of some other way to die. But Constantinians, whose mother is a rock and whose father is a bridge, are born with a spiritual deformity. They carry the seed of suicide in their genes. They're haunted by the urge to leap into nothingness, and with an over-whelming sort of melancholy that tempts them to succumb to the call of the abyss.

'However, it wasn't betrayal that killed Khaled Ben Toubal but, rather, his knowledge of it. He shouldn't have learned of it. Even so, he does learn of it – in both novels – since Warida, in the words of Marguerite Duras, had married the wind, and betrayed him with one paratrooper after another. And in each novel Khaled dies twice: once because of his Constantinian genes, and once because of his intelligence!'

What was I supposed to understand from the discourse of a man who, between words, would lay mines of silence and, between one silence and another, would give me a screwdriver to defuse them with?

Suddenly he asked me, 'Are you from Constantine?'

'Yes,' I replied, as though I were confessing to a sin.

'Since you can't change your genes, then I'd advise you not to love a woman who loves bridges. Every Constantinian love stands at the edge of an emotional slope.'

What a man he was. He'd lost the heedlessness of good health, and acquired the sagacity of illness. As for me, in vain I'd marshalled my senses to pick up on what I'd come in search of. Like other men of his generation, he had an emotional reserve about him. So he wasn't going to reveal anything to me, and I wasn't going to ask him about her.

He may have recognised me through the intuition of the heart. But from the beginning, we'd been playing dumb in a mutual pact of shrewdness, or of pride. I was as content not to know more about him as I was for him not to know more about me.

We were there because both of us were Khaled Ben Toubal, and this was the only thing both of us knew.

As soon as I got home, I called Murad on the pretext that I wanted to make sure Nasser's mother had arrived safely.

He said, 'She got here at noon with his sister, and Nasser will be spending the evening with them.'

I heaved a sigh of relief.

'So,' he asked, 'when will we be seeing you?'

Suddenly finding myself in a hurry, I replied somewhat apologetically, 'I'll be busy over the next few days.'

Then I added, 'Things are a little mixed up.'

As he said goodbye, Murad advised me lightheartedly, 'Mix them up and they'll clear up!'

He didn't know, of course, how mixed up things really were, and how helpless I was to straighten them out again!

The first question was: How, without causing more than the least possible damage and suspicion, could I manage the intertwined, overlapping relationships that had been created by our having happened, by chance, all to be in Paris at the same time – relationships on such a collision course that they needed Fate's traffic policeman to keep them from crashing head-on?

As determined as I was to see Hayat, I didn't want to lose Nasser's respect. Neither did I want to arouse Zayyan's suspicions or cause him pain, or lose my relationship with Françoise.

There was also the catastrophe of having entered the orbit of a love fraught with perils and risks, with a woman who was followed constantly by a swirl of rumours, and who, wherever she went, was preceded by bugging devices and informers' watchful eyes. I was constantly afraid of the harm they might do to both of us.

How could you have gone and fallen for a woman whose husband rules an entire country with his money and his informers? You and your exquisite, costly transgressions! What a madman you are!

I couldn't have relations with Françoise that night. My body had gone on ahead of me, looking for Hayat in one hotel after another. And how could I sleep when I was consumed with anticipation? It was as though I'd never once given up waiting for her. After being tormented by my temporary possession of her, had I missed her in order to punish myself with longing?

I knew she hadn't come to stay, and that this time, too, all I'd have of her was the dust of promises. So why was I in such a hurry?

I woke up in a good mood the next morning, and decided to melt my exhilaration in a cup of coffee. I wanted to start the day by establishing a pleasant, indolent relationship with life. I'd loosen Time's necktie, unbutton my shirt and bare my chest to the winds of chance.

I headed for the exhibition at around noon, certain that, in view of her usual lazy morning routine, Hayat wouldn't leave the hotel early.

In fact, I doubted whether she'd show up at all that day. It was her first day in Paris, and it wouldn't have made sense for her to come to the gallery to see Khaled's exhibition on her first jaunt through the city. At the same time, I didn't want to miss the chance of seeing her in the event that she did pass by.

I was prepared to sit on Time's chair for a good long while – prepared to dupe the hours as they passed lest Patience's rosary break, scattering its beads every which way. And I held out no hopes of any reward but the eagerness of a first kiss.

I adore Love's lovely extravagance. I have a passion for all sorts of mad prodigality when it comes to matters of the heart. Besides which, I'm a man of boundless patience by virtue of my profession.

But was I the only one waiting for her as I went wandering lost among those paintings? It had occurred to me that we were waiting for her together, his paintings and I, he and I. And this was another remarkable coincidence.

It was as though life had unravelled the fabric of his story and rewoven it by replacing him with me in every situation. This was the way things had happened in the novel I knew by heart, and by dint of Fate's practical jokes.

This was the way he himself had been waiting for her in the beginning of *The Bridges of Constantine*, hoping she would visit his exhibition again, this time by herself.

With the same determination, despair and hope he'd paced around the hall where he'd put on his first exhibition, and which was now witnessing his last. He'd described himself as a man who is 'loyal to places in times of treachery'.

Since then, how many paintings had been displayed in this same hall before 'Hanin' – the first painting he'd done after losing his arm, and a painting the same age as Hayat – came back and took her place on a wall? It was as though, as far as this work of his was concerned, time had been suspended, just like the bridge it depicted.

Another reason for my happiness on this particular morning was that I had bought the painting after making that crazy deal with Zayyan. He knew, without my explaining anything further to him, that he had no one but me to bequeath it to.

She was mine, then. In this exhibition hall I was a king, and she was my crown. I felt the exhilaration of going bankrupt in return for a piece of fabric crucified on a wall, and I had named it 'Constantine'.

The time crept by.

After three hours in the exhibition hall, I decided to go to the café across the street and have a cup of coffee. I chose a table near a front window so that I'd be able to see her if she came. To my surprise, however, some time later I saw Murad going into the gallery.

I thanked God I wasn't still in there. If I had been, he might have stayed with me the entire time and, if she'd happened to come, ruined my encounter with her.

I was surprised to see him, since he wasn't in the habit of visiting exhibitions more than once, and he had no interest in either Zayyan or his paintings. If he had stayed for a long time, I would simply have thought he'd changed his habits. However, he seemed to have come for some other purpose, or to meet a certain someone who, I suspected, might be none other than Françoise.

My suspicion was confirmed when I saw her bidding him a warm farewell at the door. As she did so, he planted a kiss on her cheek and wrapped his arm around her waist with a more-than-innocent friendliness.

She must have thought I'd left the gallery and gone home, and he surely hadn't expected me to be right there to witness his treachery.

A cloud of melancholy passed over me, and I realised why he was always asking me when I planned to go back to Algeria.

After finding out that I only had a tourist visa and that I'd been staying in Françoise's apartment, he'd begun asking about my travel plans on the pretext that he wanted to send something back with me. He personally didn't want to live with Françoise so much as he hoped that, between her thighs, he might find residency papers in France and, just possibly, a way of getting himself a red passport!

I gulped down the free glass of water the waiter had brought me with my coffee, as if to help me swallow the lump in my throat.

Then I left the café without going back to the gallery as I'd intended to. As I headed for the Metro station, having decided to go straight home, the sky suddenly let forth torrents of rain as though it were weeping on my behalf. With no umbrella, I went wading through the mud of human emotion.

When Françoise got home that evening, she said irritably as she took off her coat, 'I hope I don't find this kind of weather waiting for me in Nice. God, how I hate rain!'

'When are you planning to leave on your trip?' I asked her.

'Friday morning. I'll spent the weekend there and come back on Monday morning.'

I didn't say anything. I just handed her the photo of her mother with the frameless glass cover I'd made for it.

She gave me a flustered kiss on the cheek. 'Oh, thank you! It's better this way!'

Stroking her auburn hair, I said, 'You know, it used to make me sad that I couldn't make smells visible in a photograph. But I don't feel sad any more now that I've developed my camera in another way.'

'Really?' she exclaimed credulously. 'How?'

'Now, for example,' I explained, my sarcasm undetected, 'you don't need to talk. What your closed lips conceal, I can pick up with a lens inside me.'

I didn't expect her to understand, so I wasn't surprised when she replied, 'So have you invented an X-ray photo?'

'No! I've invented a tragedy photo.'

Suddenly I missed Zayyan. Only he would have been able to understand a statement this painfully sardonic. After all, he'd already invented 'the tragedy painting'. He'd also shared the same house with a woman who couldn't feel distressed over anything but the weather forecast!

I asked her if she'd prefer that I stay somewhere else while she was away. 'Of course not!' she protested. 'How could you think such a thing!'

'In any case,' I said, 'I'll be going back to Algeria in two or three weeks, and I'll definitely be leaving the apartment before Zayyan gets out of the hospital. I don't want him to know I've been staying here.'

'By the way,' I added, 'I'm planning to buy myself a mobile phone that you can call me on since, as you know, I don't answer the landline for fear that it might be Zayyan calling. He'd recognise my voice.'

'That's a good idea. Anybody who calls me while I'm away can leave me a voice message.'

When we shared the same bed after that, I found myself unable to take her into my arms without tremendous effort, or to kiss her thin lips without having to turn for help to the dullness of the senses.

I took comfort in the fact that night fell on millions of households with the same degree of sexual hypocrisy as it did on ours, and that like me, millions of people wondered how to escape from the night's scandalous betrayal of their physical alienation from the person closest to them.

I thought about my wife, who had managed to extort a child from me on the pretext of our sharing a conjugal bed.

You may happen to collide with someone who sleeps next to you, or touch a part of him that happens to be within your body's reach. But when you loiter in the side streets of fate, you might collide with a woman's love in a 'traffic accident' of the emotions, whereas it's another woman who conceives by you in a 'car crash' of the bed!

I've always taken a dim view of gaiety, and I'm suspicious of the deceptive merriment that accompanies holidays. After all, a holiday is nothing but the preparations we make for it, and the same would be true of the encounter I was so anxiously awaiting.

When I set off for the gallery at noon, the city was decked out as if a holiday were on the way. I felt it was mocking me somehow. Had the end of the year come that quickly? Or was it just that entrepreneurs are always in a hurry to sell you a holiday that isn't really yours? We create our own holidays, our real holidays, when the official ones aren't looking.

Hadn't she always said that we needed a third city that was neither Constantine nor Algiers, neither my city nor hers, a city that lay off the Arab map of terror where we could meet without fear?

So here was Paris, and a love that belonged to winter: to roast chestnut vendors, to hurried nightfalls, to rain unceasing, to storefront windows dusted with a sprinkling of cottony snow with happy new year's wishes traced in it.

This white joyousness that promised a bitter cold winter intensified my longing for her.

*If only it would snow while she's here, O God of winter! If only snow-
drifts would pile up outside the door of a house, locking us in, so that snow
could wreak its lovely savagery outside while we snuggle by the fireplace of
yearnings!*

But she didn't come, and the snow went on falling inside me as I
waited for her at the gallery. My thoughts scattered every which
way as I contemplated cynically one possible scenario after
another. Even so, I kept guarding a certain fragile possibility by
continuing to wait.

Given her dreadful, searing absence, her tantalizing, frosty
absence, she was a woman about whom you could say that she
was doing you a favour even when she stood you up.

When I'd given up hope of her coming, I felt a renewed need
to see Zayyan. I could hear his news and, just maybe, some of
hers. I begged God not to bring the three of us together in the
same room for fear of a coincidence from which none of us
would emerge unscathed.

It was four in the afternoon when I went to see him.

I was surprised to see a bouquet of flowers, chosen with the finest
of taste, next to his bedside table. The room was filled with
joyous vibrations created by the coupling of the yellow and violet
roses.

I found him cheerful, though it may have been the cheerful-
ness of someone leaning, with a forlorn smile, against the
ramshackle remains of his life. He seemed bankrupt and light,
although it was impossible to know exactly what thievery it was
that had left him so full of disdain.

He started to get up to receive me, but I told him not to get out of bed. He laid a book he'd been reading on the table next to him. As I leaned down to kiss him, he said, 'Welcome. I've missed you, man. I thought you'd drowned in a lake!'

Lest I be suspected of enjoying a happiness that a sick person might perceive as an assault on his grief, I replied, 'I've just been drowning in problems, but I'm sure you can relate!'

It was a typically Algerian reply, the kind that conveys a barrel-load of discontent the reasons for which one isn't obliged to explain as long as the one listening 'can relate' since, being an Algerian himself, he's sure to be drowning in the very same problems!

As if to find out more about the source of my problems, he surprised me by asking, 'Are you married?'

'Sometimes,' I said sarcastically.

'And at other times?'

'Other times, I'm a homeless romantic.'

Then, as if to reassure him, I added lightheartedly, 'But I'm a cautious man. I stick to my own territory!'

He laughed. 'You remind me of a friend of mine who made it his profession to take calculated risks. In other words, he wasn't a philanderer, but he wasn't faithful, either. He was afraid of the diseases going around, and whenever he made claims to virtue, I'd say to him, "Fidelity based on a fear of illness is like peace based on a fear of nuclear war – it won't last. So choose which side you're on, man, and stay there. Either be a traitor worth your salt, or a loyalist from the heart!"'

This was the first time he'd asked me about my personal life. In so doing, he'd granted me the right to ask him about his.

'And are you married?'

144

He laughed again. 'Since I hate infidelity, I've refused to get married. A successful marriage needs a bit of infidelity to keep it afloat. Marriage owes its survival to infidelity, just as infidelity owes its existence to marriage. There's nothing more depressing than feeling you own somebody forever, or that somebody owns you forever.

'I refuse to own anything. So how could I agree to own a person and demand that she pledge me her neverending fidelity based on some official piece of paper? I don't think I'm capable of promoting marital tedium between the sheets of hypocrisy.'

After a pause, he added, 'You know, the most wonderful thing in life is fidelity enveloped in desire, and the most miserable is desire wrapped in the shroud of fidelity!'

Where had he gotten the clarity of mind to arrive at such wisdom when he sat surrounded by medicine bottles and platitudes? When had he experienced these things, and with whom?

His eyes shone with a beauty borne of chronic fatigue. Yet he didn't appear despondent.

'You seem happy today.'

'Really?' he said with a chuckle. 'Well, what's the use of being in torment? Don't believe people who tell you that suffering makes you stronger and more beautiful. Only forgetting can do that. You have to greet memory from a safe distance, since all your sufferings come from paying too much attention to yourself.'

As he poured himself a glass of water, I took a closer look at the book that lay on his bedside table. A small book with an ordinary-looking cover, its title was *Les jumeaux de Nedjma*, 'Nedjma's Twins'. Curious to know more about the reading habits of a man on whose table I'd never seen a book before, I instinctively picked it up and started leafing through it, utterly unprepared for the surprise that awaited me. Although he seemed surprised by my behaviour, he said nothing as I took the book off his bedside table.

I contemplated the title. Then I opened the book unthinkingly to the first page, only to find myself faced with a dedication in her handwriting! Feeling his wordless gaze following me, I didn't read what it said, contenting myself with a glance at the date written at the end. His proud silence made me uncomfortable. Maybe he was testing me to see how tasteless I could be, or whether I had the audacity to spy on his big secret.

Concluding that she'd visited him that morning, I realised where the beautiful bouquet of roses next to his bed had come from, as well as the box of fancy chocolates. I also picked up the message that underpinned this exquisite gift when, arguing for the virtues of chocolate as he insisted on giving me a piece, he said, 'Chocolate doesn't just give you a "high" and a rush of creative energy. The pleasure of eating it helps you to swallow any bitterness that might come with it. It makes it easier to die the moment the bullet hits you. When Hemingway wrote to his stepmother asking her to send him his father's shotgun – the one he'd used to commit suicide – she sent it to him with a box of chocolates, knowing that the reason he wanted the gun was that he intended to . . . commit suicide!'

He watched me put the book back on the table. As if to take our conversation away from the topic of the woman we'd both loved, he remarked, 'It's a nice book. It contains amazing details about Kateb Yacine's death that I'd never known before. I was jailed with him on 8 May 1945 in Kidya Prison, and I lived with him through the birth of his novel *Nedjma*, from start to finish. We were of a generation with similar lives, with devastating disappointments, with patriotic dreams we had yet to grow into, with fathers we'd never gotten to know, and with mothers crazy with worry over us. Nearly all of us were alike in every way. The only thing that distinguished us from each other in the end was our deaths.'

He reached into the drawer of the small table to his right and took out a cigarette that he didn't light. Holding it as though he'd lit it, he said, 'I belong to the generation of bizarre, unexpected endings. When I read in this book about the details of Kateb Yacine's death in France, which coincided with the death of his cousin, Mustapha Kateb, and then about how his funeral was held in Algeria, I thought about a saying of Malraux to the effect that the things that happen to a person aren't what he deserves, but what fits him the best. And Yacine's death fit his life. Like his life, his death was painful, disturbing, theatrical, full of protest, provocative, ironic.

'Imagine...when Yacine died in Grenoble, France on 29 October 1989, there was an earthquake in Algeria. However, the national radio's news broadcast that evening included a religious edict issued by Mufti Mohamed Ghazali, Head of Constantine University's Islamic Council and President Bendjedid's advisor at the time, saying that such a man wasn't worthy to be received by Algerian soil and forbidding his burial in an Islamic cemetery. But even after he died, Yacine went on thumbing his nose at religious edicts, and at authorities of all sorts. His bier was the first to be carried by women as well as men. In fact, his pall bearers consisted of an entire theatrical troupe!

'His final joke was that the Peugeot 504 that was taking his body to the cemetery broke down under the weight of all the actors it was carrying. So they got out of the car and took him the rest of the way on foot to the sound of cars honking, ululations, and people singing the left-wing anthem "L'Internationale" in the Berber language.

'Neither the country's religious leader nor its government officials could do anything to silence Kateb Yacine, whether in life or in death. Nor did they manage to prevent Fate from having him buried on the first of November, the anniversary of the outbreak of the Algerian revolution. He was the first person ever to bring anarchy, democracy and ululations into a cemetery, just the way he'd brought them before that into prisons!'

'What a remarkable death!' I exclaimed. 'I'd never heard these details before.'

'That in itself isn't so remarkable,' he corrected acerbically. 'The really remarkable thing is the strange coincidences of fate that have marked the deaths of people in our generation. I have two friends, both of whom were men of history and leading freedom fighters in the revolution. One of them died grieving, and the other died laughing. Can you believe it? You must have heard of Abdelhafid Boussouf?'

'Of course. He was Head of Military Intelligence during the revolution.'

'That intractable man, who was infamous for his inscrutability and his merciless liquidation of friends as well as enemies – do you know how he died? He keeled over from a heart attack in 1980 when he was laughing at a joke a friend had told him over the phone! He'd withdrawn permanently from political life after Algeria's independence, refusing any leadership positions, which was what made it possible for him to die laughing!

'Wouldn't you say that the end he met was preferable to that of Suleiman Umeirat, his comrade-in-arms who died of a heart attack while he was reciting the Fatiha over the body of Mohamed Boudiaf, another comrade-in-arms who'd been assassinated? Even those who've died as martyrs and heroes haven't escaped this curse. The bad fortune that had afflicted his generation, he passed down to his successors, including, for example, the hero and martyr Mustapha Benboulaïd, whose son Abdelwahhab was killed at the age of fifty on 22 March 1995, exactly thirty-nine years after his father was assassinated at the hands of the French. Some thugs stopped him at a sham checkpoint when he was on his way to his hometown of Batna to take part in the annual commemoration of his father's martyrdom.

'This death in particular may embody the tragedy of our whole generation – the tragedy that Algeria would present a man like Mustapha Benboulaïd, a symbol of our resistance, with his son's corpse on the very day when he himself had been martyred. What kind of a homeland is this??'

Just then the tape ran out. He noticed that I'd opened the recorder, and as I turned the tape over, he said, 'Leave the tape recorder alone, man! Bloody history does its own recording!'

In an attempt to assuage his bitterness, I said jokingly, 'History records, but I publish! I want to publish this interview as a testimony to that period.'

'What "period"?' he scoffed. '"That period" hasn't ended, man. Algerians are caught in a dialectic of self-destruction. When they don't find an enemy to do it for them, they're programmed to self-destruct and make an example of themselves. Do you think criminals should be given the credit for innovating the practice of murdering writers, judges, doctors, cinematographers, poets, lawyers and dramatists? Algeria already has a tradition of killing its intellectuals. I was a freedom fighter when, in a kind of psychological warfare, France insinuated to Colonel Amirouche that some of his men were working as informers for the French army. So, in July 1956, after a hasty trial, he had 1,800 of his men liquidated in what's now known as "La bleuite". In no time, fingers of accusation had been pointed at intellectuals, that is, at students who had left to join the front, and whose loyalty was suspect in the view of the National Liberation Front because of their knowledge and their French educations. They were murdered by their fellow freedom fighters, most of whom were illiterate villagers who, from the start, had held these men's superior knowledge and learning against them. And nothing has changed since: Every ignoramus avenges his ignorance by trying to prove he's more pious than his educated compatriots by casting doubts on their patriotism, and finally by killing them. So here we are now, still taking up collections to help victims' families.'

Suddenly he stopped and asked me, 'Have you bought that painting?'

Before I could reply, he opened the drawer in search of something. Then he brought out a lighter and lit the cigarette he'd been holding in his hand the entire time.

Even though I hadn't said a word, he could tell I was shocked to see him smoking in the hospital. 'Don't worry,' he joked. 'I belong to a generation that was born to disobey!'

Then he rephrased his earlier question: 'What are you going to do with that painting?'

'I'll take it with me to Constantine when I go back in two or three weeks.' Then, afraid he might have changed his mind, I added, 'It will be at your disposal, of course. You can see it when you come to visit.'

'I've stopped visiting Constantine. I've got nothing and nobody left there. The last time I went there was a year and a half ago to attend the funeral of my brother Hassan's son, and as far as I could tell, the only place for it any more was on picture postcards and in paintings. Her bridges looked decrepit and worn out, as though they'd aged and lost their stones the way people lose their teeth when they get old. And people crossed them with no expressions on their faces. Sometimes they were in a hurry, other times they dragged their feet. But they were all lost and confused, like someone who's waiting for a disaster to happen.'

'Maybe that's because you visited it at a sad time.'

'I've never made a visit there that was happy. I've always left it feeling bereft. I refuse to make a pact with the mud that covers everything now, and I don't want to be there when Constantine sheds her last stones and slips into the abyss.

'Believe me. Since Boudiaf was assassinated I've hated even to travel to Algeria. When he died, something in us died, too. When they begged him to come back to be president and save the country, they didn't think that this man, who had been enervated by prisons, exile and the treachery of former comrades, was really fit to strike a deal over others' dead bodies, so they turned him into a dead body too so that we'd take a lesson from it.

'Don't you see all the stones that have fallen on us since he died? Now we can go on pelting each other with questions. However, the question is no longer: Who killed Boudiaf? but, rather, Where is this mudslide taking us? And what kind of a quagmire is history sucking us into?'

A pained silence ensued.

Then – I don't know how it happened – I went over to the bed and, like someone grabbing onto a rock for fear of being washed

151

downstream, I put my arms around him and, to my amazement, started crying.

They must have been pent-up tears that had collected inside me, like a cloud heavy with rain looking for the right time and place to drop its burden.

As if to justify my blunder, I said, 'Khaled, I love you.'

He didn't object to my calling him Khaled, nor did he seem surprised that my love for him would give me a reason to cry.

In fact, he acted as if it were a normal thing for a man to cry, and held me without trying to understand what was wrong with me. He might have understood more than what I'd told him. However, he didn't cry. I suppose he was the type who only tears up.

'Don't be sad,' he said. 'Dreams were made not to come true!'

As he held me, a shiver went through my body as I came up against the empty space that had been left by his missing arm. I was experiencing what it must have been like for him to hold her, and how it was possible for a man with only one arm to press another human being to his bosom. I didn't know any more: Was I crying over her, in him? Was I crying over him, in her? Or was I crying over myself between the two of them?

She who had been where we were, and sat in the chair where I'd been sitting – it was as if she were still among us, and I could smell the perfume of her absence.

When, after that, he wanted to get out of bed to see me off, he inadvertently knocked the vase of flowers to the floor as he was trying to lean against the table. Sorry to see what had happened, I bent down to gather everything up.

'I've gotten clumsy of late,' he muttered apologetically. 'Everything I pass, I bump into! Don't worry about gathering them up. The nurse will come and do that. They're only roses, and they were wilting anyway!'

Then, with an irony of which he alone was master, he added, 'Even if my arm falls off, beware of picking it up.'

'You're reversing that poem by Mahmoud Darwish: "If my arm falls off, pick it up, and if I fall next to you, pick me up."'

'And,' he broke in, '"strike your enemy with me…"'

'Do you know it?'

'Do I know it?' he repeated with a grin. 'I know it, and then some! It was my friend Ziyad's favourite poem. He used to always say, "If only I'd been the one to write it." To which I would reply, "Don't worry. If you fall, I'll pick you up with my one arm." With Ziyad, I knew which enemy I'd throw his body at, but if you picked up my arm, who would you throw it at?'

'By the way,' he went on genially, 'when I get out of the hospital, I'll show you some of Ziyad's poems.'

'Do you still have them?'

'Of course. I'd sooner give up my paintings than give up those poems of his. I've always had a problem with martyrs' bequests.'

We parted that day without my knowing whether he'd been happier than usual, or sadder than usual.

He behaved with the disregard of someone who's got nothing to lose. He smoked, knowing full well that cigarettes were bad for him. He would ask me to bring him miniature bottles of whiskey, the type they serve on aeroplanes that fill one glass, ignoring the fact that he was forbidden to drink it with his medicine. He would even forget to take his medicine, since he knew it wasn't doing him any good. And he would eat things that were bad for his health to lift his spirits, which thrived on things forbidden.

I think he was happy, although his happiness had nothing to do with the bouquet of flowers, or with the fancy chocolates she'd brought him (some of which he stuffed into my pocket as he bade me farewell), or with the book he'd received from her the way Hemingway had received the shotgun from his stepmother.

The reason he was happy was that the doctor had given him permission to leave the hospital the coming Wednesday, since he'd been planning to do a lot of things, the first of which was to visit his exhibition and gather up what remained of his paintings.

As for his bitterness, the most likely, albeit undeclared, reason for it was that after he'd recovered from her, the woman he loved had come to visit him and seen him in the ugliness of his final illness. He himself had told me once that when he felt he'd become ugly in a relationship he would end it and run away, even when the other party was a home-land. But where could he run away to when he was trapped in a sick bed?

He seemed to have had his 'emotional appendix' removed, and to be testing his ability to beautify ugliness by the use of sarcasm. One day, for example, he apologised jokingly for not being able to get out of bed and sit with me the way he usually did since he was flat on his back with an IV needle in his remaining arm.

He commented in bitter jest, 'It was in this position that Michelangelo painted the ceiling of the Sistine Chapel. He lay naked on the scaffolding for several months with his right hand raised towards the ceiling. Determined to finish the work by himself, he refused help from assistants. He was in such physical pain that he once said, "I'm in hell as I do a painting." The pope used to climb the wooden ladder to watch him and give him his blessing!

'Sometimes a person is honoured in a humiliating situation. It reminds me of a memorable statement made by a certain freedom fighter who was led away to be hanged. When, before his execution, he was asked whether he had any last words, he replied, "I have sufficient reason to be proud, since I'll die with my feet above your heads!" But the humiliating thing isn't for me to be in this situation. What's humiliating is to be here sharing a bed with death, when all my life I've gone to bed to do battle with love!'

On my way back to the apartment, I stopped in a bookstore to look for the book *Nedjma's Twins* by Benamar Médiène. I wanted to know why she'd given it to him.

As soon as I'd gotten home and finished the light supper Françoise had surprised me with, I excused myself and went to the bedroom, in a hurry to start reading it. Even though she was busy watching a television programme, Françoise didn't seem pleased to see me leave her and go off by myself to read. It's really strange – I've never met a woman who doesn't consider books her number one rival in the house. She'll try with all the womanly powers at her disposal to steal me away from reading and hatch plots against my books, even if it means borrowing them from me on the pretext of reading them herself, as though my preoccupation with them were an insult to her femininity.

To make matters worse, I was in the habit of reading in bed, a fact that made books into veritable co-wives. I was always inviting the books I loved into my bedroom in my belief that a beautiful book is like a beautiful woman: you can't be content to sit with her in a living room, and you're bound to feel the urge to be alone with her in a bedchamber. Living rooms were made for the venerable, sedate sorts of books that line a bookcase, that measure their reputations by how much they weigh and compensate for having reached literary menopause with their fancy bindings and the gold lettering on their covers.

I unintentionally think of books in the feminine, and categorize them as such. There are the 'easy' ones that slip into your pocket, the books of waiting and boredom that, like women with whom you have chance encounters, are only good for a single reading. There are others that are good company. They go to bed with you, then end their night exhausted on the floor, sprawled on their stomachs like a woman after a night of love. Then there are the fancy ones, printed in glossy paper, that skulk behind display windows tempting you to buy them but which, like the prostitutes in Amsterdam, might infect you with the contagion of their poor quality.

I think that for many years, the only happy relationships I formed were with books. In their passion and their rituals, some of these relationships were almost comparable to marital infidelity, which is why I would sometimes indulge in them secretly to clear myself of suspicion. Sometimes I'd spend hours in bed oblivious to the wife sleeping next to me, so engrossed was I in reading a book that provided me with more enjoyment and suspense than her body which, married folks that we were, I knew like the back of my hand.

In the house where, being the eldest son, I spent my early years of marriage with my stepmother and my divorced sister, I enjoyed sneaking books into a bedroom that had originally been meant as a boudoir where my wife could hide her things from others, or – more precisely, from other women.

While smuggling a book into the marital chamber on the pretext that I needed to read it for professional reasons, I would often think of my father who, during Algeria's War of Independence, had discovered a fail-safe way to bring his paramours into the house undetected. Given his status as a leading freedom fighter and the fact that we lived alone in a huge, Arab-style house, he would sometimes lock me, my grandmother, and his new bride into one of the house's large rooms, claiming that he needed to receive fellow fighters who occasionally spent the night at our house engaged in 'consultations' before going back up into the mountains.

I was only six years old at the time. Even so, I noticed that my father had started locking us into the room, whereas his custom before had been just to cough loudly whenever he brought a strange man into the house and, walking several steps ahead of his guest, say, 'Make way! Make way!', at which point the women would rush into the nearest room and shut the door until the men had passed.

One night I looked through the keyhole, which was just slightly below eye level at the time, and saw him coming in with a woman in a black malaya. When I told my stepmother about it she seemed shocked. My grandmother intervened, scolding me roundly and, so as to contain the scandal, claiming that it was the custom for freedom fighters to disguise themselves as women.

From that day on, my stepmother, who hadn't bought my grandmother's story about freedom fighters dressing up as women, started spying through the keyhole herself, and would see women of various shapes and sizes passing through the house.

However, this discovery of hers didn't change her behaviour in the least. She wouldn't have dared tell my father that she knew he was lying to her. She was afraid he'd get angry and send her back to her family, in which case she would have exchanged the honour of being married to one of Constantine's leading men for the ignominy of being one more number in the divorce court's files.

So it was that she went on preparing the most delectable repasts for the fighters (both the 'brothers' and the 'sisters') who'd come down 'from the lofty, breathtaking mountains', using the most beautiful embroidered sheets in her trousseau, and sleeping in the guest room next to her baby girl while my father fought his battles of liberation in her marriage bed just metres away. As she tossed and turned, she may have been searching for faces and names for the shameless women who came into her house under cover of the modesty of the malaya and the righteousness of jihad to copulate with her husband in her very presence.

I had to reach the age of contemplation to realise that on the day when I put my eye to that keyhole, I'd been discovering none other than Constantine herself, and that that old house was simply a reflection of her hypocritical traditions.

All at once I'd come to see that fathers lie, that freedom fighters aren't sinless, that the women who wear the malaya aren't above suspicion, that the women who cower in the abodes of marital injustice aren't as deceived as I'd thought they were and that, accordingly, the victim isn't innocent of its own blood!

As I grew older, I began to see that my father's behaviour at that time had a 'Zorban' aspect to it that had contributed to his legend as freedom fighter and lover.

By virtue of his education and upbringing, he was a man for all fronts. He'd gone to battle not only against colonialism but also against the institution of marriage, which he'd never believed in but had associated himself with at my grandmother's insistence. He'd needed a wife to raise me after my mother's death, so his mother had presented him with a relative of his who'd been trained to be a good housewife and mother.

In reality, his passion for freedom had given him a penchant for liberated women, and he had an abiding weakness for foreigners due to the fact that they were educated. His good looks, which he'd inherited from Constantine's first Andalusian inhabitants, enabled him to win the hearts of the fair-skinned and dark-skinned alike. He wrote his first poetry serenading a certain French teacher. And then there was the Jewish widow whose husband worked as a guard in Kidya Prison, where my father had been held. My grandmother would go to the man's house whenever she wanted to send something to my father behind bars and when, two years later, famine struck and my father was assigned by the French Administration to distribute food vouchers to Constantine's Muslim residents, he would make surreptitious visits to her and some of her Jewish neighbours and give them some of the vouchers. In those days people of different religions and nationalities lived side by side, and my father had been accustomed to helping any acquaintance or neighbour who requested his aid.

Being his own version of Zorba, he was accustomed to surrounding himself with widows and spinsters: with women whose roses were about to wither and for whom he was their only gardener.

He was responsible for all the women on earth without distinction as to age, religion or beauty. He was responsible for their bodies and their dreams. He was concerned with educating them and managing their futures even to the point of finding them husbands. Indeed, he was responsible for all the hungry on earth, wherever they sought sustenance, and for all the oppressed and colonised, wherever their land or their cause. So, as the saying goes, 'he lived without a fortune, he died without a bequest.' It didn't matter to him to possess as much as it did simply to live.

After independence he rented a spacious apartment. We occupied the larger part of it, while he lived in just two rooms: his lavish golden sitting room where he received politicians and old comrades whose numbers dwindled every year, and a sumptuous bedroom whose furniture he'd bought from some French colonists who had left Algeria after independence. Dating back possibly to the end of the nineteenth century, it included an enormous, hand-carved wardrobe covered with large mirrors and decorated with tiny waterwheels. Next to it was a high bed whose headboard, bearing the same engravings, was topped by two three-dimensional copper angels that looked as though they were flying towards each other. The bed was flanked by a pair of small marble-topped bedside tables, while across from it sat a four-tiered chest of drawers with handsome copper handles, on top of which was mounted another mirror with a similarly engraved frame.

The sitting room was my father's punishment. A little-used room prepared for guests that never came, its door, which was opened only on special occasions, reminded him that the comrades of yesteryear had scattered from around him.

As for the bedroom, which had been his kingly realm and what remained of his former glory, it came to be *my* punishment after he was gone. For sentimental reasons, selling its furniture was out of the question. Consequently, I found myself commencing my married life there just the way it was. The room had a smell which conjured up the time of the dead, and which spoiled my own time. It's a difficult thing to start your married life on a bed that your father occupied alone. He'd slept continuously on its left side to the point where time, colluding with his body, dug a grave in the wool mattress so that you couldn't share it with anybody without one of you rolling onto the other.

With its high bed and its wardrobes' heavy doors, it was a room that would have served better as an antique shop than as a love nest. But maybe my father had wanted it to be that luxurious in order to compensate for the absence of love in his life. My father wasn't wealthy, and he hadn't bought the furnishings for that room in particular to be seen by anyone but himself. Even so, it reminded me of bedrooms that have been furnished with such sinful extravagance, it's as though their owners want to convince whoever sees them that rich people aren't bad lovers!

Imagine starting out your married life in an elderly person's bed haunted with nightmares born of troubled sleep, and being obliged, for silly sentimental reasons, to learn how to dispose of a life that your father lived before you. His scent is here, clinging to the wood, the curtains, the wallpaper, the crystal in the chandelier. You're at a loss, not knowing how long his scent will go on seeping into you. And you wonder to yourself: is this entire room nothing but a resting place for his scent?

I'd thought in the beginning that I'd only be staying there temporarily, that it was just a wayside inn and I a mere bedfarer. Then one day, in the place where I slept, and at the moment I least expected it, I was overwhelmed with the scent of absence. It was the scent that, from the very start, had spoiled my relationship with my wife's body, so thoroughly that I insisted she take birth control pills lest we become parents to a little one afflicted with hereditary, bed-borne malformations!

After that I found my happiness in escaping to Abdelhaq's house, where my desires found an illicit bed for themselves with Hayat. You have to constantly invent your counterfeit other life in order to rescue your lacklustre actual life.

I'd married a woman I thought could do the housecleaning inside me, who could sweep up the destruction other women had left in my life. I'd used marriage as a kind of prophylactic measure, thinking it would set up barricades that would protect me from life's slips and slides, only to find that it had snuffed life out. The reason is that someone might blackmail you without saying a word. It's the silent blackmail of the weak individual that gives her the right to dispose of your life however she pleases once you've fallen into her grip by virtue of a legal document.

She might do you harm not because she means to but, rather, by possessing you to a hurtful degree. She may pin her happiness on her right to make you miserable by virtue of the fact that she's your life partner. As for you, you start to feel that life with her has become your death, and that there has to be an unpleasant confrontation with this person who hasn't knowingly hurt you or betrayed you but who, nevertheless, is slowly destroying you.

162

You want to resign from the role of the good, happy husband that you've played for years as a way of avoiding arguments and disagreements. You want to give up the Oscar you might have won for your lead role in the film *Married Life*, not for lack of ingenuity – since you'd still be capable of telling more of the types of lies that a woman will swallow without the least effort – but because you're weary, because life is too short to spend it spinning lies, and because the terror you go through every day is too awful to add to it the fear of your wife.

It may have been for all these reasons that I chose to go live in Mazafran. It provided a way of postponing the decision to separate from my wife since, in spite of everything, it pained me to hurt her.

In any case, I succeeded that evening in reading the little book I'd bought before Françoise slipped under the covers beside me. As I drew her to me, I thought about how there are women you live with without being truly intimate with and how, unlike all the rest, there's one woman whose phantom you need to be intimate with when you doze off, and to think about in your moments of deepest isolation. In order to survive, you need to know that you still live in her memory, and that she's certain to come.

That night as I shared a bed with Françoise, I embraced someone else, and went to sleep with my head pillowed on the arm of a rendezvous.

Chapter Six

THEN SHE CAME.

The doors of anticipation were unhinged as her light came suddenly streaming in.

In she came, and for a moment the world stopped turning, while the heart skipped a beat.

A hurricane approached in a fur coat.

O Divine Providence, be merciful to me!

So at last we had met.

Mistaken are those who say that mountains can never meet, and those who build bridges between them so that they can shake hands without bowing or curtseying understand nothing about the laws of nature. Mountains do meet, albeit only during earthquakes and major seismic tremors, and when this happens they don't just shake hands – they're transformed into a single mound of dirt.

Could we have avoided the disaster? We'd come together where happenstance had arranged an encounter for us in the last strongholds of sorrow.

A good morning to you, o beautiful lady bearing a curse!

So here she was. How could I disengage from her eyes when all I wanted to do after that long absence was to look at her?

When she saw me, she made me think of a lemon tree whose blossoms had fallen off out of sheer surprise. The last place she would have expected to see me was an art gallery in Paris, at the exhibition of an artist whose existence – outside of a book, that is – she had always denied.

'Unbelievable,' she said.

'It's a life we owe to chance encounters.'

In a pleasant astonishment not without a tinge of alarm, she blurted out, 'O my God, I never would have expected to see you here!'

'What can I do if everything brings you back to me?' I asked with a twinkle in my eye. I was alluding to something she'd once said, namely, 'Everything brings me back to you,' which I'd corrected at the time, saying, 'And everything keeps me in you!'

She commented shrewdly, 'I thought you'd moved addresses since that time!'

'As you can see,' I quipped, dusting off my jacket, 'whenever I'm about to leave you, I stumble across you again!'

Then I continued, 'By the way, the nicest things that happen to us aren't things that we find, but that we stumble across.'

Here also I was echoing something she'd once said, namely, 'No love is more wonderful than the kind we find when we're looking for something else.'

How can you free yourself from a love that's taken you over to the point where it's infiltrated the ways you express yourself, and where one of the things you enjoy about it is unveiling language's mysteries?

The intoxication of being with her was a linguistic state of being. It was as though I were dancing with her through words: clasping her about the waist, making her fly through the air, scattering her, gathering her in. The steps our words took always found their rhythm from the very first sentence.

In every conversation we were a pair of dancers who went gliding over mirrors of ice in festive attire, our feet clad in the music of words.

One time she'd said, 'I dream of opening the door to your house with you,' to which I'd replied to the rhythm of a tango, moving her dreams two steps back, 'And I dream of opening the door... and finding you.'

However, life had reversed our roles for us. Here she was, opening the door of a gallery to visit an exhibition, and finding me. It wasn't time for a tango, but for a Viennese waltz, with its feverish spinning, its sentences with hands clasped around one another's waists, and its faltering first steps with their rapturous, interlocking declarations. It was time for the puckered lips of a woman who, during my absence, had turned thirty years (and a few more kisses) old, and who would need to add seven more kisses to reach the age of my sadness – an age documented in a certificate that took no account of my birth at her hands in a café one October thirty-first at a quarter after one in the afternoon.

With her, things always begin the way they end: on the brink of the last quarter of an hour!

She studied me in awkward surprise. After two years of being apart, we were hastily sizing each other up, and entering into a silence amid lengthy tête-à-têtes that had never been.

I asked her if anyone had come with her.

'No, I came by myself,' she replied.

'Well, then, I suggest that you take a look around the exhibit, and then we can have something to drink at the café across the street.'

I deliberately let her tour the exhibit on her own. I wanted to preserve the beauty of the distance, since this way I could see her clearly, and spy on that memory of hers that hung suspended on more than one bridge.

As I'd expected, it wasn't long before she headed towards that particular painting. I saw her stand in front of it for a long time, which wasn't surprising if she hadn't seen it for an entire ten years.

I went casually over to her. She was looking through the exhibit guide. I asked her if she'd liked the painting she'd been looking at.

As if to conceal some cause for suspicion, she said, 'I was just thinking how odd it was that the artist had sold it. I see a red "sold" sign on it.'

Seizing the opportunity, I asked her if she knew the artist.

'No, not at all. But it's most artists' custom to keep their first painting. Based on the date written on it, this was his first painting. In fact, there's more than a quarter-century gap between it and the rest of his work!'

'Were you interested in buying it?'

'I don't know,' she said after some hesitation.

Then she continued, 'In any case, it's been sold, and I'll have to choose another one. In any case, I can't concentrate on anything as long as you're with me, so I'll come again some other time to pick out a painting or two.'

Wanting to lure her into a confession of sorts, I said, 'I still can't believe we're together. What on earth would have brought you here?'

I, who didn't put much store by her answers, wasn't concerned about how to word my questions. It was enough for me to see how flustered she was, like a woman holding onto her skirt when the wind blows. She had the ability to captivate with a sudden silence in lieu of a confession that had nearly been sent flying by the winds of surprise. So, between two sentences that were retreating in deceit, she pulled down the skirts of language without a word.

'It was just a coincidence. My brother Nasser gave me a card announcing this exhibit since he knows I love art. I left France ten years ago, and from that time on I stopped following the local cultural scene.'

I couldn't understand why she would insist on denying this man's presence in her life at some earlier time. Was it because of his handicap? His age? Or was it just that, like all authors, she didn't like her characters to be exposed as real people?

It was obvious that Nasser hadn't made any mention of me, nor had Zayyan, of course, so that she thought I'd been at the gallery merely by chance. In view of the difference between the name of the artist and the name of the character in her novel, she may have thought I'd fallen for the lie, especially since she knew Zayyan was in the hospital and that, as a consequence, I couldn't possibly have seen him.

I guess that was the moment when a certain crazy idea was born in my mind, and I excitedly began planning out its details, having decided to pull a prank on her memory as huge as her denial!

When we were alone at the café, Hayat was very quiet, and seemingly distracted. As though she were recalling something, or expecting someone to come, she kept looking over at the gallery, which was visible to us through the café's front window on the other side of the street. She hadn't changed.

Her love existed in a kind of overlapping time zone: It was as though, when she was with you, she was carrying on with a man she'd loved before you, while getting ready to love the one who would come after you. She was in such a never-ending state of romantic attraction, she no longer experienced the kind of panic women feel at the beginning of a love relationship, or the bereavement experienced by former lovers when they've been left emotional orphans.

I, on the other hand, might take a full two years to mourn a love lost. How idiotic! How plebeian! How could I have had such patience with a woman for whom the end of a love affair is no different than the passing of royalty? No sooner has the king died than, with the announcement of his death, his successor is announced. No sooner is one love declared dead than the next man to ascend the throne of her heart is ushered in.

I once asked her why she'd written only one book. She replied sarcastically, 'There's only one love that I've ever put on mourning for. In order to write, you have to enter into a state of mourning for someone or something. Life gets shorter as we get older, and we've got no time for this sort of extravagant waste. Mourning is just a betrayal of life.'

Maybe what she meant was that loyalty to a single person is a betrayal of ourselves. However, she avoided saying so, since at the time, I'd happened to be the person she loved!

When the waiter brought our orders, I lit a cigarette and asked her, 'Have you written anything over these past two years?'

By means of this question alone, I could find out what had happened after me.

My question must have surprised her, at the very least for the way it anticipated questions to come. Clever woman that she was, I think she'd figured out our 'lovers' code'. So she knew that what I was actually asking her was whether she had put on mourning for me, if even for a while.

'No,' she replied in an absent voice.

She added nothing to this word, no justification that might have softened its impact. A pang went through me, as I took the confession I'd just received as an insult to our love. Hadn't there remained enough of the conflagrations of that lovely time to ignite words in a book?

Had she not really loved me, then? Was the only thing she'd loved in me Khaled Ben Toubal, the man I reminded her of and who, or so she had claimed, was one of her literary creations? Or was it Abdelhaq, the man she'd mistakenly imagined to be me, and who would have succeeded me to her heart's throne if death hadn't beat her to him?

One love passed her on to another, and she had no time for loss, the loss that fills a writer's inkwell.

After a long silence on my part, she asked me, 'What are you thinking about?'

'About a play entitled, *Mourning Becomes Electra.* Try doing a bit of mourning. You might end up writing some nice things.'

'I've quit writing novels. Writing novels is like gambling – it gives you a false sense of having gained something. While you're busy managing others' lives, you forget to manage your own. I mean, you forget to live. What a novel adds to others' lifetimes, it steals from its writer's. It's like frittering away a life on the pretext of managing its affairs.'

'So,' I asked acerbically, 'do you kill off your characters to save yourself the trouble of managing their lives?'

'There are characters who grow so big inside you, they don't leave you any room,' she quipped, 'so in order to survive yourself you've got no choice but to kill them off. Some novelists have died at the hands of their characters because they didn't expect that a creature of ink would be capable of murder.'

After a pause she continued, 'Take Khaled, for example. If I hadn't killed him off in a novel, he would have killed me. Every time I've measured another man against him, my situation's gotten more disastrous. He had to go. His beauty exposed others' ugliness, and unsettled my emotional life.'

I felt the urge to tell her that, in spite of it all, Khaled was still alive, breathing in Paris's air along with us. But I held my peace. It wasn't time yet for that confrontation.

Yet, for some reason unbeknownst to me, talking with her only made me want her more. A writer who's too busy devouring life to write any more novels will whet your appetite to devour *her*. Besides, her capacity for subterfuge gave me an added excuse to lure her into an encounter in which her novelistic masks would come falling off.

Here she was. And here I was, distracted by her, from her. I'd forgotten everything I'd ever held against her. I'd forgotten why we'd parted, and why I'd hated her. I wanted her now, without delay, and with the same extremity as before. I was going to say, 'Light the tunnel of anticipation by setting a time we can meet.' But I feared that this might come across as a kind of begging that wouldn't sit well with a woman who only liked men who found it next to impossible to express emotion. So I rephrased the thought in a form that would leave her no choice but to do what I wanted her to.

I said, 'What time will I see you tomorrow?'

'Are you in a hurry?'

'I'm in a state of plenitude.'

Then, as if to correct a deliberate slip of the tongue, I added, 'I've got a lot of words for you in my quiver.'

'Why dissipate yourself being prolix with me? What you've got in your quiver might be the stuff of a novel.'

She had a kind of innate womanly guile, the charm of a woman who conspires against you with your tacit approval. She was a difficult, seductive woman whose beauty resided in an impossible half that blocked the way to another half that might give you the mistaken impression that she was open to the possibility of fulfilling your desires.

She was the criminal by design, the charmer as if by accident. You made a pact of fidelity with her, knowing that you were concluding a bargain with a cloud, and that it would be impossible to predict where or when it would burst.

She was a woman who knew how to clothe herself in someone else's persona. She could identify herself with women who ran the gamut from the extremes of chastity to the extremes of wantonness, from the extremes of innocence to the extremes of criminality.

I said, 'Our conversations need to take place behind closed doors.'

'I don't like boring bed chatter.'

Ready with an answer I was sure would persuade her, I said, 'You won't get bored. I'm preparing you a bonfire for which you'll be the firewood.'

I uttered this statement with a smile on my face, since I alone knew what I meant by it.

Then, in a different tone, I continued, 'How can you endure this rain alone? We're in Paris. So, if you aren't defeated by your hankering for me, you'll be defeated by the weather forecast – unless, that is, you've brought someone in your luggage who can keep you warm!'

She sank for the first time into a long silence. Finally, as though she were talking to herself, she murmured, 'Shame on you.'

And she added nothing further. In her voice I detected a note of sadness that wasn't quite like her.

As for me, I felt the sadness of someone who's done harm to a butterfly, and I couldn't see any reason to have been mean to her. Maybe it was because I was so in love with her. Or maybe, since I realised I'd have her only for a short time, I couldn't restrain myself from this sort of amorous aggression.

'Forgive me,' I said contritely. 'I didn't mean to hurt you.'

After a pause she said, 'What hurts me is that you still don't realise how much I'd be willing to pay for a time together with you. My husband's spies are planted everywhere, yet I'm sitting with you in a café, not caring if I die because of you in some "accident of love". And if I haven't died yet, it's because I gave up on both love and writing, the two things my husband has never forgiven me for.'

As I took her hand to kiss it, her wedding band came into view, so I put it down and picked up the other one, planting a long kiss on it and murmuring as if to myself, 'My darling...'

As I withdrew my lips from her hand, I asked, 'How did he allow you to travel without him?'

'I came with my mother on the pretext that I wanted to see a gynaecologist who specialises in treating infertility. We're also here to meet with my brother Nasser. He's come from Germany especially to see us. I've been afraid my mother would die without seeing him again. This thought has become my constant dread. She's aged rapidly since he left.'

Still holding her hand, I said, 'How I've wished I could meet your mother. I've often thought of her as my mother, too, not just because I'm an orphan, but because I feel as though my body overlaps with yours somehow. Sometimes I feel as though we came out of the same womb. Other times I feel that your body is the one that brought me into the world, and that I have a right to settle there. Give me a nine-month residence permit inside your womb – I'm applying to your body for emotional refugee status!'

She smiled, her cheeks flushing like a virgin's. Some locks of hair fell out of place, and she looked as though she could be my little girl.

Sometimes what I loved about her was her brazenness, and other times, her girlish modesty. I loved that proud, self-contained femininity that you couldn't compromise unless you'd received permission born of passionate affection.

Unhurriedly brushing a strand of hair off her face, she said, 'With you I want to be eternally pregnant.'

'In that case,' I said jokingly, 'I won't be able to ask you to have a little girl who's pretty like you. Do you realise what a loss it would be for you not to be repeated in another female? The amount of femininity in the world would suffer a decline!'

'Rather, I know what a loss it is to run my fingers over my belly in search of you, and wonder why you still haven't penetrated me. You'd have to be a woman to imagine the grief of a womb that hasn't conceived by the one it loves. Only a woman could understand that.'

After a pause I asked her, 'Hayat, did you love me?'

'I'm not going to answer that. Your question is an insult to me, and my answer to it would be an insult to you. Feelings that beg to be expressed are half-lies. Verbal disclosures are a kind of psychological undressing that violates others' intimate spaces. This is something I learned from you. I used to beg you for some confession of your love, and you would say, "A mouth-watering verbal revelation is bound to be spiced with hypocrisy. Silence is the only thing that's free of all deceit."'

'So when did you memorise all that?' I asked, amazed.

'In the days I lived at the foot of your sofa with the patience of a cat, lapping up every word you uttered from the bowl of infatuation.'

I retorted with a chuckle, 'And when the cat was full, she'd turn me into a ball of yarn. Sometimes she'd play with me, and other times, she'd fray my strands with her claws. How many times did you dig your claws into my kindheartedness, then make my pain even worse by licking my wounds?'

We laughed together with the collusiveness of a lovely era past. When I saw her look at her wristwatch in an announcement that she was late, I said, 'I want to see you. We've got to arrange a time to meet.'

'I don't think I can outmanoeuvre both Nasser and Mama. One of them is bound to tag along wherever I go.'

'Why are you a novelist, then?' I asked, laughing.

Once I'd given her my mobile number, we parted in the café for fear that we might bump into one of the Algerians frequenting the exhibit.

I had her leave a few steps ahead of me, and as she was waiting for a taxi I headed for the Metro to go home, fearful of losing the beauty of a happy excitement that might give my secret away.

My other reason to be happy was that Françoise would be leaving on a trip the following morning. When I got back, I found her packing.

Exhausted after two days of working at the institute, all she wanted was to sleep so that she could get up early the next day.

I was glad she hadn't approached me for sexual attention. My mind was entirely on Hayat, and, unbeknownst to me, her mind was on another man!

I stayed up late that night watching television. I couldn't sleep. Then I thought of calling Nasser out of politeness to ask about his mother.

When I called, he welcomed me heartily as though he'd missed me, and insisted on inviting me for dinner the following Saturday at Murad's house, since his mother would be coming to make Constantinian food for them.

I asked him about her health. With a tinge of sadness, he said, 'The misery Ma went through at the hands of the French when my father was a wanted revolutionary leader was nothing compared to what she's suffering at this age on my account. Imagine an older woman having to endure the hardship of travelling to see her son because his home country has closed its doors in his face, and having to choose between his being dead, or homeless.'

I didn't want to tell him something that, on the pretext of consoling him, would only have made his pain worse.

What he had said reminded me of something I'd heard once about the mother of Ahmed Ben Bella who, despite her fragile constitution and tiny frame, astounded the French with her courage. When they imprisoned her son and brought her to visit him in order to destroy his morale and torment him with the sight of her, she surprised them with her reaction. When she saw him in shackles, her only response was to say, 'The free bird doesn't thrash about as if it were in a trap.' Later they realised that by quoting this proverb she'd been urging her son to be a mighty eagle, a predator, not a meek little sparrow that trembles with fright in the hands of the enemy.

Meanwhile, life was preparing another test for her. After Algeria's independence, Ben Bella emerged from the enemy's prison as a political leader, only to find that the prisons in his home country had opened their doors wide to receive him for another seventeen years. His ageing mother wasn't allowed to see her son until a full two years after his arrest. On that day, to humiliate her son, she was stripped naked and searched, then left to tremble with cold within sight of the revolution's guard dogs. Given her advanced age, she didn't hold up against the chill winds of history, and she died not long afterwards of misery and cold. And it all happened in full view of heartless spectators, and a homeland that could mutate mighty birds of prey into frightened sparrows.

In his prison cell, the eagle known as Ben Bella had become a trembling, orphaned sparrow now that his wings, whose feathers had grown in French prisons, were no longer able to carry him to his mother's funeral procession.

He would have to wait fifteen years before the prison doors were opened grudgingly once again and he could alight, brokenwinged, tearfully on her grave.

I don't know why, but somehow I suffered pain on the very day when I'd been the happiest. I had called Nasser in hopes of catching a whiff of his sister, only to find myself weeping over his mother. So haunted are we by our sufferings that we turn even love into sorrow.

The next day I got up early to have breakfast with Françoise, to give her the requisite warm send-off, and to receive her final instructions on how to manage household affairs in her absence. When I headed back to the apartment after carrying her suitcase to the front entrance, a strange feeling came over me as I locked glances with the doorman, who eyed me with a curiosity that betrayed a certain unspoken hostility.

I felt as though, rather than living in the apartment, I was hiding out there like some undocumented immigrant. I'd established an illicit relationship with this residence, and for as long as I skulked there I had to be careful not to attract the neighbours' attention. I wasn't to open the door for anybody since I wasn't 'anybody' in this place. Nor was I to answer the telephone for fear that 'he' might be on the line. After all, I was in the wrong place atop the mines of memory. And when that same telephone rang and rang without my answering it, I discovered that I'd been there at the wrong time, too!

The only thing I could muster any enthusiasm for was the project that had fallen to me given a certain bizarre intersection of chance happenings: I'd decided to lure Hayat to the house where I was staying as a way of forcing her to confess that once upon a time she had passed this way, and that a particular man actually existed.

She had once commented that memory has a variety of tricks, one of which is writing. But what she'd meant by 'writing' was 'lying'. By giving me the false impression that novel-writing always involves fantasy, she thought she could get away with smuggling this fact into a book. She who so loved to document her crimes of passion, how could she have failed to describe his house down to the last detail, including a certain statue of Venus in one corner of the living room, the paintings of hanging bridges on the walls, the balcony overlooking Pont Mirabeau, and the art studio whose shelves were piled high with the outcomes of years of toil? After all, she'd never imagined that one of her readers might, some day, be destined to reside in her book's secret chambers.

I was aware of what a privilege life had granted me. Consequently, I decided to spend my day at home, enjoying my detainment in the labyrinths of a novel into which I'd been thrust as one of its main characters.

Actually, something in me was anticipating her voice, something that kept waiting for some part of her, and this apartment was the only place I knew that was suited to the state of tension I was in.

I was waiting for her voice the way I was used to waiting for a photograph. When you're sitting on the bench of squandered time, not waiting for anything at all, you find that things are waiting for you, and life gives you a picture of a scene that will never be repeated.

When you wait without waiting, without knowing you're waiting, that's the moment when the picture comes. Like love, like a woman, like a telephone call, it comes when the place is filled with possibility.

I myself was filled with that house, living amid dust-covered objects that reached out and touched me in their noiseless din, reminding me that I was just passing through. So I got my camera and began, in my own way, to document my fleeting time in their presence. I'd grown accustomed to firing a stream of flashes at anything I felt was in danger of vanishing, as though I were killing it in order to rescue it.

I'd learned to seize fugitive moments and halt time's flow in a shot. A photo is a desperate attempt to embalm time.

When the roll of film was full, I was surprised to find myself feeling like a father. It was as though the camera that had been my life's companion had turned into a woman who was carrying my children inside her. The fleeting, mysterious moment when shadow and light intersect to create a photograph is no less miraculous than the instant of conception between a man and a woman.

I don't know why this idea occurred to me. Maybe it was because, given my orphan complex, I'd always been obsessed with women's bellies and breasts, in constant search of a womb to which I could entrust a child.

Like Venus, Hayat had the fresh resilience of a belly that's never carried a child, the sadness of a woman who coyly conceals the tragedy of her emptiness. Every time I had inter-course with her, I would pray to the gods of fertility to liberate the womanhood that had been taken by force in the beds of the military. In a never-ending state of erection, my memory rebelled against the idea of her womb growing old without revealing our secret.

One time I said to her jokingly, 'You'll never get pregnant by anybody but me. Since the death of Fascism, women have stopped conceiving under duress, capitulating to the brute force of their dictators. One time I read about a woman who said, "When I saw Mussolini passing by in his motorcade, I felt as though I'd conceived by him." Talk about the miraculous charisma of power! Now, by contrast, the fires of passion have melted the royal seals on princesses' closed wombs, and blue bloodedness has lost its appeal to would-be royal mothers.'

I was so preoccupied with her, I nearly forgot I was waiting for her.

I was still busy bringing her to mind when my heart jumped to the sound of the gadget that had been waiting for her voice.

I ran to look for my mobile where I'd left it in the bedroom.

'Good morning. I miss you! Why did you take so long to answer? Are you busy gathering firewood?'

How was it that, with so little, the gentle rain of her voice could awaken all those sweet storms inside me?

Lord, have mercy. I'm helpless before the power of a voice that, with a few words and half a laugh, launches a romantic attack on me!

Stunned with joy, and in a nod to memory, I replied with a name I used to call her. 'Madame, "bearer of lies",' I said, 'we won't be able to rekindle the flames without bearing more firewood.'

Rejoining with words from Ahmad Shawqi's play, *Qays and Layla*, she said, 'Woe be to thee! Hast thou come seeking fire, or to set the house on fire?'

'Stray kitty in the Paris rain, I'm the only hearth you have to warm you. Come, and let the house catch on fire!'

I wished I could have talked to her longer. Her voice had a body. It had an odour and a texture. It was all I needed to survive, all I needed to remain in a state of bliss.

She told me she'd had to sneak in a call to me while people were distracted with other things, and that she wouldn't be able to meet me that day because Nasser and her mother had her hemmed in on all sides. But then she shared an unexpected piece of good news that hit me like a joyous thunderbolt: 'It would be hard for me to see you during the day, since it wouldn't be right to leave Nasser and Mama alone. However, I've figured out a way I could spend tomorrow night with you. Imagine it being easier to see you for an entire night than for half an hour during the daytime!'

Not believing my good luck, I said, 'How did you manage to pull off a miracle like that?'

'It just fell into my lap – a gift of coincidence. But, in keeping with your advice, I used my novelistic talents to make it happen.'

With a giggle she went on, 'I used to waste my literary energy on ruses like this. But a novelist who can't come up with a lie that will fool the person closest to her will never succeed in marketing her lies in a book. Novel-writing takes daily practice!'

Laughing, I thought about how she couldn't possibly know I'd be bringing her to this house to confront her with a lie that hadn't fooled me – assuming, that is, that I was 'the person closest to her'.

'So,' I asked with excited curiosity, 'what's the idea you've based this novelistic ruse on?'

'It's a simple idea and, like all convincing lies, it's based on a bit of the truth. Mama's going tomorrow to the place where Nasser's staying to fix a Constantinian dinner for him and his friends, and she'll probably spend the night there. As a married woman, I can't go with her to a strange man's house and spend the night there. I can't stay alone at the hotel, either. So I've suggested that I spend the night with Bahiya, a relative of mine that I haven't seen for quite some time. She's actually my paternal cousin, whose house I stayed at when I was a student. She lives in Paris, but her husband is always away on business, and he'll be gone all week. I called her, and we've agreed to say that I'll be going to visit her. She's been my accomplice in mischief ever since we lived together ten years ago.'

I concluded that the gathering she'd mentioned had something to do with the dinner Nasser had invited me to at Murad's house. But I went on playing dumb, of course.

In a serious tone she added, 'I prefer that we not meet at my hotel. You choose the place, provided, of course, that there aren't any Algerians around.'

Laughing, I said, 'You can run, but you can't hide! They're everywhere – from the fanciest hotels to the seediest! So I suggest that you come to the house where I'm staying. That would be safer.'

'And where is this house?' she asked, as if to reassure herself that it was in a decent neighbourhood.

I wanted, of course, to avoid giving her the address. 'Don't worry,' I reassured her. 'It's in a quiet location on the West Bank of the Seine.'

'Give me the address, and I'll take a taxi there.'

'I prefer to wait for you in a café at the Metro exit and escort you there. What time do you expect to be here?'

'At around seven thirty.'

'I'll be at the Mirabeau Café at the Metro station exit from seven o'clock on.'

She was silent for a moment, as though the name of the café had aroused some sort of reaction on her part.

'Don't go on being like a frightened squirrel. We're off the Arab map of fear. Don't turn coward when life gives you a coincidence this wonderful.'

'Maybe it's because it's so wonderful that it scares me so much. We get used to the wonderful things in our lives being accompanied by a feeling of fear or guilt.'

Love for her was an exercise in danger, and it would have to remain thus. Simple though she was, she couldn't afford to take risks. In this respect, she was like all other women.

As I hung up the phone, I felt as though all the seasons of the year had passed through the vibrations of her voice in the course of a single conversation, and that I was lost between the sunshine of her laughter, the clouds of her silence, and the mist of her secret sadness.

That telephone call had stirred up conflicts born of emotions so unruly they bordered on the violent.

After her voice was cut off, an inexplicable sadness came over me. For all the happiness she brought me, she also had a way of unleashing waves of grief.

An old wish came back to me: if only her voice could be bottled up and sold in pharmacies so that I could buy it whenever I liked. I needed it to survive. I needed to be able to take it three times a day: once on an empty stomach, once before bed, and once whenever I had a fit of joy or sadness, as had happened just then.

Chapter Seven

To the right of memories, along the Left Bank of the River Seine, chairs awaited an encounter with coincidences, tables sipped evening ennui, and, at a café's front window in a corner prepared for two, I awaited her not far from an apartment that had come straight out of a book.

She was sure to come. After all, she had a lover here on pins and needles hotter than any fireplace, while I had desires with a pinch of cardamom, and black coffee brought to me by a neatly groomed, melancholic waiter.

I was sitting there daydreaming behind the glass of anticipation when suddenly her face illumined the place like a flash of lightning. I stood up to greet her and unthinkingly placed a kiss on each cheek, Paris being a place that lets you steal kisses in public.

She pulled out a chair and sat down across from me. Catching her breath, she said, 'I got lost in the Metro's mazes. I've gotten out of the habit of moving around in that crowded underworld! So what brings you here? I've never heard of this station before!'

I didn't believe her, of course. The only thing I could believe was the blank spaces between her lies, and I could see she needed a lot of suitcases to smuggle even one of them.

'Sorry. I thought you were good at getting around on the Metro.'

Dropping her purse on the chair next to her, she replied, 'For a minute there I was afraid you'd given me the wrong directions.'

'Of course not,' I said, grinning, 'though I'd love to go back down the wrong path with you!'

She studied me for a moment as though she were trying to decipher a signal I was sending her between the words. Then she said irritably, 'You still insist on talking to me in riddles!'

'Not at all,' I said with a laugh. 'I just meant that I'd lived a whole lifetime wrong, and the only right thing I ever did was to stumble across you.'

I'd contented myself with telling her half of what I meant. The other half, she'd discover later.

'Please,' she begged, 'don't force me to make any extra effort! I haven't got the strength to go rummaging around between the words. I'm worn out from making sure Ma and Nasser didn't change their minds and make me go with them to that dinner.'

When the waiter came to take her order, she said she didn't want anything, and that she preferred to leave the café.

Was she in a hurry for us to be alone together? Or was she nervous, apprehensive about some surprise I might have in store for her?

I paid for my coffee and we left.

She looked dazed, and seemed to be dawdling as she saw me following a route she was apparently familiar with.

I asked her if there was something bothering her.

'I've just forgotten what it feels like to walk down a street safely. I'm used to distrustful cities that wait outside your door and keep you under surveillance, whether out of curiosity or malice. It keeps you in fear's grip.'

We were turning down the street that led to the apartment when it started to rain all of a sudden. I asked her if she had an umbrella with her.

'No. I was in such a hurry, I forgot to bring one.'

'And I was so excited, I forgot to bring one, too! But that's all right. We're almost there.'

Teasing her about walking several steps ahead of me, I asked, 'Are you in a hurry?'

'I'm in a wet spot,' she replied a bit crossly as she covered her hair with her purse.

I picked up my pace as we approached the building, thinking about her oblique eloquence.

She stood beside me in speechless amazement as she watched me press in the secret code that opened the door to the building. I refrained from asking her why she was amazed, continuing to play dumb.

'Do you live here?' she asked.

'I've always lived on the side streets of your love,' I quipped.

Surprise seemed to have frozen her in place at the door. 'Come,' I said, pulling her along by the hand. 'Don't let your questions stop you short.'

Like someone who's been sleepwalking, then suddenly wakes up, she asked me, 'Where are we going?'

'You know the words from *Swan Lake*: "Come on tiptoe, placing a hand over your mouth lest you divulge the secret of the place to which I'm leading you, so that you can possess alone the jewels that stud your name."'

'Is this the time for *Swan Lake*?' she grumbled. 'I ask you a question, and you answer me with poetry!'

'Your presence always immerses me in lovely things!' I replied as we got into the elevator.

When the elevator door closed, she wasn't thinking about our first moment alone together. Instead her gaze was fixed on the elevator control panel.

Maybe she'd begun to realise which floor I was taking her to. However, she just kept staring at the control panel as though she were betting on the possibility that she'd guessed wrong.

Deliberately prolonging the obnoxious game of playing dumb, I pressed the surprise button, saying casually, 'Love always has a lofty presence, you know. It lives on the seventh floor.'

She didn't say a word, nor did I search her eyes for the effects of the shock produced by her collision with reality.

As I opened the door and turned on the lights, I felt her looking around the place to reassure herself that things were all right.

The game made me think of a situation where an artist refuses to acknowledge the person who inspired him to do a certain painting, and just when you end up believing that the idea behind the painting was his alone, the steps of fate lead you to where his secret lies hidden, and you can't resist the urge to confront him with his deception. This apartment, which had emerged from her book and matched her description of it down to the last detail, was perfectly suited to just such a confrontation.

I love that moment when I manage to silence a woman with an argument she would never have expected, then observe her naked before the truth.

I'd decided that as long as she wasn't evincing any obvious reaction, I'd take the game of playing dumb to its limit.

'Do you like the apartment?' I asked.

Choosing her words carefully, she replied, 'It has a nice cozy feel to it.'

Noticing her wet clothes, I added, 'On a day like this you should have brought an umbrella, or worn your fur coat.'

'I wore this jacket for fear that a fancy coat might cause me problems on the Metro. I hear that muggings and pickpocketing have been on the rise lately.'

'And who says you'll be safe here?' I asked as I placed a first kiss on her lips. 'There's nothing more dangerous than a lover who's been waiting for two years!'

With a kiss I swallowed her lipstick, leaving it to her to swallow her lies.

'I've missed you,' she said. 'I've waited so long for this day!'

As a matter of fact, she was still under the unsettling influence of the location, and didn't ask me how I had ended up in this house or what I was doing there.

I began studying her features following the surprise of the first kiss, which always leaves a person's face different than it was before.

Seeking relief from the embarrassment of the situation, I said, 'You get younger with every kiss. A few more, and you'll almost be back to twenty years old again!'

'And who told you I liked that age?' she countered as she headed towards the living room. 'Today I'm as old as your lips.'

'And tomorrow?' I asked with a touch of bitter sarcasm.

Surprised by the question, she replied, 'Tomorrow? I don't know. The afterlife isn't one of my preoccupations.'

'In that case,' I joked, 'I'll give you enough kisses to get you to hell in no time!'

I teased her as a way of alleviating the awkwardness of the first moments, though, if the truth be told, all I wanted to do was look at her.

I sat down on the sofa across from the fireplace and watched her as she made the rounds of the living room. She looked without comment at the statue of Venus and the paintings that hung on the walls.

I didn't want to interrupt her first private moment with memory. I was content just to gaze at her.

She was soaking wet. Something about her reminded me of Olga, my Polish neighbour, as she dried her hair in her white bathrobe.

Worried that she might get sick, I said, 'You could dry your hair in the bathroom.'

She smiled absently.

Before she headed for the bathroom, I remembered something and added, 'If you'd like to change your clothes, I have a dress you could put on.'

'Does it belong to the lady of the house?' she asked cattily.

She might have seen pictures of Françoise and her mother on the corner table in the living room.

Ignoring her provocation, I replied, 'No. I bought it for you.'

I left her standing in the middle of the living room and returned shortly with the black dress in its fancy bag.

As I handed it to her, I said, 'I hope you'll like it, and that it will fit.'

'When did you buy it?' she asked as she took it in astonishment.

'Believe it or not, I bought it more than two months ago, even before I expected to see you!'

She spread it out, obviously impressed.

'It's beautiful, really beautiful. How could you have thought of buying it for me? You must have ruined your budget!'

'Don't worry. It was a good emotional investment.'

'If I hadn't come to Paris and we hadn't seen each other, what would you have done with it, silly? Would you have given it to your wife?'

'Of course not. I bought it to bribe Fate. It's a love dress, and I'm happy to have you wear it, not somebody else.'

'And is there a somebody else?' she shot back with obvious womanly jealousy.

'No. However, it was you who taught me that we tailor every love from the fabric of a love that went before it.'

Without commenting, she went over to the mirror and held it up to herself.

'Black suits you,' I said.

Starting to put it back in its bag, she said, 'It's too pretty to wear in the house. It's a party dress.'

'And we're at a party. In Paris. Where will I see you in it if not here?'

She appeared convinced.

I suggested that she go into the next room and put it on.

She took a moment to study my face reflected before her in the mirror. Then, without a word, she took the dress and headed for the other room, to which she obviously knew the way!

Had I wanted to test her knowledge of the house? Or was I testing my patience with her, and punishing myself by having to wait for her as she bared herself to her memory in that other room?

I could have joined her out of impatience, or I could have suggested that she put it on in the living room. But, wanting to preserve the beauty of the moment, I did neither. Despite my body's hunger and haste, I took pleasure in postponing my pleasure, like when you have a piece of fruit you know is yours, but you put off taking the first bite.

I tried to make the wait easier by looking for a cassette tape suited to the occasion. The one I wanted was already in the recorder, so all I had to do was rewind it and press the button:

> In the name of God I begin to speak:
> Constantine is my passion.
> In my dreams I remember her
> As dearly as my mother and father.

I sat down with Constantine to wait for her, or so I thought, until she appeared around the corner like a black swan. It was as though whatever she put on, she wore nothing but her malaya, and what should I find but that she herself was... Constantine.

As she stood before me, I contemplated her peculiar, inexplicable appeal. She wasn't the most beautiful. She definitely wasn't the most beautiful. But she was the most alluring. She was the most splendorous. And this was something I couldn't explain any more than I could explain the uniqueness of her voice, which could cause a cosmic disturbance with a single word.

As she made a half turn in the dress to the rhythm of the music, she asked in our Constantinian dialect, 'Do you like it?'

'Do I like it? What a question!' I said, a tremendous longing welling up inside me. 'I like *you*!'

I'd always loved the way she moved, the way she turned, the way she stopped, the way she bent down, the way her shawl cascaded over her hair, the way she lifted the hem of her dress with one hand as though she were holding onto a secret, the way she went, the way she came...

During the days when she would visit me disguised in her mother's cloak for fear of curious stares and criminals who lay in wait for unsuspecting women, I remember telling her that I loved her in that black cloak. Her response was, 'You have to love what you're wearing in order for it to love you. Otherwise, it will reciprocate your apathy and dislike, and you'll look ugly in it. Some people aren't on friendly terms with what they wear, so they look unattractive even in their elegance, while others positively glow because they're wearing an outfit they like, even if it is simple and the only one they have.'

So, did she look so appealing in that dress because she loved it?

Or did she love the appeal of the situation itself, and the oddness of the fact that we were meeting in a house that took her back ten years to her first emotional labyrinth?

Mingled with sighs of longing for Constantine, the words of the song were an expression of our losses. With the rhythm of its tambourines, the music charged the atmosphere with fear – the fear of desires that generate emotions so violent that the urge to dance feels like a passage into another sorrow.

Being in an 'emotional preserve' off the map of Arab fear gives you permission to test out your madness. So I said to her, 'Hayat, dance for me.'

My request surprised her, and her reticence surprised me. With the bashfulness of Constantine's women in a time past, she said, 'I can't. I've never danced in front of a man before.'

Responding with a manly gallantry to match her womanly timidity, I said, 'I'm not just a man. I'm your man. And if this beauty isn't for me, then who is it for?'

It was as though I'd uttered the password her body had long awaited, since I don't think anyone before me had asked her such a question.

With the modesty of a Constantinian woman when she dances for the first time in the presence of a man, her body began to sway gently to and fro. She wasn't writhing. She wasn't twisting. There was nothing provocative about her movements. Her power to excite lay in her oblique allure, in a womanliness that danced beneath a din of muslin as though it were weeping, and to a song laden with a burden of sorrow.

The atmosphere was filled with the buds of wild, deferred passions that had blossomed at last outside the gardens of fear, but in a house so entangled with our sorrow that we found ourselves unable to rejoice there.

It seemed to me that, given the impossibility of our being joyful, we were making love through dance with the ecstasy of a transcendent sadness.

It was the first time I'd witnessed a dance that stokes the flames of grief. I sat across from her in silence: so sad, I was rapturous, so rapturous, I was sad, so hungry for her that I was intoxicated with her. My blood frothed within me, like grapes off the vine being pressed beneath her feet.

I loved the eloquence of her feet, dyed with men's blood, in every desire a bit of masked violence. Was this why I'd been afraid of her heels? Or was it because dancing in high heels didn't befit Constantine? I said, 'Take off your shoes, Madame. In dancing, as in worship, we don't need shoes.'

I'd noticed Venus standing erect, wearing her eternal smile. The fact that she was a goddess didn't exempt her from the requirement to appear barefoot in the presence of Louis XVIII. The day she was brought to him so that he could receive her in a manner that befits a goddess of beauty, one of his minions felt it his place to demand that she humble herself and perform the rites of obedience by coming to him barefoot as in the ancient myths.

Since her left foot was covered by a piece of fabric that hung from her waist, it's said that restoration experts at the Louvre replaced her right foot with one that had no shoe on it.

But Venus has been getting cheekier ever since. Never once have they been able to get her statue to bow, or her amputated hands to clap in applause for a ruler or monarch.

She wished she could come down off her pedestal and dance to the music herself. However, a Constantinian dance isn't done by a half-naked woman with a shawl tied around her hips. In fact, the women of Constantine have such a solemn presence, their dance is almost a rite of worship.

O goddess of beauty, it's far more beautiful than a striptease, too marvellous for words!

So grieve a little, my lady of stone. (We can't dance with some-body who's happy.) Wear a dress of velvet embroidered with threads of gold, a dress too heavy for you to put on alone, and too beautiful for no one to see you in it. Around your waist wrap a belt whose gold links your mother has spent a lifetime collecting so that you can don it on your wedding night. Around your hennaed feet draw a pair of ankle bracelets whose jangling can be heard when you walk, and only one of which can be seen when you're seated. Then come and ride in the gently swaying howdah of desire and learn to dance like a Constantinian.

Hayat bent down to take off her shoes. Then she continued dancing with her feet, and her desires, bared to the rhythm of the ankle bracelets in my head.

I was so enthralled with her that I'd forgotten about the possibility that we might be disturbing the neighbours. So when the telephone began ringing insistently in the bedroom, I expected it to be somebody calling to complain about the music.

In keeping with Françoise's instructions, I made no move to answer it, but just looked at my watch instead. It was a quarter after nine, past the hour when civilised folk put up with loud parties.

The tape was about to end, and I went over to the recorder to lower the volume.

As she sat down across from me on the sofa, she asked, 'Aren't you going to answer the telephone?'

'No.'

'Maybe there's somebody who insists on talking to you,' she suggested cattily. 'Letting the phone ring off the hook is something women tend to do more than men.'

Ignoring her insinuation, I said, 'Lovers, like worshippers, don't interrupt their prayers to answer the telephone.'

'They don't interrupt their prayers to look at their watches, either – unless, of course, they're expecting a telephone call!'

I laughed at her jealousy-driven logic. Taking my watch off and setting it on a nearby table, I said, 'On the contrary, time is a worshipper's sole preoccupation since, like the lover, he's afraid his hour will suddenly come upon him. Every love confronts us with the fear of death. Time is lovers' obsession even though, like the dead, they don't need a watch. After all, by entering into love, they've exited time as we know it!

'So,' I continued. 'I've taken off my watch, and I challenge you not to look at yours again, either!'

'Damn you,' she retorted, laughing. 'You always beat me without the slightest effort!'

Drawing her towards me, I corrected, 'But it does take an effort to counter your emotional inanity!'

I gave her a protracted kiss, a kiss so late in coming it would have to make up for a two-year wait. Nothing but a kiss can restore a lifetime that's slipped out of your grasp even though you've been wearing a watch on your wrist the entire time!

I felt the urge to ask her whether anybody had ever kissed her on this same sofa before. However, I already knew the answer, so I replaced this question with another, more urgent one.

'Hayat, has another man kissed you since me?'

Surprised by the question, she replied with a cunning laugh, a rainy laugh whose storminess I ignored.

In clarification, I said, 'I don't want a novel. It doesn't matter to me who he was, or how, or when. All I want to know is whether it happened or not.'

She usually didn't tell the truth until there was something in the truth that would cause me pain, and for once I hoped she would lie.

I was expecting an answer from her, but all she had for me was some quick-fix words, like bandages you apply in a hurry to staunch a wound.

Thinking that another question would exonerate her, she said, 'You once said that intelligence was a kind of "question-sharing". So let me be intelligent and ask you: What relationship do you have with the woman whose pictures are all over this house?'

I laughed at her question. Intelligence to her wasn't 'question-sharing' but, rather, 'question-reversal'. I'd brought her to this place to force her to confess that Khaled actually existed, and here she was reversing our roles and interrogating me about Françoise!

I decided to throw the hot embers of jealousy back her way as fast as she had thrown them my way. Interestingly, she still didn't expect me to have met Khaled, or even to know anything about him, since she thought he had left this house years before. She had, however, become acquainted with Françoise through the paintings of her that covered the walls, and she didn't understand how this woman could have stolen the two most important men in her life.

'She's a friend I've been staying with for the past month.'

Then I continued spitefully, 'After you and I parted, I fell into more "womanholes". But in every one of them, I stumbled upon you!'

'So, then, there's no need to ask you what you've done in my absence,' she said with a laugh that concealed a seething jealousy. 'And since you've stumbled upon me in every hole, I imagine you've spent a lot of time on the ground. Have you enjoyed yourself?'

She was a one-woman intelligence bureau that required you to file a report on every encounter with every woman you'd made love to before her. And like all intelligence agencies, she found satisfaction in scrutinizing every last detail.

Wanting to go on causing her pain, I ignored her curiosity. After all, she knew that any story that doesn't divulge its details is a romance, and that passing flings whisper their secrets into the ears of beds that have no memory.

Maybe this was why she'd never spoken of her love for either Khaled or Ziyad. Maybe it had been a love too big and beautiful to be described anywhere but in a book.

The more certain she became of my infidelities, the more passionate she became towards me. As I reflected on the matter, I stumbled upon a remarkable irony: that a man's loyalty to a single woman makes him all the more desirable to others, who make it their aim to bring him down and that, if he does fall, his unfaithfulness to her makes her want him all the more! I remembered Khaled who, like me, might have lost Hayat in the past precisely because he'd been too loyal to her. He'd become worthy of her jealousy only after being snatched up by Françoise, just as he'd become an artist worthy of note in Algeria only after leaving it and being snatched up by Parisian art galleries.

So, those who say we need little lies in order to preserve the truth ought perhaps to add that we need a bit of betrayal to preserve fidelity, whether to a homeland or to a woman.

Over supper we sat opposite a painting of a bridge. Wanting to make good of the situation, I tried to lure her into a conversation about Khaled.

I said, 'There's always been a bridge nearby whenever we've been together. Do you like this painting?'

Seemingly surprised by my question, she replied, 'I don't like bridges any more. Ever since Uncle Ahmed was assassinated on my account when we were on a bridge, I've hated them, especially since

I have a grandfather who committed suicide by throwing himself off the Sidi Rached Bridge. Even though his death didn't have anything to do with me, I still think of it now and then. Yesterday, for example, as I was walking past the Eiffel Tower, I thought about how we never hear of anybody committing suicide by throwing himself off a tower. When somebody wants to kill himself, he doesn't look for the highest place to jump from. Instead, he looks for a place that's full of life's hustle and bustle. That's why a person might throw himself off a bridge, since he wants us to witness his death. He wants to use the life force around him to destroy life. He thinks life might commit suicide with him since, in spite of every-thing, he doesn't believe it will go on after he's dead.'

She seemed more beautiful when she was talking about some-thing serious. So I tried to draw her into a conversation on another serious topic.

'If you hate bridges,' I said, 'then why are all your novels full of them? Can you explain this riddle to me?'

Resorting again to her usual sarcastic equivocation, she said, 'Proust once said something to the effect that explaining the details of a novel is like leaving the price tag on a gift. Like him, I don't offer explanations for anything I've written!'

'Of course not,' I said jokingly. 'I can see you're a woman who abides by the etiquette of gift-giving!'

'By the way,' I went on, 'the reason I asked the question was that I've bought a painting of a bridge by Zayyan, and I was intending to give it to you.'

'Please,' she broke in, 'don't do that. I might never hang it in my house.'

Sounding to myself like Françoise, I argued, 'I was going to give it to you so that you could hang it on the walls of your heart.'

'There's no room to hang anything on the walls of my heart any more.'

That was my last attempt to get her to talk about him, and afterwards I started to feel depressed.

Had I really loved her? Or had I loved the pain I felt in her presence? Here was a woman I didn't want, but that I didn't want to recover from. The bouts of suffering I experienced because of her had a cleansing effect that seemed almost to elevate me to the stature of a prophet.

Noticing the sadness that had come over me, she said, 'Don't be so down. This dress from you is present enough. So, since you like the painting, keep it for yourself. Forgive me. It's just that I've started to feel as though bridges are bad luck.'

I was thinking at that moment about how, after every time of pleasure, love would count up all the children I hadn't had by her. But after every deprivation, literature would rub its palms together in delight over a novelistic creation to come. This woman, who had shirked her literary duty and been content instead to 'be written', was, by virtue of being deprived of me on this day, going to give birth to her most beautiful piece of writing ever. I'd made up my mind that her pen wouldn't emerge from this house – his house – unscathed.

After supper I set out a basket of fruit and a bowl of strawberries, which I'd bought because I knew she liked them. As I put them on the table, I said teasingly, 'Beware of strawberries. Even though they're unarmed, they might spark a world war. I read somewhere that on the evening of June 5 1944, the radio station of the French resistance in London overseen by De Gaulle during the German occupation broadcast an encoded message that said, "Arcine loves strawberry jam." This was an announcement that the Allies had landed their armies on the shores of France!'

'Really?' she said, amazed.

'Don't worry.' I said, 'Their formidability doesn't lie in their strength but in their seductive red colour. Maybe that's why it's so hard to resist them when you look at them. Unlike other fruits, strawberries don't worry about protecting themselves with a rind or a peel. They're a fruit without a veil, so to speak, which is also why they go bad so fast.'

Her eyes followed my hand as it dipped a strawberry into the sugar bowl. Feeding it to her with a deliberate slowness, I said, 'I wonder who it was that first associated apples with sin. Sin isn't something that's munched on. It's something you're fed, bite by bite, and pleasure comes in the grey area between the two acts.'

By the second strawberry I'd stopped talking. I wanted to teach her the virtues of silence in the presence of this splendid fruit.

I left it to her mouth to go on thinking about a pleasure that can't last. Otherwise, I feared that, like Zorba, we might have to vomit it up in order to recover from it, since overindulgence in pleasures is a kind of Greek tragedy.

But had she realised that I was preparing her for a suspended pleasure, and that I was feeding her the fruit of farewell?

I hadn't thought love would dare abandon us here where it had led us. On the other hand, could it really have caused something to happen between us in a house teeming with the ghosts of lovers who hadn't had the time to change their sheets and gather up their things?

She wasn't herself, and I wasn't myself. We spoke a language that wasn't ours, and we were trying so hard to seem intelligent that we said stupid things. We would speak, then fall silent all of a sudden for fear of saying more than half the truth, reserving the other half of it for our pain.

We spent the whole evening resisting the weariness of questions, fighting off the drowsiness of replies. But wasn't our patient endurance entitled to a bed on which to rest our deferred desires?

A woman whose scent and nightgown I once couldn't go to sleep without, I now couldn't go to sleep with, nor did I know what I'd do when she was gone.

There'd been a time when I would have tried to get her to stay, saying, 'Don't leave! Every member of my body feels like an orphan when you're gone.' And now I was an orphan in her presence. Everything in me wept over her, and she couldn't see.

As I lavished her with breathtaking pleasure, I used to say, 'I'm going to spoil you with pleasure until you're no use to any man but me!' And when the two of us parted, I didn't think I'd be any use to any other woman. But now I'd discovered that I was of no use even to her any more. So, had I lured her here so that I could issue a death certificate for a love that had been alive when we were apart?

She lay down next to me, a woman defused. As I drew her into my arms like a meek little girl who'd come to me for protection, I thought back to the time she used to ask, terrified, 'Will you live with me?'

'I'll nest in you,' I would reassure her as my head fidgeted in search of the warmest place on her chest.

With a lover's terror she would press me, 'Will we really always be together?' to which I would reply with a lover's naiveté, 'Of course we will.'

A sudden fear of losing her came over me as I mutely repeated the same movement in search of a place for my head on her chest. My head came up against her black muslin dress, which she hadn't taken off. I sensed that Death would steal one of us away from the other, and that we would never see each other again.

Something Nasser had once said came back to me: 'What if her husband arranges a "clean" death for her, or what if she's assassinated by henchmen, for example?'

What worried me wasn't the thought that I might die, but the punishment of living after she was gone.

The thought of her actual death was a revealing test of my love for her. You can't realise how much you love someone unless you envision the ordeal of her absence.

An idea I'd benefited from during the days of assassinations and friends' deaths was that in order to love those around me in a better way, I should imagine that every time I saw them, I was seeing them for the last time.

The day I tested out the effect her actual death would have on me, I nearly died myself. My heart started racing, I became short of breath, and I thought I was done for. I dialled her number, then hung up as soon as she answered, since I'd just wanted to make sure she was alive. We hadn't spoken for a long time, but when I got my breath back I felt hostile towards her, since I saw that Death might snatch me away without her knowing, and she would go on squandering words that she'd deprived me of when I was alive to build a monument over my tomb in a novel.

We lay with our clothes on in Françoise's room, surrounded by paintings of her.

As if she were about to cry, Hayat clung to me and asked, 'Don't you love me any more? Are you thinking about her?'

I didn't reply.

In situations like this, words don't make it to their destination alive. It's only the ones you don't say that escape the stray bullets of divulgence.

I held her close, kissed her and said, 'Go to sleep, sweetheart. And may you wake to the writing of a book!'

We woke the next morning to the disaster of light.

As when you're developing film in a darkroom, light was a disaster.

'What time is it?' she asked in a panic.

'I don't know,' I bantered. 'On orders from you, I decided not to look at the clock!'

She glanced over at a clock on the bedside table. 'Oh, my God!' she shrieked. 'It's eight fifteen!'

She jumped up and headed for the bathroom, straightening her dress as she went.

Just like that, the time had run out: with a cunning day lying in wait for a happiness that, still yawning, had yet to wash its face, an unmade bed after a night of love that wasn't, and her scent's fleeting passage through the bedchamber of another woman.

She put her clothes on. Then, as she put the black dress back in its bag, she said, 'Could you call for a taxi for me?'

'Stay to have morning coffee with me. Then go.'

'I can't. I prefer to get back now. It's safer that way.'

It made me really sad to hear her say this, I'd waited so long for a morning that I could begin with her.

As I escorted her out to wait for the taxi with her, I complained, 'What's the use of modern technology if we still haven't been able to devise a machine that stops time? How I wish we could have had breakfast together some morning!'

205

'And what's the use of inventing a machine to stop time if we're going to spend the time we gained on nothing but having supper and breakfast?' she rejoined in a tone that betrayed the bitterness of her disappointment.

I liked her astute riposte, which I received with a silent smile. She was right.

I put my hand in my jacket pocket to warm it from the cold, only to find the chocolates Zayyan had given me when I visited him in the hospital.

Just then I had a sneaky idea that gave me a feeling of smug satisfaction. I was still thinking about the best way to carry it out when I saw a taxi coming down the street in our direction. All I had time left to do was kiss her goodbye and give her a couple of them with the words, 'Here are some chocolates that were given to me by a friend I visited at the hospital. They'll tide you over.'

She stood there for a moment staring at the two pieces of chocolate. She was sure to recognise them from their distinctive brand, but she didn't say anything.

She got in the taxi in stunned surprise, yet without understanding how I'd ended up in Zayyan's hospital room, or how the chocolates I'd given her had ended up in my pocket.

As I walked back to the house, I felt the elation of someone who's won a gruelling chess match at the last moment. However, it was an elation tinged with a painful bitterness, the kind you feel when you realise something beautiful in you has died.

Don't be sad, I told myself. She hadn't come to stay, but just to make you aware of the enormity of her departure. What can you do against a woman who approaches love with a magician's paraphernalia, who contrives deceptive arts especially for you, who turns things upside down in front of you, concealing some things, causing others to appear, and turning everything around you into a big illusion? She puts you in a glass box and, in a dazzling magical display, splits you in two, one half being you, and the other half being a copy of another man. Then she puts you back together again in a book.

Sorceress that she is, you don't know whether you've emerged from her hands rich or poor, happy or unhappy. Are you you, or somebody else? Have you come out of her magic hat a white dove, a frightened rabbit, or tear-stained coloured scarves?

As I put my watch back on, it occurred to me that Love is a magician who begins his show with the illusion of stripping his victims of their wristwatches. Is it only when the false-hoods of magic and conjurers' tricks vanish that we can look at the clock?

It was nine thirty on Sunday morning. Drinking bitter black coffee alone at Love's funeral, I was confronted with a temporal vacuum I didn't know how to fill on such a rainy day.

I put on some music, then began covering the tracks of what hadn't happened now that my visitor had left, slamming dream's door behind her. I began by inspecting the bedroom. I'd always hated odourless beds, and women who are obsessed with hanging out their laundry for everyone to see. This time, however, I would have to take precautions against women's ability to sniff out betrayal, since Françoise would be back the next day.

When we review our lives, we find that the nicest events were the ones that happened by chance, and that big disappointments always come on the lush carpets we've rolled out to receive happiness.

I decided sorrowfully not to plan for anything any more, with the exception, of course, of moving out of the apartment before Zayyan's discharge from the hospital the following Wednesday. I would have to be sure not to leave any telltale signs of my having passed this way. While I was thinking about it, I went to get the tapes of Constantinian songs so that he wouldn't find them in the recorder.

While I was thinking about all these details, I remembered that I hadn't visited him for a couple of days. I also recalled how, as he handed me the chocolates, he'd said he would have preferred that they'd brought him some *zalabia* or *qalb al-lawz*.

'But Ramadan's still a long way off!' I teased him.

'True. But being sick is like fasting. When you're sick, you spend your time craving all sorts of food, especially the ones you associate with childhood or nostalgic memories.'

I decided to go to one of the Moroccan neighbourhoods that don't recognise French holidays and buy him some Algerian sweets before going to the hospital. It seemed the best possible way to spend a Sunday, especially since I was feeling increasingly guilty towards him.

I bought him a small box of dates and a loaf of Algerian flat-bread. Then, when the vendor told me that a certain lady made these loaves every day and that they ran out fast, I bought one for myself.

I was astounded at this world I'd known nothing about: another Algeria that had been transported whole, complete with its products and customs, to a neighbourhood in Paris occupied by brown-skinned faces. It made me think of a sarcastic remark Murad had once made, that, 'Apart from your mother and father, you can find anything in this country!'

208

After that I stopped at a humble-looking café that claimed to serve 'Royal Couscous', and since I was so hungry I managed to convince myself that it was so. In actuality, I'd also stopped there because I wanted to kill some time while I waited for visiting hours to start.

I got to the hospital at around two o'clock, and it was unusually busy because of all the visitors that come on holidays.

I was happy to have come, since this way, Zayyan wouldn't feel even lonelier on this day in particular. I was also happy about my 'homemade cargo'. It was the first time I'd brought him food instead of newspapers, which only made him feel more careworn.

I knocked on the door, excited at the prospect of surprising him. Then I opened it as usual and took a step inside the room. But to my surprise, I found his bed occupied by an elderly woman hooked up to an IV. Emaciated and wan, she cast me a vacant stare which, when she caught sight of me, turned to a pleading expression as though she were asking for something that she couldn't put words to, and which I couldn't identify.

For a moment I stood there looking at her in a daze. Then I apologised and quickly left the room.

I went to the nurses' station on the floor to ask about the patient in Room 11. I tried to calm down, reminding myself that they might have taken him to do some tests or X-rays. Or they might just have moved him to another room. I remembered him telling me more than two weeks earlier, 'You might not find me in this room, since I may be moved to another ward,' to which he'd added jokingly, 'I'm a bed-hopper around here!'

I expected the nurse to tell me his new room number. Instead, though, she asked me if I was a relative of his. 'Yes,' I replied.

'We called the telephone number we have yesterday evening to inform you that there had been a sudden deterioration in his condition. We left a voice message asking his relatives to come, but no one contacted us. We called the number again this morning, but there was still no answer.'

Between terror and haste, I asked her, 'When was that?'

'At around ten thirty this morning.'

That was the time when I'd been out shopping for food.

Referring to a large notebook in front of her, she said, 'The first call was made at nine fifteen last night.'

'And would it be possible for me to see him now?' I asked her anxiously.

With the tone of someone who's had years of training in consoling strangers, she said, 'I'm sorry, sir. He's deceased.'

I felt as though she'd uttered the news in Arabic. My heart had translated it instantaneously into the language of tragedy, reducing the entire sentence and the dutiful words of condolence that followed it to a single, five-letter word – *death* – that descended upon me like a thunderbolt. I couldn't understand how five letters strung together in that context could be so painful. It was as though the 'h' at the end was nothing but a hearse.

The possibility of his death had been there. But I hadn't expected it to come this fast, or with this particular timing. All these coincidences taken together were too absurd to be mere happenstance. Rather, they had the insistence of Fate about them.

Moved, the nurse said, 'It's painful to think that he died just two days before he was scheduled to be discharged. He seemed so happy about leaving. I myself was surprised when someone told me this morning that he'd spent last night in the intensive care unit.'

After seeing me stand there stunned for a few moments without saying a word, she asked me if I wanted to see him. I told her I didn't. She handed me a paper to sign if I intended to receive his things. After opening the closet and glimpsing the box of fancy chocolates on top of a pile of his clothes, I told her I preferred to leave that until later.

I left the hospital in a state of emotional paralysis, as though my tears had been stored in a freezer that now contained what had once been 'him'.

I took the Metro laden with my bag, with all the things I'd brought him but which he no longer needed.

Wanting to be rid of it, I tried giving it to a homeless man at one of the Metro stations. Suspicious, he showed no enthusiasm, preferring that I give him a ten-franc coin that he could buy some wine with. So I ended up giving him the bag and ten francs to boot, to persuade him of my good intentions.

The master of irony and ambiguous silence, he hadn't given me a chance to tell him the final lie I'd prepared to justify being too occupied to come see him.

Maybe he'd needed to hear the things I'd kept to myself for fear of hurting him. Maybe he'd needed the truth. So by his death he'd exempted me from the need to go on lying. He'd decided to pass on to his spiritual 'bed' while I was occupying his earthly one.

He'd given me his house, his women, his things, yet he hadn't left me a chance to give him even a few pieces of *zalabia*, thereby to fulfil the final, simple wish of someone who was fed up with life in a foreign land and who had nothing left but his hunger for home.

I recalled his sardonic air, and that distracted presence that precedes absence's completion. There were so many things I would have said to him that day if it hadn't been for the fact that, since the time when all this blank space came between us, I'd grown weary of words. And I wondered how long he'd been headed for the realm of wordless silence.

As I walked into the apartment, I felt the full weight of the calamity, the shock of reality that pushes you under the wheels of a train you boarded with the intention of dreaming. I flung myself onto the living room sofa, exhausted as a race horse.

First I had to stop running for a bit, to sit down and figure out what had led me to this house. I who'd amused myself by trifling with literature, had I unknowingly been trifling with fate?

The situation was so bizarre, it had left me completely disoriented. I began reflecting on the scene as though I weren't its main actor, and as though I'd seen it at some time in the past.

When I read this artist's life story, I'd found myself identifying with him in so many places, I wished I could repeat his life as intelligently as it deserved to be repeated. But who can claim to be intelligent over 'what is written' – the predetermined fate that, for me, had started with a book that no one can read and come out unscathed?

Was that where the curse had come from? Or had it come from Hayat (whose name means 'life')? In keeping with the Arabs' custom of calling what they see to be evil by a name that conveys its opposite, she was a woman who was the very converse of what her name signified.

Or did the curse lie in the bridges, one of which still hung across from the sofa on which I lay? It was here that Zayyan had confronted the reality of the death of Ziyad, who had missed being Zayyan's match by a mere three letters.

In the presence of these bridges, I burst into dance to the rhythm of the one-armed Zorba on the day they informed him of the assassination of his only brother.

Is it mere coincidence that bridges are constructed from cement, a substance that, like someone plotting against you, conceals a dark rage and unspoken evil? For a long time I've been suspicious of bridges' intentions – ever since I noticed a resemblance between bridges and escapees, since they both have two opposite sides to them, and you don't know which side they belong to.

But Zayyan wasn't an escapee. Rather, he was someone who wanted to facilitate the escape – the liberation – of what he thought to be a homeland.

How stupid of the man! Between what he thought to be a bridge and what the bridge thought to be a homeland lies your dead body. After all, a bridge isn't measured by the distance that separates its two ends, but, rather, by the distance that separates you from the abyss beneath it.

When you're born atop a rock, you're doomed to be a Sisyphus whose lofty dreams doom you to a lifetime of towering losses.

We who climbed the mountains of illusion, who picked up our dreams, slogans, projects, writings and paintings and carried them, panting, to the peak, how have we rolled back down the slopes of defeat one generation after another? And who will pick up all we've dropped in the foothills?

When France, after standing meekly for seven years outside the gates of this citadel as well fortified as an eagle's nest, at last entered Constantine, the city's cavalrymen, unaccustomed to the ignominy of captivity, jumped off the bridges on horseback, returning to the valley's womb. Death by jumping off those steep slopes was the final victory for these men whose sole source of pride was that they were sons of the rock.

With them the era of beautiful death came to an end, and Wadi al-Rimal became a sewer bed for the offal of history where, along with the city's refuse and news of its respectable thieves, floated the corpses of its beautiful, wretched sons.

Nothing can prevent you from climbing 'the bridges of death', not even the 'safety belt' with which, after too many cases of suicide, they wrapped the bridges' waists. The railing might prevent you from looking down on death, but it can't prevent death from looking down on you where you are in the depths of your failures.

Suddenly, like Hayat, I'd begun to consider these paintings a bad omen, and I felt as though my sitting in front of them was a silent provocation of a fate I had no strength to face.

I was glad that I'd be leaving the apartment soon, and that the paintings would stay where they were. Then I remembered the painting I'd bought, and which would remain in the exhibit until it ended. I thought of having Françoise bring it. Then I thought about how strange it would be for me to travel with Zayyan's corpse in the company of that painting. My stream of consciousness finally brought me to my suitcase, which I needed to pack, and to Zayyan's things, which I would have to sort through quickly, since I didn't know when my flight to Constantine would be.

I found myself recalling what I'd experienced two years earlier after Abdelhaq's assassination. I'd had to get my things out of his house, where I'd stayed from time to time during that period when journalists had to keep constantly on the move. Abdelhaq himself hadn't had a fixed address since the time he began feeling himself in danger.

Maybe things had been easier back then, since my only concern had been to gather my own things, whereas I'd left to his wife the miserable task of taking care of his. Even so, I'd been pained on account of all the things Hayat had brought. Through successive visits, the house had come to be occupied both by Abdelhaq's humble possessions and by those other, high-class items that she used to smuggle out of her house. She pitied a house that was such a far cry from the opulence of her own residence, not realising, of course, that she was furnishing not my home but my friend's!

At first I'd been planning to explain the situation to her. But then I'd started to enjoy the romantic misunderstanding we'd gotten ourselves into, and I was tempted to hold on to the ambiguity that had brought us together.

Whenever he passed through, Abdelhaq could see how often she'd visited by the new additions to the house, from beautiful towels, elegant sheets and a bathrobe to crystal ashtrays and kitchen utensils. I'd gotten used to seeing her arrive laden with everything she could get her hands on at home, including even imported cheeses, chocolate bars, and packs of cigarettes. In fact, so incorrigible was she in her sentimental criminality that she once gave me some clothes and jewellery she'd bought for my wife!

She was generous in everything: the way she worried about you, the way she busied herself with you, the way she craved you, the way she pleasured you, and even the way she caused you pain.

It was the kind of adoring generosity that, when you lose it, you feel the same ache you felt when you were orphaned the first time, since you realise there isn't another woman in the world who will ever love you to the same degree, or in the same way. You can see that during your infatuation with her she wrought havoc in you with her wanton ardor and liberality. She corrupted you, ruined you, pampered you and shaped you to the point where you'd be of no use to any other woman.

When Abdelhaq died, the question arose as to what I was going to do with the things Hayat had brought to his house. Should I leave them there for his wife to deal with however she chose, or should I take them to my house to punish myself with them?

Even more difficult than coming up with a convincing story for my wife to explain where the things had come from would be having to live with them every day, since every one of them was associated with a memory that stirred up sorrows, and took me back to a happiness that bore the seeds of my approaching misery.

This woman's love had been an ongoing punishment. Never did I meet a woman after her but that she brought a kind of chastisement, never did I use anything she'd given me but that I tormented myself with it, and never did I draw another woman close but that I felt chilled to the bone.

How was I to escape painful comparisons? She who had bestowed on me more than any other woman ever could: had she secretly hoped, in everything she gave me, to cause me pain? After all, everything romantic love gives you contains the seeds of its future retribution.

Which is more merciful, then: what the dead leave you when they depart, or what love leaves you after the departure of the living?

I put out my questions in the ashtray of anguish and headed for Zayyan's room.

Behold life, with its 'things' that never die. Behold the things that you think you've won, only to find that they've defeated you, since they're bound to outlive you.

The task I faced with Zayyan's things was reminiscent of the one I'd confronted with my father's things and the bedroom he bequeathed to me, with a wardrobe containing suits, clothes and items suited to a man his age: his nightshirt, two house robes – a thick one, and a light silk one – his underwear, which was always the same French brand, his calendar, his woollen house slippers, his glasses, his watch, his sweaters, and his medicines, of which he had a three-month stockpile, since he thought that by buying large quantities he was buying a longer life for himself.

In my father's bedroom, then in Abdelhaq's house, and now in the presence of Zayyan's things, I saw that we're of less value than anything we own.

Otherwise, how could an ashtray that cost ten francs live longer than you do? How could the hands of a 500-franc watch go on turning, oblivious to the fact that your heart has stopped? The same goes for a bed, a chair, or a pair of shoes. How is it that a pair of socks still damp from your sweaty feet cares nothing about your demise?

How is it that the things you paid the most for are the first to betray you, and that the ones that nearly cost you your life go to someone else the minute you die?

The same question had come back: How was I to face the unjust presence, the terrible, frigid presence of those things that had no interest in someone whose corpse was still warm? Of course, there's nothing more malicious than innocence. So I've learned not to be deceived by things' seemingly ingenuous, familiar presence. However sad they might appear to be, they're gloating in secret, reminding you that even though their owners are gone they're the ones that will survive. They might even go to their former owners' enemies, the way a dead soldier's boots go to a miserable adversary on a snow-swept battlefield.

If you want to test things by your death, close the door and leave.

The first crafty thief is the dust that will place its gloved hand on your things without moving them from their place. Without anyone noticing, they'll become his by virtue of your absence.

The dust that advances, sweeping over every place from which you've absented yourself, is nothing but a rehearsal for what will happen after your death.

At that point, your things will go to whoever snatches them up, not with the diffidence of dust but with the insolence of a thief. It makes me think of a scene from the story of Zorba. As a certain old lady is dying, she sees that the people who've come on the pretext of consoling her are vying to pilfer her things, taking advantage of her inability to defend the possessions she's striven all her life to protect. Faced with a painful quandary, she doesn't know how she should expend the meagre strength she has left – by clinging to her last breath, or by holding onto her last hen?!

In death, the most miserable role falls not to the person who's passed away and has nothing more to worry about. Rather, it goes to those who have to witness the fate of his possessions after he's gone.

Sad though she was, I didn't think Françoise would put up with having things' cadavers in her house for very long. Based on what I knew of her, they'd be gone in no more than two or three hours – the time she would need to gather up Zayyan's papers and books so that she could hand them over to the next Arab who came into her house.

As for the other things, she might put them in bags, which would take their place on the ground floor next to the rubbish bin. Or, at best, she might keep them in her garage to wait for the next Red Cross collection.

Françoise was obsessed with charity initiatives. It was as though she'd devoted herself to helping *les misérables* of humanity who, depending on the latest tragedies in the world, took turns occupying her heart and her bed. It had even occurred to me that her intimacy with Zayyan fell under the rubric of her charitable activities.

Depending on the most recent news report, I would see her rush to answer calls to provide aid to this group or that. She would gather up clothes she didn't need, shoes, curtains and sheets – some worn out and some not – into big plastic bags which she would take down and deposit next to the concierge's station, where they would wait to be picked up by the Red Cross.

Françoise combined kind-heartedness with Westerners' naiveté in relating to the Other. It was a naiveté governed by a media-driven logic that oversimplifies things by dividing the world neatly into good guys and bad guys, civilised and backward, necessary and unnecessary.

One day when I saw her going downstairs with some bags to donate to victims in Sarajevo, I confessed that I envied her the courage to get rid of everything so quickly, and her ability to throw things into a bag to give them away without regret, hesitation or nostalgia, unconcerned about things' memory or sentimental value. I told her I wished I could be like her – that I could gather up my memory into a bundle and set it at the door. That way, I could get rid of my load and travel light the way she did.

'So then,' she asked, 'what do you all do with things you don't need any more?'

'We don't have anything we don't need,' I said jokingly. 'Even when our stuff gets old and worn out, we need it in our wardrobes or storage sheds, not out of stinginess, but because we love to weigh ourselves down with memory. If we give charity, we prefer to give money rather than our things' dead bodies. That's why we always need big houses.'

Then I continued with a laugh, 'Isn't that catastrophic?'

Behold the catastrophe! O Arabs weighed down with your loads, another bequest awaits you! But what will you do with the ill-fitting foreign identity of a man whose homeland hadn't found room for him, and who left you what he'd imagined to be a homeland: books on poetry and Algerian history, pictures he'd taken with people who may have been family or friends, who may be dead or still living, an old copy of the Qur'an, several years' organisers filled with addresses, appointments and names, medical prescriptions, used train, Metro and aeroplane tickets, posters from art exhibits he'd put on, cassette tapes of Arab music, house coats, and small items associated no doubt with memories known only to him, such as an empty Chanel No.5

bottle that lay in a far corner of the wardrobe, bathed in a kind of fragrant sorrow as if loyalty were sobbing in apology for all women's infidelities?

You gather about you fake imitations that you call a homeland. You surround yourself with strangers you call family. You sleep in the bed of a transient whom you call a sweetheart. You carry in your pocket a little black book filled with the numbers of people you call friends. You invent holidays and occasions, symbols and customs, and frequent a coffee shop the way you'd visit a friend.

As you're tailoring an ersatz homeland, your foreign-made identity gets so loose on you that it feels like a burnoose about to fall off your shoulders. You treat a foreign land as though it were home, and home as though it were a foreign land. You've got to realise, man, that your foreign-made self is a tragedy that you only become aware of in stages, and your awareness of it is only complete when the coffin lid closes over the unanswered questions of a lifetime. By that time, of course, you aren't around to find out what a stranger you were, or what an exile you'll be henceforth!

I was still thinking about what to do with all these things when suddenly I glimpsed a pair of shoes under the dresser. It was his only pair of shoes, or, rather, the only pair left here, since he was sure to have had another one that he'd worn to the hospital.

I didn't know why he'd chosen that other pair for his final journey. He might have left these here for a nicer occasion, since they were new, and looked as though they had never been worn. Even so, they looked more forlorn than the others, hiding under the dresser like an orphan boy afraid to catch someone's eye lest he be thrown out . . . or killed.

So, can shoes be orphaned, too?

They looked as though they were clinging together like the legs of that terrified little boy. When I reached over to bring them out of their hiding place, I recalled the small boy whose picture I had taken. He had spent a night hiding under a bed only to discover, when he woke up the next morning, that he'd lost his whole family.

I, who had decided not to cry in the face of death, found myself dissolving in tears before a pair of shoes whose shine was now covered in dust.

Zayyan was a man who had respected the distance between himself and others, who had worn a modest air of feigned inattention. It saddened me to be violating his secrets, to be loitering in a world that hadn't expected a stranger to enter it after he was gone. It pained me that his possessions hadn't preserved the sanctity of his absence but, instead, had begun talking behind his back, chattering away to the first passerby.

I remember how, during one of my visits to the hospital, I had to leave the room and wait outside until the nurse finished serving him. When I came back in, he apologised for the wait, and talked about how demeaning it is to be sick, since it makes your body public property and gives others the right to violate your privacy.

He said, 'This is the first time I've been in a hospital since my arm was amputated more than forty years ago. I hate the humiliation of being sick. What's saved me is that throughout my life I've gotten used to coping with the looks that strip my handicap naked by playing dumb. And I've just gone on doing the same thing here.'

Then he continued, 'The ability to play dumb is a skill I acquired from being an orphan. When you live as an orphan, life teaches you different things than it does other children. It teaches you inferiority, since the first thing you realise is that you're less important than everybody else. You see that there's nobody to protect you from other children's blows, or from the blows life deals you later on. Like a willow tree on a wind-swept plain, you're alone and exposed to whatever fate brings your way, and you have to defend yourself by acting stupid. When other children bully you, you pretend you didn't hear or understand, since you know they have fathers to stand up for them, and that you don't.'

After a pause, he said, 'Everyone who's inferior learns something from the experience, whether he's generous or tightfisted, violent or peaceful, trusting or suspicious, single or a family man. Every orphan is afflicted with a kind of presumed inferiority which he treats himself for in whatever ways his psychological aptitudes allow. But the worst sort of orphanhood is orphanhood of the limbs. It's a kind of naked inferiority that's on display for everyone to gawk at. And there's no cure for it. Whenever you see anyone, your eyes are drawn right away to what he has and what you lack, since it takes a hell of a lot of playing dumb to lie to yourself!'

I'm thinking back now to what he said, and to a saying by Mu'awiya Ibn Abi Sufyan, namely, 'one-third of wisdom is perspicacity, and the other two-thirds are deliberate inattention.'

I'd only been able to glean the remaining two-thirds of his wisdom when I began gathering up his things after he died, in the course of which I suddenly happened upon a copy of *Chaos of the Senses*. It looked worn-out from having been passed from hand to hand, and no one had written a dedication on its front page. He'd probably bought it himself, since the price, 140 francs, had been pencilled in on the inside of its front cover. The price's three digits summed up the woes of a man whose lover had removed him from the heart of a book of which he was the principle character and turned him into a stranger who had no place even in a dedication on its first page. He'd paid 140 francs to learn her news, tracking her infidelity between the lines.

So, then, he knew who I was, and was relating to me with the same feigned ignorance he'd practised all his life!

The discovery descended on me like a thunderbolt, and froze me in place. I began leafing through the book and rereading certain pages at random, in search of what he might have found out about me through it.

In his desire to find out her news, how could he have failed to buy a book she'd published after they parted?

And she, who, like a typical Arab regime, made it her profession to document her crimes and interrogate her victims in a book, how could she have failed to reveal me to him just as he had been revealed to me in *The Bridges of Constantine*?

So, then, each of us had learned everything about the other, yet without realising that the other knew this.

Like someone trying to unlock a big secret by piecing together a mosaic of little secrets, I set about trying to identify when exactly he had realised who I was, and which particular detail had enabled him to recognise me. Was it the name Françoise had given me when she made an appointment for me to see him?

If I hadn't introduced myself as Khaled Ben Toubal, would he have recognised me, for example, from the handicap in my left arm? Or would he have recognised me because, as in the novel, I'm a photographer, and from Constantine? Supposing that, when I visited him in the hospital, I hadn't said anything at all, would he have known who I was by a lover's intuition, or by the suspicion one man harbours towards another?

Besides, he might have recognised me and found out everything about my relationship with Hayat from that book, which didn't matter in the end.

But had he known that I was living with his girlfriend in his house, and that I'd met Hayat and brought her there? Had he known that the reason I hadn't visited him that day was that I'd had an appointment with her, and that she'd been dancing for me as he breathed his last?

Might he have chosen that particular moment to die as a way of taking 'playing dumb' to its ultimate extreme?

I still can't believe that the timing of his death was mere coincidence. I can't see any reason for his health to have declined so suddenly. When I saw him two days earlier, there had been nothing to indicate that his life was in danger or that he was suffering a relapse.

In fact, I'd never seen him as jocular as he was that day. However, I know how sneaky this particular illness can be. Right before it does you in, it might give you a feeling of amazing well-being, and everyone around you will confirm the feeling by telling you how well you look.

I know this from my father. But from my uncle I also know that a person chooses the timing of his death. Otherwise, how could he have died on 1 November in particular, the anniversary of the outbreak of the Algerian Revolution that he'd helped to lead?

I found confirmation of this in a scientific article I once read. I kept a copy of it since, when I found it, I felt as though I'd happened upon conclusive evidence for a heartfelt belief.

The subject of the article was a series of studies done by Metchnikoff, a scientist who at the turn of the twentieth century proposed a theory having to do with how human cells function. According to his theory, an individual dies only if he or she truly wants to, since organic death is nothing but a response to an urgent psychological demand. If this theory is correct, it means that the Algerian Revolution ended my uncle's life with a bullet whose lethal effect was delayed by forty years. It also means that I was the one who had persuaded Zayyan to crave death so thoroughly that he summoned its presence, thereby putting himself out of his misery.

This idea only intensified my grief. So as soon as Françoise got back to the house, I asked her whether she had told Zayyan that I was staying with her.

'Of course not,' she replied, taken aback. 'I would never have done that after you begged me not to.'

'Thank you!' I murmured.

I heaved a sigh of relief. My God, what a hard thing it is to feel you've offended the dead!

Surprised at me, Françoise went on, 'Zayyan knew I had other relationships, and he didn't interfere in my life. This was clear between us from the beginning. So why are you worried?'

It would have been a long conversation indeed if I'd explained all the reasons for my anxiety. But in situations like this I would see how alien she was to me and what an absurd dimension our talks tended to take on. Even so, when she heard the news of Zayyan's death, she was so upset that she collapsed on the sofa, saying over and over, 'It isn't possible. Oh my God…'

As she listened to the messages on the answering machine, she asked me how I hadn't been aware that the hospital had called.

Surprised by her question, I told her I'd been out that evening. Then, in a reply that surprised me even more, she said, 'Oh, that's right. You must have been having dinner at Murad's.'

I kept quiet for a few moments, having concluded from her tone of voice that she was in regular contact with him, and that they even called each other every day.

It wasn't the right time to give too much thought to the fact that a friend had betrayed me while I was busy with the details of another friend's death. It was good, at least, to have it confirmed to me that death takes a variety of forms. There are the dead we bury under the ground, and there are the living dead that we inter in the mire of their infamies.

I was a man who could understand a wife's unfaithfulness, but I couldn't forgive the unfaithfulness of a friend. A wife's unfaithfulness might be a passing fancy, whereas a friend's unfaithfulness is premeditated treachery.

Françoise's last statement had put an icy distance between us. She might have interpreted my coolness towards her after that as a sign of my grief over Zayyan's death, not realising the size of the cemetery I carried in my heart.

That night I contented myself with holding her in my arms as I thought about some night to come in which Murad would take my place, a transient in this resident bed.

Since I hadn't slept, I left the house early the next morning to take care of some last-minute tasks that had arisen out of recent developments, and in preparation for my imminent return to Algeria.

When I got back that evening, I told Françoise I'd gone to the Air Algérie office, and that there was a flight to Constantine in three days' time. I asked her if I could count on her to take care of administrative procedures while I took care of other things. After a pause, I added, 'It's going to cost 32,000 francs to transport the body.'

'Do you have that amount?' Françoise asked.

I found myself smiling as I replied, 'No. I used what I had to buy that painting!'

'Damn!' she muttered. 'Half of the proceeds from his paintings went to charitable societies, and the other half, which went to him, we can't dispose of. Since he's passed away, all his assets are frozen pending a determination of the heirs.'

She continued as she lit a cigarette, 'If only you hadn't bought that painting. It went for the highest price of all. Zayyan usually insisted that his paintings be sold at reasonable prices so that they'd be within everyone's reach. Maybe he put a higher price on that one because it was the dearest to him.'

'I'm the one who put a price on it. He didn't ask anything of me. I wanted to spend all I had left of that prize money on it, and set my mind at rest.'

After a pause she said, 'Don't you think it's remarkable that Zayyan had always wanted to keep that particular painting, and that its price is around the same as the cost of transporting his body to Constantine?'

A shudder went through my body. My God! I thought. Where did she get that idea?

A feeling of terror came over me. It was as if, by buying that painting, I'd stolen his grave from him, or as though I'd bought my own. My thoughts started going in all directions, and I recalled the way Hayat thought of bridges as a bad omen.

Without mentioning my concerns to Françoise, I found myself asking, 'Do you think we could find a buyer for it in the space of two days?'

With no sign of either dismay or surprise at my decision, she replied, 'It might be possible as long as it's on display. All we'd need to do would be take the "sold" off of it. Every gallery keeps a list of prominent clients who are interested in acquiring paintings by this or that artist, and it contacts them in cases like this.'

Selling it would make me as sad as it would to keep it, so I didn't know any more which was the right thing to do, especially in view of the fact that I'd spent my money on it because I loved it, and because I knew I was the only person who appreciated its sentimental value. In the event that I kept the painting, the question would be: who would I borrow the money from? From Nasser, who was too honest to have an account with that much money in it? Or from Murad, whom I didn't want any more dealings with, and whom I wouldn't have expected to offer much help to begin with? The only solution, if I decided to borrow the money, would be to contact Hayat. I figured she'd be able to come up with this kind of sum, and that would have made me happy had it not been for the fact that the only money she had belonged to her husband. So borrowing the money from Hayat would have been an insult to Zayyan, who'd spent a lifetime refusing to be sullied by white collar thieves' filthy lucre. Alternatively, I could try to borrow the money from the Algerian embassy. However, Zayyan would also have refused to ask help from a state whose only gesture towards the dozens of creative geniuses who had been assassinated at the hands of criminals was to provide national flags to cover their corpses. So how could I even think of asking the embassy for help?

A man of scruples with a sense of dignity, his would-be corrupters had presented him with untold numbers of low doors which, in order to go through them, his pride would have had to stoop and he would have had to relinquish his self-esteem. Now that his stature was spread out lengthwise in a coffin, would he go through a door he'd refused to go through when he was alive?

So the matter didn't require much thought. Having been entrusted with this man's remains, I was determined to conduct myself in a way that befit what I knew of him. I couldn't imagine that he would have been pleased if I had begged for the money I needed to take his body home when he, during his lifetime, had given away in charity enough money to guarantee himself a decent burial. Wouldn't it be more dignified for the remains of this lofty man of sorrow to travel at the expense of one of his paintings than at the expense of a benefactor, or thanks to the generosity and charity of the pirates of pillaged homelands?

Françoise interrupted my train of thought, saying, 'If you want to put the painting up for sale I'll need to inform Carole right away, since time is of the essence. Sometimes things don't happen quickly, especially since we're nearing year's end, and during the holiday season people don't have money to spend on purchases like this if they're relatively pricey.'

Lighting a cigarette and heading for the balcony, I said, 'Call her.'

The next morning I woke up exhausted from a night filled with bad dreams. I must have talked in my sleep or tossed and turned a lot, since Françoise had relocated to the sofa in the living room.

Embarrassed, I planted a kiss on her cheek and apologised.

'It's no big deal,' she said sweetly.

Then she asked me, 'Why were you so upset?'

'I was having a nightmare,' I said as I headed to the kitchen to make the coffee. The painting, my conversation with Françoise, and the whole previous day sorting Zayyan's things had probably all collected in my subconscious, then come out in the form of a nightmare: as I was about to cross one of Constantine's bridges, people on both sides started shouting at me to stop. People were rushing to get their things out of their miserable dwellings perched on the heights, screaming at whoever didn't already know it that a landslide was starting and that all the bridges were going to collapse. Everyone was terrified, not knowing which bridge to take to get out of Constantine.

Being a logical man, I could also think of another explanation for the dream, namely, an article I'd read when I was in Algeria, then forgotten about, and that seemed to have resurfaced in my consciousness that day.

Handing me a French newspaper, a colleague of mine had said jokingly in the capital's dialect, 'Be careful, brother. Constantine's a goner. One of these days you're going to wake up and find yourselves at the bottom of a ravine!'

The title of the article, written in bold, announced that Constantine was slipping downward, and was preceded by a line in small print that asked, 'What is the government waiting for?'

The article, which presented numerous alarming facts, asserted that the city was now sinking at a rate of several centimetres annually, and that at least 100,000 impoverished residents, who had come to the city from all over the country, were living within the danger belt in homes that had been built in haphazard fashion on rocky slopes. This had further endangered the Sidi Rached Bridge, whose situation was already precarious because it rested atop twenty-seven stone arches.

Al Kantara Bridge, which, ever since being built by the Romans, had been toying with danger, promised to fare no better. Despite being considered one of the most remarkable structures in Constantine, Al Kantara Bridge had remained out of use for five centuries until Salah Bey brought in one hundred workers from Europe to restore it under the supervision of a Spanish engineer. Then, in the nineteenth century, the French tore it down and built the bridge that stands today.

Everyone who's ever invaded or ruled Constantine has established his glory by rebuilding its bridges without even a passing nod of recognition to those who had built them before him! As a consequence, Constantinians' hopes hung, like their bridges, on what would be decided by the American, Canadian and Japanese experts who, according to the newspaper article, would consult over the best way to rescue a city that had lived for 2,500 years as well-ensconced as an eagle's nest on a towering cliff: a miracle created by rock, and ruined by human beings.

I didn't tell Françoise about any of this. She had enough nightmares ahead of her that day.

We divided up the list of obnoxious death-related details. Françoise went to follow up on the administrative procedures, which included passing by the hospital to pick up Zayyan's things, while I went to finish up last-minute tasks and check on my flight reservation.

That afternoon I got an unexpected phone call from Françoise.

'It's good I found you,' she said happily. 'The painting's been sold! And I managed to get you the money in cash, since you wouldn't have been able to cash a cheque for several days.'

Before I had a chance to say anything, she added, 'You can come by to pick up the money right away, since you've got no time at all. I won't be here when you arrive, but Carole will take care of it for you.'

Not knowing whether she was delivering me news of a gain, or a loss, I didn't reply.

'Now don't tell me you regret it!' she chided me. 'We've been lucky, since we might not have been able to sell it for several days.'

Everything was settled, then, and I didn't want to get into a debate over what might have happened. Keeping it short, I said, 'All right. I'm coming.'

On my way to the gallery I was assailed by conflicting emotions. I realised as I went there that I would be seeing the painting for the last time, yet without forgetting that it was in that very place that I'd seen Hayat for the first time after a two-year separation. And I wondered how it was that, in the space of just a few days, a single place could join the most beautiful of memories with the most painful, the former because I thought I'd recovered a lost love, and the latter because I realised that I'd lost a homeland.

I had gone to such extremes trying to make a fool of Love, it had started coming to me disguised in forgetfulness when I least expected it. How can you kill Love once and for all when it isn't something that existed between you and a single person but, rather, between you and everything that bears any connection to that person?

At the gallery door I was met by the exhibition poster, which featured a reproduction of one of Zayyan's paintings depicting an old, half-open door. A black ribbon had been placed at the painting's top left corner to announce the painter's death. I stopped and stared at it for a few moments as though I wanted to make sure it had really happened.

I was received warmly by Carole, who was affected by Zayyan's death, having known him ever since he came to France. She invited me into her office, expressing her sadness over the fact that he wouldn't be there at the close of the exhibition as he usually was. She handed me the same sum I'd paid for the painting, saying, 'I'm sorry. You didn't even get to enjoy owning it for a while.'

'Maybe it's better this way,' I said. 'I might have gotten used to it, or it might have gotten used to me. In any case, it changed its owner without budging from its place, and it changed hands without even noticing!'

I didn't try to find out who had bought it. As I thanked her and left, I thought about how, by recovering this sum, I was recovering not the value of the painting but, rather, the value of that prize, which I seemed to have won so that, by means of a prize-winning picture of death, I could finance the tragedy of another death. Death had prospered so much among us that it could finance itself now!

As I made the rounds of the exhibition, I wasn't surprised not to see any other visitors. It wasn't a time for going to art exhibits, nor a time for dying.

It was four o'clock in the afternoon, at the beginning of a week, at the end of a year, and people were busy getting ready for their festivities. So, had he made a point of dying at a time when life was too busy for him, so that he could slip out of its grip unnoticed?

It didn't sadden me to see the gallery empty. In fact, it made me happy, since I had it all to myself. I felt as though I owned every one of those paintings for a time, albeit in anticipation of losing them all. After all, the wealthy refuse to let someone own a painting through the eyes of the heart.

I was happy because I was there to do the only thing I'd ever hoped to do, but hadn't been able to: to tour the exhibit with Zayyan himself. I knew he would come, since there was no way he would miss an appointment with paintings that were longing to be taken down off walls of steel and returned to their painter's arms.

Everyone was too busy for him, and now, at last, he had all the time in the world, so we'd be able to stop and have a long talk in front of every painting. We would have been able to, that is, if it weren't for the fact that now *I* was the one who didn't have the time – although I didn't know how to justify my busyness to him – and the fact that I would have to leave him before the Air Algérie offices closed.

Then he'd curse the airways and ask me, 'And what are you going to do in that country? Would anybody be idiotic enough to spend the New Year's holiday there?' to which I wouldn't have any answer. Then, when he couldn't keep me any longer, he'd bid me farewell in his usual fashion, saying, 'We'll continue our conversation tomorrow,' and, after a pause, 'that is, if you have time.'

'...if you have time' – that phrase was his way of sparing himself the humiliation of begging for a visit.

But the hour of departure draws near, my friend. The time of 'the greater visit' has come to an end. There isn't even enough time for those programmed hospital visits. Ordinary time is dead, my dear. You're now in 'frozen time'.

Had he known that?

In his last paintings he seemed withdrawn from life, as though he were painting things that had abandoned him, or that he had abandoned: the corpses of things that were no longer his, but that he continued to treat with the goodwill born of intimate association. He painted them with light strokes of colour as though he were afraid they might be hurt by his brush – the same brush that hadn't been afraid to hurt him.

He painted the tragedy of things or, rather, their silent betrayal in the face of tragedy. Take, for example, the doors that occupied so many of his paintings: unused doors discoloured by time. Doors closed in our faces. Doors ajar, stalking us. Safe doors with cats napping on their sills. Doors of fabric separating one home from the next, exposing us while claiming to conceal us. Doors with footsteps sounding behind them, or hands knocking on them. Narrow doors through which we flee, only to find that they lead our pursuers to us. Doors we hide behind for protection only to find that they incite aggression against us, and doors unhinged that deliver us to our murderers. We rush away from them in terror, or we die of treachery on their thresholds, leaving a single shoe behind. After all, isn't a single shoe, in its aloneness, a symbol of death?

When I saw all these paintings for the first time, I asked Françoise what secret lay behind the prolonged conversations Zayyan appeared to have had with doors. She said, 'When an artist enters into a phase in which he draws nothing but the same subject, it means that this subject is associated with some significant event or suffering.'

236

I didn't ask her what suffering lay behind the paintings, nor do I think she would have known the answer. The day Murad and I got into a heated discussion about the door paintings, in which Murad saw nothing but women's thighs, some spread wide and others ajar, she'd been so impressed with his theory that she seemed to share his opinion, though she said nothing. Only now, as I moved among them, absorbed in their minutest details, did I feel I'd discovered the answer to my question. The answer was based on a conversation I'd had with Françoise some time earlier. The day she told me about Zayyan's illness, she had said, 'His nephew's murder devastated him so completely, I think it's what caused his cancer. Cancer is nothing but the body's tears. It's a known fact that it tends to appear after some sort of tragedy.'

After that I looked for an opportunity to ask Zayyan about the details of his nephew's death, since I sensed that this event had destroyed him more than even death itself could have.

We'd been talking about the incredible variety of ways in which people in Algeria were dying when, with a kind of macabre humour, he said, 'We should issue a catalogue of Arab death, so people can choose from a list of the available ways to die. After all, Arabs have outdone themselves in developing the culture of death. So, instead of dying a Kurdish death, sprayed with chemicals like an insect, you might choose to have the honour of dying by a golden revolver from the god of death himself, or one of his sons. Or, rather than being mangled live by ravenous dogs and your innards paraded around a prison yard as happened in certain Moroccan prisons, you might prefer to dig your own grave and get into it of your own accord so that your murderers can slaughter you while you lie in the final position of your choice.

237

'You also have the option of not dying all at once, since there are Arab regimes that offer death by instalment, beginning with having your fingernails pulled out and your fingers burned with acid – if you're a journalist – and ending with having your eyes gouged out and your belly split open, depending on your butcher-executioner's mood.'

He spoke with bitter scorn.

Gathering my courage, I said, 'I was so sorry to hear about your nephew's assassination. How did it happen?'

'Salim?' he said, surprised by the question. After a pause, he continued, 'He died more than once. The last time he was shot to death.'

It was obvious that I'd placed my hand on a fresh wound. I said nothing more, but left him the freedom to stop there, or go on.

Like a vessel overflowing with grief, he gushed forth, 'Of all the deaths I've lived through, Salim's was the most painful to me. Even the death of his father, who was my only brother, didn't hit me as hard. When security forces killed his father in the 1988 demonstrations, Salim was a young man. He started studying night and day so that he could begin supporting his mother and two brothers right away. He was such an outstanding student, he was accepted into the Personnel Training Institute. He was so passionate about learning, the government sent him to study in France for six months so that he could install computer information systems in Constantine's customs departments.

'At the time when he started his job, gangsters had begun killing off government employees. After a couple of his colleagues were murdered and he started feeling himself in danger, he asked the government to provide him with a safe house. They ended up giving him a house way out on the outskirts of Djebel al

238

Wahch. He wasn't comfortable there, of course. Imagine a "safe house" without a telephone, and at the edge of a forest! Then he started saving up out of his salary to buy an armoured door for his house. The amount required was a small fortune, and if he'd chosen to he could have gotten ten times that amount by demanding a commission on all the equipment he'd been assigned to bring back from France. But he was honest and self-respecting by birth, content with what he had. And he loved Algeria. So, in the age of ideologically justified looting and thievery, he was setting aside part of his hard-earned salary for a security door to protect him from murderers.

'But they came just when he thought he'd secured himself against them. It was eleven at night, just after the curfew had begun, when the death squad stationed itself outside his armoured door. They were confident that nobody would come to help him at that hour of the night. They also stood to gain from the general state of confusion that prevailed, since, if there was a commotion, nobody knew whether it was security forces trying to enter a house where terrorists had barricaded themselves, or terrorists attacking the house of their next victims.

'Like some American horror flick where the victim stands defenceless behind a door secured from the other side by human beasts, they'd come armed with the equipment of death, and screamed at him to open up. But he didn't, confident that his armoured door would protect him.

'Death wasn't with them. They *were* Death. Four and a half hours went by with Death outside the door, defying him to the rhythmic clanging of axes and picks and the sound of curses and insults. "Open up, you pimp, you good-for-nothing. We've come for you, you infidel, you enemy of God!"

'His heart responded from behind the door with prayers for protection from the Master of Doors. Neither his wife's sobbing nor his little boy's wails did him any good, and none of his neighbours came to help. The police didn't hear and neither did God, in spite of the deafening noise being made by the instruments they were using to get the door open. Having died more than once before, Salim started preparing for his final death. As the hours passed and death approached, the murderers went into a frenzy, threatening more and more loudly to make an example of him.

'With everything in him trembling, afraid of everything and afraid for everything, where would he find the courage to open the door and be done with it? Where, at a moment of terror, would he find the wisdom to know how he was supposed to act? And what could he salvage before death opened the door for him?

'He was shaking so badly, he couldn't pick up his three-year-old son, so he collapsed onto a chair as his little boy clung to his leg. Every now and then he would think of something to tell his wife to do after he was gone: to kiss his mother for him and ask her to forgive him and pray for his soul, to give me his greetings and ask me to look after his son, or to apologise to a colleague of his that he'd borrowed money from, and to pay it back if she got any compensation from Customs.'

At this point I saw Zayyan tear up for the first time.

'Imagine a man as needy as he was, instructing his wife in a situation like that to repay a debt for him after he dies while leaders with a steady income of dead bodies are plundering a homeland.'

'And how was Salim killed?'

'At three thirty the next morning, Death managed to break down the door. Salim collapsed onto his knees and begged them not to kill him in front of his little boy. They dragged him outside and sprayed him with bullets. That was their way of appeasing Death, which had been insulted by having to wait four and a half hours outside that well-secured door.

'His body was like a sieve, and in the days that followed, our battle was with the cement that had clung to his blood.'

Now I wonder whether the key to unlocking these paintings might lie in the story of a man who spent his entire savings on an armoured door to ward off Death, only to find that all he had bought was a prolongation of Death's torment. Perhaps Zayyan had wanted to suggest that behind every door, Death lies in wait.

My heart didn't have room for any more pain, nor did I have time to start a conversation with each individual painting. So I headed straight for that particular one. I felt as though I were going on a date with a woman who was married to someone else, the way I used to feel with Hayat. So, do paintings also belong to the institution of matrimony? Are they the property of the one who owns them, or of the one who sees them? Do they belong to the person who loves them? Or to the one who can afford to buy them? And what if they belonged to somebody who had lost them precisely because he was the only one who had ever truly wanted them?

Could I have avoided this loss? The most I could have done would have been to postpone it. After all, I'm nothing but a hand in the life of all the things I own. Someone else's hand preceded me, and someone else's will follow me, and each of us owns them only for a time.

It would be better if we consulted things the way a judge consults a couple's children when they divorce, asking them which parent they want to go with. What a violation it is of things' rights for them not to be entitled to choose their owners! And so many problems might be resolved if, instead of seeking verdicts from people, we sought them from the things people disagree about and go to war over.

I stood there gazing at the painting as though in apology for not having been able to keep her, as though, by looking at her long enough, I might be able to entice her to run away with me, the way a girl about to be married against her will might elope with her true love.

Now that she belonged to someone else, a more pleasant role had fallen to me – the role of lover. She was Constantine who, nestled for the last twenty-five centuries in history's arms, would comb her hair and engage in long tête-à-têtes with the stars from atop her throne. Constantine needed a lover to woo her, to henna her feet as they dangled in the ravines, to pamper her, to kiss her to sleep at night. She didn't need some sadistic husband that would come home every night in a terrible mood to bicker with her and beat her to a pulp!

Hadn't Abdelhaq once bemoaned Constantine's fate, saying, 'She's too enchanting to belong to anyone, and too much of a legend to have to carry one random foetus after another. So how did they bind her to these mountains? How did they prevent her from slipping out of her rapist's grip?'

The two of us were engaged in a silent debate. Like the women of Constantine, this painting was too spineless to decide her own fate. At the same time, she was the type that stares right through you until you turn into a painting yourself. At a certain point it seemed to me that she wasn't a bridge any more, but that I'd been transmuted into a bridge. It made me think of the artist René Magritte, who drew a pipe and called the drawing 'This is not a pipe'.

Would Zayyan have needed another lifetime to realise that this entity he had drawn more than thirty years earlier wasn't a bridge, or a woman, or a city, or a homeland, since – according to some people, at least – a homeland isn't a place on earth, but an idea in the mind? If this is true, then it's on account of an idea, not a land, that we go to war, die, and lose our limbs and our relatives and our possessions. Does a homeland consist of soil? Or does it consist of what happens to you on that soil?

Are we imprisoned, humiliated, scattered from our homes, assassinated, and forced to die in exile, all for the sake of an idea?

For the sake of this idea, which survives even when we die, we're willing to sell the most precious things we own just so we can ship our remains back to an illusory homeland which, if it weren't for this deceptive idea, wouldn't even exist!

I was thinking: What is it that made this painting so important to Zayyan? The only answer I could find to the question was something he'd said once, namely, 'We don't make all our paintings with the same part of ourselves. A long time ago I stopped painting things with my hand or my heart. The geography of spiritual homelessness has taught me to paint with my steps. This exhibit is the map of my inward journey, and everything you see in these paintings is the tracks of my sandals. Picasso used to speak of going to his studio the way a Muslim goes to prayer, leaving his shoes at the door. As for me, I walk into a painting with the dirt on my shoes. I draw with the dust of homelessness that clings to my sandals.'

This, then, was the painting Zayyan had done with his heart, and with all his heart he'd hoped to lie down on it like a bridge, and go to sleep.

With it had begun, and with it had ended, the story of the old man and the bridge. He was a man who had lived his life under bridges' spell. To him belonged the wind and all the unhinged doors that covered the walls in his absence. The wind blew through them in the evenings, but to everyone who stopped to look at them they would say, 'Don't go on knocking at these doors. The artist isn't here any more!'

His questions were voiced through bridges and doors. Whenever he stopped in front of one of his paintings, I would imagine him, with his whimsical seriousness, answering a question it had asked him: 'Why did you stop painting?'

'To forget. To paint is to remember.'

'Why did you stop using watercolours?'

'Because oils allow you to correct your mistakes. To paint is to recognise your right to be imperfect.'

'O master of blackness, why are you wrapped in white?'

'Because white is colours' ruse. When they were leading Marie Antoinette to the guillotine, they asked her to change her black dress, so she took it off and put on the whitest dress she had.'

'Why are you in a hurry?'

'I walk through one country, while my sandals grope the soil of another.'

'Why are you sad?'

'I regret committing all those acts of heroism at my own expense.'

Then his paintings asked him, 'What can we do for you as we hang here, orphaned?'

'I'm tired! You can prop me up against the pillars of illusion so that I can imagine myself dying standing up!'

That evening I went back to the apartment carrying a fancy bottle of wine and a bottle of perfume wrapped in pretty ribbons to present to Françoise.

The Christmas and New Year's season was in the air. I'd been so engrossed in pain, I'd forgotten what it's like to live in a culture of celebration, so I decided to spend what was left after buying the plane ticket on some recreational shopping.

As she opened the door, I could see that Françoise was surprised at what I'd brought. She asked me if I'd gotten the tickets.

'Yes,' I assured her. Then I added, 'This perfume is for you.'

'Thank you!' she said, giving me a kiss. 'How could you have thought about a present in the middle of all this sadness?'

'Today is the last day I have to thank you for all you've done.'

Given the extreme sorrow called for by the situation, I'd decided, for one night, to take a vacation from tragedies. I've always had a hard-to-understand urge to experience either pure misery or utter happiness. In either case, I want to take the moment to its ultimate limit, to season my sorrow with generous amounts of madness and irony. I want to sit down to the table of losses with the spirit of celebration that befits it, to sip fancy wine, and to listen to beautiful music after having had no time to listen to anything but news broadcasts.

Sarcasm and dry humour are the only things that can overcome the illusion of antagonism between death and life, gain and loss.

Before sitting down to my glass, I called Nasser to inform him of Zayyan's death. I'd put off calling him so that I wouldn't have to talk to Murad, who was finished as far as I was concerned. This way also, Nasser wouldn't taint the sacredness of my sorrow by relaying the news to Hayat, since I'd come to feel that Zayyan's death was my concern alone.

'To God do we belong, and to Him shall we return!' he cried. 'I can't believe it, man. I was just with him this past Friday, and he seemed to be doing fine. This bitch of a world takes the good ones and leaves the bad ones. He was the best man I've ever known.'

I told him that the body would be taken next day to Constantine and that we'd be at the airport at six in the evening if he wanted to recite the Fatiha over him.

He said he'd come, of course. He seemed sorry that Murad wasn't there, as he'd travelled to Germany two days earlier. As far as I was concerned, that was the best news he could have given me.

He asked me if someone from the embassy would be there. 'I don't think so,' I said.

'So, then, I'll see you tomorrow.'

Françoise had ordered in pizza, so I went to the kitchen to make a salad and fry up a plateful of sausages I'd bought a couple of days before from a butcher that sells halal meat. Full of weird contradictions, an Algerian will insist on eating halal meat even when he's drinking wine along with it!

When she saw me setting the plate on the table, Françoise said, 'My God, there's a lot of rich stuff on that plate! Don't you know that frying oil is your number one enemy?'

I smiled. How was I to rank my enmities by order of degree, and where would my other enemies rank if rich foods were my number one foe? How can you compare the enmity of oil, the plotting of butter, the perfidy of cigarettes, the conniving of sugar, and the machinations of salt to the betrayals of friends, the envy of colleagues, the injustices of kinfolk, the hypocrisy of comrades, the intimidation of terrorists, and the humiliation of the homeland? Aren't all these enmities too much for one person to bear?

I remembered Zayyan asking me to close the door to his room one day so that he could light a cigarette.

Amazed, I asked, 'Isn't it forbidden to smoke in the hospital?'

'Of course,' he replied with a smile. 'In fact, it's tantamount to a crime. But, as Amal Donqol said to his doctor from his deathbed, "Laws were made to be broken." Besides, man, you can't live and die obedient, or go on being such a wimp at the age of sixty-seven that you're afraid of a cigarette!'

I contemplated his ashtray, which lay hidden in his bedside table drawer. It was full of cigarette butts that were so long, it looked as though he'd only taken a single drag from each one – like fires that had been set, then hurriedly put out.

He dissipated life the way he wasted cigarettes just for the fun of lighting them. There was no sign of a match in the ashtray. After all, a man with one hand can't use a match box. So was that why he was so enamoured of lighting fires?

He said scornfully, 'Don't believe anybody who tells you that things are bad for your health. The only "things" that are bad for your health are people. They do you a lot more harm than the stuff the Ministry of Health warns you against. So as I've gotten older I've learned to replace people with things, to surround myself with music, books, paintings, and good wine. At least they don't conspire against you or stab you in the back. They deal with you straight. And more importantly, they don't play the hypocrite with you or put you down, and they don't care whether you're a rubbish collector or a five-star general.'

Warming to his subject, he went on acerbically, 'I read some time ago that a rubbish collector in France lost his arm when his glove got stuck in the teeth of the truck's compressor. I thought about how this man who lost his arm in the "dirty" battle of life as he struggled to make a "clean" living would never enjoy the prestige of a military officer who'd lost his arm in a battle to take over someone's homeland. Limbs are only worth as much as their owners. General Antonio López de Santa Anna, who ruled Mexico as a dictator several times, held a solemn official funeral for his left leg after losing it in the so-called "Pastry War". So, between the rubbish collector's arm and the general's leg there's a difference of five stars. It's only before objects that we're truly equal. Unlike the people around him, that general's wooden leg couldn't care less about his stars!'

More than his art, it was this man's wisdom that impressed me, and his voice followed me wherever I went. On one occasion after another, it would come in the form of some dimly lit statement, and whatever happiness I now enjoyed came from listening to our recorded conversations in which, as I lay in bed hooked up to the elixir of memory, he would talk to me about the convictions he had settled into over time.

He had died and left me his voice. That voice of his, between the clouds of language and the clear skies of silence, would dissipate my illusions, training me in the art of exposing life's ruses and sweeping away its mines.

I stood looking for a song that fit my mood, a song that, like ice cubes, was missing from my glass. I wanted it to be in Arabic, since grief in situations like these, like rapture, can only be in Arabic, and I asked Françoise's permission to listen to it.

She asked me about its lyrics. I didn't feel like explaining the song to her, but out of politeness I said, 'The singer is talking to a woman he'd been in love with, and who ditched him without a thought for his feelings.'

How could I translate a song that conspires to make you break down and cry, a song in which the kamanja rips you to shreds as its bow is drawn back and forth over the strings? What other language, what other words, could possibly convey the agonised longing in the lyrics, 'Ahhhh, how you've wronged me ... for your sake I would have left my own children orphans!'

It came as no surprise that the woman Fergani was bewailing resembled Hayat, as though every song in the world, whoever happened to sing it, was crying over her and her alone. She was the number one suspect in every love song, the traitor in every story, the villainess in every schmaltzy film, the woman on whom you could pin all the romantic crimes ever committed.

'Are all Arabic songs this sad?' Françoise wanted to know.

'No,' I said a bit defensively, 'not all of them.'

As if out of courtesy, she replied, 'Maybe this sadness is the secret behind the Arabs' romanticism and their emotional generosity.' I retorted derisively, 'We're emotionally generous, my dear, not because we're sad, but because we're orphans. There's no one more generous than an orphan. There may be a lot of us, but we're an orphan nation. We've been this way ever since history abandoned us. As Zayyan says, an orphan never gets over his feeling of inferiority.'

I paused briefly, then continued, 'The perfume I gave you – Chanel No.5 – is evidence of this. Even after Coco Chanel had achieved success and fame, she went on suffering from her orphan complex. She named her first perfume with the number she'd been given in the orphanage she grew up in. Note the simplicity of its bottle, with its glaze-less, unadorned square shape. That's what orphanhood is like: naked and transparent. It doesn't even have a name. It has a number instead. The miracle of Coco Chanel isn't that she was able to create such a wonderful-smelling perfume, but the fact that she made orphanhood into a perfume, and a number into a name.'

'Amazing!' exclaimed Françoise. 'I never knew that!'

'It's something that isn't known to many people, maybe not even Marilyn Monroe, who never used any other perfume. When she was asked once, "What do you wear to sleep?" her answer was, "A few drops of Chanel No.5."'

'My God, where do you get all this information?'

'This, my dear,' I bantered, 'is the culture of orphanhood.'

Then, in a more serious tone, I went on, 'I'm talking to you about Marilyn Monroe because I thought of her today at the exhibit. It's said that she was so sensitive to the fact of being an orphan that she could pick another orphan out of a whole roomful of people. The same sort of feeling came over me all of a sudden today as I walked into the gallery. I felt sure that any visitor, with or without a sixth sense, could have identified that particular painting as the orphan in the crowd.'

'I would never have believed until now that a painting could be an orphan. In any case, there wasn't anybody in the gallery to notice it.'

'Don't worry,' Françoise said reassuringly, 'people are just busy with their holiday celebrations, and a lot of them haven't heard the news of Zayyan's death yet.'

Then she added, 'By the way, did you know that the gallery sold that painting for 50,000 francs? It made a 20,000-franc profit without the painting even coming down off its hook. All Carole had to do was call one of our clients and tell him that the artist had died for the price nearly to double!'

'That's the cunning of art dealers for you,' I said angrily. 'They wait for an artist to die to make their fortune off a piece whose creator couldn't even make a living off of it, or even guarantee himself a decent burial.'

Out of curiosity I asked her, 'Who bought it so fast, and for that price?'

I expected to hear that the buyer had been one of those wealthy expatriate Algerians who, now that their bank accounts were bloated with looted money, had made it a practice to burnish their reputations by rushing to buy up every available piece by leading Algerian artists. They were the only ones I could imagine being able to come up with 50,000 francs to buy a painting offered for sale over the phone. Once in a gathering I'd heard one of them justify his sudden passion for art, saying, 'Making money is a talent, and spending it is a sign of cultivation.' So, now that he'd proven by what he'd pilfered that he was 'talented', all he had to do was prove by what he'd acquired that he was 'cultivated'!

But then Françoise countered all my expectations by saying, 'He's a wealthy French *pied-noir* who owns rare paintings, including a collection by Les orientalistes, and another by Mohammed Racim. He recently bought paintings by Jean-Michel Atlan that had been offered for sale. You must have heard of Atlan – a Jewish painter from Constantine who was considered one of the big names in abstract art and who died in the 1960s. He was famed for his passion for Constantine, and was imprisoned more than once for supporting liberation movements.'

I was still in shock when she added, 'Carole told me he'd wanted to buy more of Zayyan's paintings, but the gallery wasn't authorised to sell any of them – other than yours, of course, since it had been sold while Zayyan was still alive.'

Seeing how downcast I looked, she came over and sat next to me to try to cheer me up. 'Don't be so sad,' she said. 'He's a man who loves art, and who's known for his obsession with everything related to Constantine. When Zayyan visited Constantine for the first time, he brought some little things back for him. I think he was a childhood friend, and that they studied together or something like that.'

My voice all but gone, I asked her, 'But do you think Zayyan would have sold him the painting?'

'I don't think so, actually,' she confessed. 'Zayyan had rejected the idea of selling it to anybody under any circumstances. If it hadn't been for his confidence in you and his sense that he was going to die, he wouldn't have sold it even to you. I think he would have liked to keep it for himself. At the same time, he wanted to leave it to somebody, and there was nobody to leave it to. One of his nephews was murdered in a horrible way a couple of years ago, and another nephew disappeared some time back, and it's believed that he either died or joined the criminals. As for his only brother, he was assassinated ten years ago in the 1988 demonstrations.'

There's nothing harder for an artist at the end of his life than not to find anyone he feels he can entrust his works to.

I said with rueful cynicism, 'Did you know that the name *pied-noir* – "black foot" – was used to refer to the French colonists who were sent to settle in Algeria after the colonialist invasion in the mid-nineteenth century? They were so called because they used to wear thick black shoes as they oversaw work in the plantations.

I'm sure this wealthy man didn't expect to carry on the tradition of wearing history on his feet. Nor would he have expected to see the day when this painting had no relatives left but him. But its family have been wiped out in senseless wars, and he had to wait until they'd finished each other off so that he could receive a full inheritance.'

Possibly not having understood what I said, she commented, 'In the art market, it's just a matter of time. If you just wait, with a bit of patience and the necessary funds you'll end up getting whatever painting you want. All you have to do is grab the opportunity when it comes along. Sometimes you have a stroke of luck and you end up benefiting from some momentary lapse of attention, as on this occasion, when people were preoccupied with their holiday celebrations, and the news of Zayyan's death hadn't yet gotten out.'

Pouring a bit of wine, I said, 'Of course. All of history is the outcome of momentary lapses of attention!'

I wasn't Boabdil, surrendering the keys to Granada. So why cry? They were losses that no one could gloat over, since I'd chosen them of my own free will.

When Hayat used to visit me for an hour or two before rushing back home in a panic, I once said to her, 'I'm not interested in owning you in instalments. I refuse to win you for a few hours after which you go to somebody else. Little wins like that don't make me any richer. I'm not the neighbourhood grocer. I'm a lover who prefers to lose you in style. What I want with you is a win as devastating as a loss.'

What I didn't know was that serious wins generate successive losses, like that prize that, ever since I won it, I'd been spending on my losses.

The situation took me back to Zayyan, who, like a maimed Greek hero and in this very place, had danced with his one arm amid the shambles of his life on the night when he turned most of his paintings over to Françoise and went to bury his brother.

How I wished I didn't identify with him in this final, absurd scene. I'd come to France to receive a prize. But had Fate brought me here simply to be the hand that surrendered a painting and received a dead body?

I put on Zorba's music and sat down to drink a toast to him.

Good evening, Khaled.

Now that you've become part of this beautiful ruin that's like nothing you've ever known before, you'll need to do a lot of dancing, friend. So dance, and don't worry about disturbing the dead.

Don't say it's too late, since you're living in a 'detemporalized zone' – a zone stripped bare of Time. And there's no point in looking at your watch, since it isn't here to tell you what time it is, but to place Time's remains between us. Everything's over now, and Time is of no concern to you any more, since eternity is the flipside of nothingness.

And now that you've come to see things clearly, you can't paint them any more. You've entered the no-colour zone, headed for the soil.

The soil you used to long for, and which you called your home-land (your homeland?), you can go to now at your own expense without sprucing yourself up the way you would normally do before an appointment. There's no point in being stylish, since all bodies are alike as far as maggots are concerned. And there won't be anybody to notice your injury – the stub that, whenever you got undressed, you hid from sight.

This soil that welcomes you and the maggots that feast on you will poke fun at the women who loved you and whom you were too proud to satisfy. You refused to seduce a harlot by the name of Life, and you've come today to give your ageing body to the worms.

You fool, from now on whatever depravity others are accused of, you'll be the one who committed it. Whatever sin someone else is taken to task for, you'll be the one who's guilty of it. Whatever wisdom comes out of a man's mouth, you'll be the one who uttered it, and whatever woman conceives, you'll be the one who snuck into her bedroom.

Now that it's all behind you, you're wiser than ever. So get up and dance.

Dance, because a woman you once loved betrayed you with me, and will betray both of us with others.

Because a house that was once yours now belongs to someone else.

Because paintings that you once made have passed into unexpected hands.

Because bridges that you glorified have shut you out, and a homeland that you loved with a passion has abandoned you.

Because silly things that you once despised have outlived you.

Because your brother Hassan will be close to you from now on.

Because his children whom you raised have fallen into the trench of hatred and won't be at your funeral.

Because Constantine, the city so dear to you, has averted her gaze the way the Greek gods turn away from the sight of a dead body.

Françoise got up, cleared the table, and started towards the kitchen with the plates. Turning up the volume of the Zorba music, I called her, saying, 'Please, Catherine, come sit next to me. Before long we're going to be having some severe air turbulence.'

'But I'm not Catherine,' she objected.

'Oh, that's right,' I rejoined lightheartedly, 'you didn't read that novel. If you had, you would have realised that I'm not Khaled, either.'

After coming back and sitting down beside me, she said, 'You're drunk, aren't you?'

'Is that what you think? Because I told you the truth? The truth, my dear, is taken from the raving of drunkards. Did you know that the Tuaregs choose their names by casting lots? And I became "Khaled" by coincidence.'

Undeterred by her skepticism, I went on, 'At a time when heads and pens have gone flying, we journalists haven't done well at finding pseudonyms to hide behind from our would-be murderers. We just choose whatever new name we happen across. I, for example, took the name of a character from a novel I liked.'

After a brief pause, I continued, 'If you want to know the truth, I'm not Khaled Ben Toubal. Zayyan is. But that's another story. Khaled Ben Toubal was his name in the novel I mentioned, and then it became my name in real life. In novels, too, we need to borrow names that don't belong to us. So, as we move back and forth between fiction and reality, we often don't know who we are any more. It's the game of masks in the carnival of life.'

'So what *is* your name?'

'What difference does it make what my name is as long as you know who I am from the things I say and do? Whenever a part of me affects you, it leaves its signature on you, so to speak.'

'Fine. But what's the name written on your birth certificate and your passport?'

'I don't want you to be like a detective who wants to investigate the identity of some passerby. Suppose we'd met at one of those seaside resorts where, for the sake of creating the illusion of happiness, visitors are required to give up their real names for the duration of their stay and be called by the names of oysters, Greek gods, or even just numbers. After all, it's a cruel punishment to have to carry your real name around like a ball and chain all your life!'

I envy people in Arab countries who live without names, like football players who go by numbers instead of names, members of parliament who go by the names of their districts, government officials who are known by their titles, singers who only perform as part of a band or a choir, and the dead who lie in mass graves where official visitors lay a single wreath for them all. They're in history's 'seaside resort', where they've all been reduced to anonymity. Governing is a process of reduction. There's a blessing in being 'nobody' that you realize only when a ruler comes along and nationalises all names, or when death comes and scatters you in all directions.

Zorba had begun trembling as he danced, and I thought about Borges when, at the end of his book *A History of Eternity*, he talks about how, when you die, you become nobody. I decided to put my arm on Zayyan's shoulder and begin dancing with him. Zorba's dance is more beautiful when it's performed by two men with the vigour of those who've lost all, opening their arms wide to embrace nothingness.

Come on, Zayyan. Everything's finished, so dance. When you dance, as when you die, you become the master of the world. Dance so that you can mock the grave.

Hadn't you wanted to write a book for her? Dance so that I can write it in your stead. Get yourself a pair of legs for your last dance, and come barefoot. When we dance, as when we die, we don't need shoes!

Chapter Eight

D EATH ESTABLISHES AN ORDER to human relationships.
In spite of the time we'd lived together, Françoise went
back to being a stranger. She drove me to the airport and bade
me farewell with a bonhomie that had never been love. Then she
drove away, leaving me – who'd come into Zayyan's life by mere
happenstance – to be his only family.

She offered to stay for the ceremony that would accompany
the body's placement on the aircraft, but on a sham religious
pretext I persuaded her not to. The fact was, I expected Hayat to
come with Nasser, and I didn't want anyone to ruin the aesthetic
of this tragic scene.

I finished checking my small bag after a long wait in lines of the
living. Jostling to and fro, they were laden with cargo of the most
peculiar sorts – their booty from life abroad – from blankets,
ironing boards and flower pots to cooking pots, prayer rugs and
miserable-looking bags of every shape and size. From here I
went to where there were no lines crowding me from all sides,
and where people themselves were the cargo, sealed and
numbered, in the underbelly of the plane.

I stood in the room where everything that was ready for shipping was deposited in preparation for being sent in one direction or another. On one side of the room lay stacks of huge boxes ready to be conveyed out to the aeroplanes. Airport employees with their blue uniforms and yellow caps rushed to drag the boxes onto trolleys, which periodically produced a loud racket and brought in ice-cold drafts of air.

Somebody directed me to the other side, where I went to wait for him.

Then he appeared.

Strangers came carrying him on their shoulders, a dream in a wooden casket. Crowned with a loser's pride, he approached in a funeral procession perfectly suited to his derisive wit. I nearly shouted at them, 'Don't go too fast! You might trip over his laugh!' Slow, deliberate man that he was, beware of rushing him. Self-possessed like one deep in meditation, listen to his mockery as he passes across his last painting. He traverses his fate from one shore to another the way he would traverse a bridge, borne by people who have no idea how often he had drawn this very pathway.

When an engineer designs a bridge, his sole concern is that it provide safe passage. As for the pleasantness or unpleasantness of the passage, it's determined by a Greater Engineer, who alone possesses the right to plan out the steps of Fate.

O God of bridges, O God of the final passage, do not wake him! Those who lived their lives as wayfarers are entitled to rest.

O Goddess of beds, a bedfarer he was, wherever he alighted. So grant him respite in his final resting place, constricted though it be.

And you, O God of doors, no safe grave awaits him. So do not let them unhinge the door to his slumber!

In his presence I discovered that I'd lost the ability to cry. All I could do in the face of grief was to give a mute moan, like the call of a whale in the darkness of the ocean.

In the face of death he was doing what he'd always done in the face of life: scoffing! And since I found no tears in my eyes properly suited to his mockery, I began sharing in his smiles.

Suddenly I glimpsed her with Nasser. She'd come, then. But was it really her? Clad in a long fur coat, the woman approached with measured steps, her head wrapped in a black muslin scarf. Even though it was bitterly cold, I didn't like her luxurious mourning garb.

As she came nearer, I thought about how her coat must have cost more than that painting had, and how, if she'd been willing to give it up, it would have been enough to make Khaled feel a little less cold.

All she lacked was a dark coat and a red rose and she would have become Nedjma. Didn't she have a simple coat in her closet that would have been appropriate to such a heartrending occasion?

I convinced myself that the woman wasn't Hayat. She must be Nedjma, that beautiful, fugitive stranger who'd gone fleeing from poems and fallen into the clutches of history. A woman like her would have had the face of every woman, and every name in the world. Nevertheless, today she'd taken off the black malaya she'd worn in mourning for Salah Bey, and had put on a fur coat that had been acquired for her by one of history's highway robbers.

After all, who's going to call a pirate's wife to account if she wears some of his booty?

She was walking with an unaccustomed slowness. Had her hennaed feet grown weary? Ever since her wedding day she'd been walking towards this lifeless body.

Nasser introduced me to his sister, though it would have made more sense for me to introduce her to him. The woman in the fur coat said nothing, perhaps as a way of concealing her hesitation and the awkwardness she felt when it came time to shake hands.

Not for Nasser's sake, but for Zayyan's, we avoided looking too long at each other, as we wouldn't have wanted him to witness, after death, what he had known to be true when he was alive.

In his presence we washed our hands of our romantic memories as though we underestimated the intelligence of the dead.

As Nasser held me in a long embrace, one of his tears clung to my cheek. He mumbled something bleak-sounding, and burst into tears. It seemed as though he'd grown old, as though he, too, was no longer himself, as though he'd become Taher Abd al-Mawla. In him I saw his father's features as they'd been immortalised in pictures of the revolution.

What peculiar fate had brought Nasser, who'd refused to attend her wedding when he was in Constantine, all the way from Germany to attend Khaled's funeral here in Paris? Was our gathering around his body a last wish he'd wanted to snatch from the scornful jaws of death?

It had been a death so rigorous in its precision, so unexpected in its timing, so astute in its choice of witnesses, that our meeting seemed to have taken place on command.

There's no misnumbering or mismanagement in this unjust world. Rather, there is what René Charles refers to in one of his poems as 'the chaos of precision'. It's the kind of monumental, turbulent death that you find in a Greek tragedy.

What a tragedy it is to leave behind something this traumatic! And what a comedy to witness it!

We were standing before the legend of an ordinary man with epic-sized dreams – a man by the name of Khaled Ben Toubal who, from the time we gathered around him, had reclaimed his original name and who with this name was returning to Constantine. His death had changed his name, and revealed ours.

I remember him asking me one day with a kind of shrewd cynicism, 'Khaled . . . are you still Khaled?'

Like him, I nearly asked the woman in the fur coat, 'Hayat . . . are you still Hayat?' And the reason was that since she entered this place, she had become 'Nedjma': Nedjma, the object of passionate love, the desired, the revered, the woundress, the causer of sorrow, the wronged wronger, the ravished, the savage, the loyal traitoress, the virgin after every rape, the daughter of the black and white eagle over whom everyone fights, and around whom alone they come together.

She is the wife that bears the name of your enemy, the daughter you didn't conceive, the mother who abandoned you. She is the woman whose love was born intermeshed with the homeland, synchronous with its tragedies. She is none other than Algeria.

The story of Nedjma is one of Algeria's most famous love stories, and in its legendary dimension it was born following the 8 May 1945 marches – the first ever to demand Algerian independence – for which Constantine and the surrounding cities paid with the deaths of more than 30,000 demonstrators.

Kateb Yacine, sixteen years old at the time, was led away to prison with thousands of others. While on his way to his first detention, he saw young men in handcuffs being dragged by trucks to unknown destinations, and others being shot to death on the road.

He was placed in a huge, overcrowded cell to which military officers would come periodically to collect men that no one would ever see again. When, some months later, Kateb Yacine left prison, he found no home to receive him. Thinking he'd been killed, his mother had lost her mind and been committed to a mental institution. The young man sought refuge in the house of his two maternal uncles, both of them teachers, only to find that they had been killed. He then went to the house of his grandfather, a judge, only to learn that he'd been assassinated. But the greatest shock of all was his discovery that in his absence, the paternal cousin he was in love with had been married off to someone else.

Nedjma, the girl whose love would never lose its grip on him, had been taken forcibly away, and he'd been doomed to a life-time of mad raving in which 'Nedjma' became all women. So whenever a woman in one of Kateb Yacine's plays dropped her veil, 'Nedjma' would appear.

On his last birthday, and following the death of his mother after thirty-six years of silent madness, he said, 'I was born on 8 May 1945. I was also murdered on that day alongside the people whose bodies lay dead in the streets, and alongside my mother, who ended up in an insane asylum. Then I was born anew with "Nedjma". She was my first love, my painfully impossible love. But I'm happy in my sadness over her. She's the one I write about, and, like one gone mad, I've never written about anyone else.'

He, the playwright, would never have expected the woman he had loved for fifty years, and whom he wouldn't have recognised in her old age, to attend the final scene of a real-life theatrical production that had begun when he first saw her half a century earlier.

He would never have believed that a playwright's final text could be improvised by Fate, and that Death would be the one to assign the roles of actors and spectators alike. There are no three sounds of a gong to announce the rise of the curtain, since Fate doesn't tell you when it's your turn to go on stage. Nor does it tell you which side of the stage you'll be on, or who will be in the audience that evening.

She was weeping diffidently now, seeking refuge from memory in her fur coat. But when she visited Zayyan in the hospital and gave him that book, had she known that she was handing him his fate, revealing it to him as one would a prophecy?

On its first page she had written, 'I loved this book, and I'm sure you will, too.' What was it in *Nedjma's Twins* that she'd wanted him to see if not the uncanny death of his friend Yacine? Had she, the novelist, not expected that, like Nedjma, she would find herself by happenstance attending the final scene of the death of a man who had loved her passionately and drawn her like a madman only to have her abandon him to old age and illness in a foreign land?

I couldn't get over the similarity between the two situations. Like Nedjma, Hayat couldn't have attended Khaled's funeral if her brother hadn't been with her, the difference being that Nasser was standing among the funeral goers, whereas Nedjma's brother lay shrouded next to her sweetheart in a transit lounge for the dead, just like this one!

In the strange, 'theatricised' death of Kateb Yacine and his cousin, Mustapha Kateb, there was something that surpassed theatrical imagination itself. What made it even stranger was that both brothers had been men of the theatre. Mustapha Kateb, whom I'd known personally, had been director of the National Theatre during the 1970s before illness destroyed him, while Kateb Yacine had headed the opposition theatre and staged his works at workers' gatherings in colloquial Arabic and Amazigh.

And whereas Yacine had been a wiry, testy fellow who'd come to know the inner geography of prisons and detention camps followed by mental institutions and pubs, Mustapha Kateb had been a god-fearing, sombre writer. He'd also been endowed with an aristocratic Constantinian handsomeness, his silver hair and quiet smile making him look all the more distinguished.

Given their differences in belief and temperament, the two men had lived cut off from each other nearly to the point of estrangement, each of them orbiting his own sun, until the day when death brought them together and placed them side by side in a lounge like this one at the Marseilles Airport before their final voyage to Algeria.

This time the actors weren't on stage; they were in coffins. And the one directing this final scene of the play was outside the theatre. After all, the theatrical space was too huge for any mere human to have been able to manage it. This time, too, there was no competition among the actors, since the only actor in Death's drama is Death itself. And since there was no place for applause, the actors wouldn't come out to greet the audience before their final withdrawal.

Isn't it fate that caused Kateb Yacine to die in Grenoble on 28 October 1989, and his cousin Mustapha Kateb to die just one day later in Marseilles? One newspaper even ran a headline that read, 'Kateb + Kateb = Maktub [decreed by fate].' Thus it was that Kateb Yacine's body was brought to Marseilles Airport to be placed on the same aeroplane with the body of Mustapha Kateb.

Benamar Médiène talks in his book about how, being Kateb Yacine's best friend and the person responsible for escorting his body home, he found himself witness to a bizarre series of events in the course of which the transit lounge for luggage and dead bodies in coffins at Marseilles Airport was transformed into a stage with no boundaries or curtains, a stage on which everything was real, and where everything evoked a Greek theatre.

Suddenly he saw a woman approaching with unhurried steps. Clad in a long dark coat, she held a long-stemmed rose in her black-gloved hand. Her eyes were hidden behind dark glasses, while her upturned coat collar concealed most of her features.

The woman came up to the two coffins and read the name written on each one. Stopping next to the one in which Mustapha lay, she bent down and kissed its edge. Without removing her gloves, she passed her hand quickly over Yacine's coffin as well. Then, after holding onto the rose for some time, she placed it on her brother's coffin and retreated.

She was 'Nedjma'!

Like the protagonists of novels and plays who step out of their texts and come to bid a writer farewell, 'Nedjma' had come. However, she hadn't come to bid farewell to the writer who had made her a legend and a symbol of the nation, the poet who had made her face into a thousand faces, her name into the name of every woman, and her story into a classic of world literature.

Rather, she'd come to say goodbye to her brother. She was Zuleikha Kateb who, now in her seventieth year, might well have forgotten after all those years that she was 'Nedjma'. After all, she too had gone by two names, one in real life, and the other in legend. Consequently, she hadn't expected life itself to remind her before Yacine's dead body that, despite her old age, she was still 'Nedjma'. But legends never grow old!

When life starts alternately imitating theatre and literature, it can become so outlandish that it makes you look like a liar. After all, who would believe you if you told them about a woman like a black tulip, sometimes referred to as Hayat, and other times as Nedjma? She's a woman who always shows up at the last moment, in the last scene, to stand in front of the coffin of a man who'd waited for her so long, his time had run out.

She's a woman who, like your homeland, doesn't bother to do anything but pass her gloved hand over your coffin or, at best, grace it with a rose. How many times do you have to die to be worthy of her warm embrace!

It made me think of Somali writer Nuruddin Farah who, justifying his reverse emigration from Europe to Africa, said, 'I'm in desperate need of warmth. That's what dead bodies need.' I nearly took that woman's coat off her so that I could use it to cover Khaled's coffin for its long journey back to the homeland's frosty chill. I nearly shouted at her, 'Don't be Nedjma! Keep him here with a kiss! Keep him here with more tears! Say you loved him! Scandalise yourself with him a bit. Is there anything more wonderful for a lover than the scandal of death?'

Place your hand on him: the hand that kills, the hand that writes. Pass it over the top of the coffin as though you were massaging his shoulder, the site of his orphanhood.

Don't worry that he might be scandalised somehow. He isn't afraid of anyone any more, nor is he in danger of anything. He's simply on display to satisfy the curiosity of others. His closed eyes keep the secret, and his rib cage, where he held you as his little bird, is forlorn and cold since you left it. So cover him up.

O woman filled with dread and hesitation, fling yourself onto the wooden box that holds him the way you used to fling your-self into his lap as a little girl, back in the days when he would play with you, draw you to him with a single arm and hold you close.

Here he is, prostrate before you. Who has been yours since him? Who, besides him, has ever been yours? Kiss his coffin. Kiss it. He's bound to know it. Don't believe anyone who tells you that wood isn't a good conductor of heat, since death doesn't recognise the laws of physics.

While the living aren't looking, fulfil those final wishes that we snatch off Death's corpse, and give him a kiss of the sort that brings the dead back to life.

I, who'd learned her geography like the back of my own hand, knew her volcanic regions, her mercurial regions, her igneous regions. I'd discovered her glacial region as well, and the topog-raphy of her studied sadness, a sadness calculated not to exceed its proper bounds.

As I saw her in that staid sorrow of hers, I knew for a certainty that things had reached their conclusion. And, having witnessed her icy composure, I realised that if I were to die, this was the way she would relate to my corpse as well!

269

After we'd finished reciting the Fatiha, the three of us moved to a far corner of the lounge. I took the opportunity to hand Hayat a bag containing some small notebooks in which Zayyan had recorded scattered thoughts over the years, as well as some other papers he'd kept in an envelope and which I assumed were his in view of their masterful poetic form of expression and the difference between her hand-writing and his.

The bag also contained her two books, without dedications, which he'd kept the way they were down the years apart from a few sentences he'd underlined. Nor had I forgotten, of course, *Nedjma's Twins*, which she'd given him a few days earlier during her last visit to him.

In this way I'd divided Khaled's bequest between two women, confident that one of the two would be quick to throw most of her share in the bin and keep nothing but his paintings for their monetary value, and that the other, having lost his paintings, would turn her loss into a book.

All I kept for myself was his watch, not realising that I would fall into its snare later on. How can you approach life from the point of death, as though the hands of time were turning against you, with every rotation hastening your annihilation? To justify to Nasser my having given that bag to his sister, I said, 'These are some papers and writings Zayyan left behind, and I thought they might be of some use to Madame Hayat if she decided to write something about him.'

'Don't worry,' Nasser replied wryly. 'The press will be sure to shroud him in newsprint!'

She didn't open the bag. She didn't even take a peek at its contents. She must not have expected to find herself in such a peculiar situation. However, she turned to me for the first time and asked me, 'With regard to the paintings, what have you all done with them?'

'I think most of them have been sold,' I said.

To which Nasser added, 'When Hayat called to tell me he'd died, the first thing I thought of was the painting you told Murad and me you'd persuaded him to sell to you. At first I'd thought you were crazy for spending everything you owned on a painting. But later I thought about how there are certain things that are irreplaceable, and that a person shouldn't think about how much they cost if he has the chance to acquire them.'

'What painting are you talking about?' she asked curiously.

Before I could say anything, Nasser replied, 'It's a painting Mr Zayyan made in his early days as an artist and that was really precious to him. It depicts the Sidi M'Cid Bridge.'

With an innocent-sounding politeness that placed a sham distance between us, she said to me, 'I wish I could see it. Might you leave me a phone number or an address I could write you at in case I need anything related to Zayyan's works?'

She knew my habit of disappearing suddenly from her life, and this was apparently the only way she could think of to ask for my address in her brother's presence.

Replying in a way that would give her to understand that I hadn't changed, I said, 'Sorry, I don't have a permanent address yet.'

Then, after a brief silence, I added, 'Besides, I sold the painting!'

'You sold it?!' the two of them cried in unison. 'Why??'

'Why?' It wasn't the right place to explain to them 'why' I'd sold it. Zayyan might have been listening in on us, and he already had one tragedy to deal with. Besides, one question was bound to lead to another. 'Why?' would become 'how?', 'for how much?' and 'to whom?'.

'For how much?' was nothing by comparison with 'to whom?'. Once they knew that, it would look as though I was a traitor who'd sold Algeria and the entire Arab nation to the West. It would be because of me that Granada had fallen and Jerusalem had been lost. After all, some grand plot must have been woven against the Arab nation and carried out by the gallery in cahoots with the hospital, especially in view of the fact that most of the doctors there were Jews. Indeed, was anything that had happened to us for centuries attributable to anything but a conspiracy?

They went on standing there in shock, waiting for an answer from me, but I didn't know what to say. Sometimes you have to write a book the size of this one to answer the single-word question: 'Why?'

And I couldn't help but wonder: Was she really in such shock over the loss of that painting that she'd lost her voice?

I think she was about to say something when a voice came over the loudspeaker inviting all passengers travelling to Constantine on Air Algérie Flight 701 to go to Gate 43. She seemed to take this summons as an excuse to prepare to leave, so there was nothing left to say.

I thought of something Malek Haddad once said to the effect that the voices that come over the loudspeakers in train stations, bus stations and airports address 'the gentlemen travelling' to such and such a location, since 'the ladies' never go anywhere. In his day, women were forbidden to travel, so they stayed cooped up at home. Today, by contrast, they don't accompany a loved one who's travelling in a coffin simply because they don't have the time.

Nasser pressed me to his breast, saying, 'May the Lord comfort you in your loss, and protect you. Believe me: If I were allowed into Algeria, I'd go with you. But you know how it is.'

Then he stopped in front of the body for a few moments and murmured what appeared to be a prayer. I saw him wiping tears away as he rested his right hand on the coffin.

Had Nasser's prayer awakened something inside her? Had the voice over the loudspeaker reminded her that I and the person shrouded for burial would be going away together, and that she had lost us both?

She extended her hand to me in farewell. Then, for the first time, I saw her burst into sobs in front of his lifeless body.

I feel contempt for people who, despite their misery, haven't got the guts to risk a breathtaking happiness, a happiness that carries a steep price. It's the kind of happiness that you have to seize when you can, since a great love is something you experience at that moment of extremity when you're about to lose it.

It's the moment of glory for the brilliant lovers who show up just when we've given up on them, who hijack a taxi to get to the airport in time to buy the last ticket on a certain flight and reserve a seat for coincidence next to someone they love.

I wanted a love that would arrive just minutes before takeoff and change my travel plans, or reserve itself a seat next to me on the plane. But, instead, she just left me with him and went on her way.

She didn't say a word. She just cried. Meanwhile, Khaled remained shrouded in the chill between us. I'd managed to get him the price of a ticket, but I hadn't managed to get him a coat.

As the voice over the loudspeaker repeated its call, it cemented the awareness that a farewell was in the offing, but no handkerchiefs are big enough for the big goodbyes.

I was the only one with him when they came to take him away. They picked him up and carried him to a place where he'd be a human being surrounded by luggage, while I boarded the aircraft where I'd be a piece of luggage surrounded by human beings. So, though we were both taking the same aeroplane, we parted ways there.

My last travelling companion was gone, and I trembled, not knowing how to close the door behind a man who had lived, as he had died, on a history-swept bridge.

Like salmon, those who've lived their lives in a foreign land look for a waterway that will take them back to where they came from, and they cross a bridge to get there. However, the bridge doesn't exist on account of the river, if there is one. Like citizenship, it was only created because of a hoax known as 'the homeland'.

So, friend, sleep like a painting. Your bridge isn't a bridge any more.

In every airport, leave-taking wins the day, and lovers' rosaries break and are scattered on the floor.

Airports call you with feverish persistence, repeatedly announcing the number of the flight that Fate itself has reserved for you at a travel agency that specialises in final journeys.

So, lonely traveller in the tightly sealed box – with no ticket in your pocket, and with all paths leading to where you're going – why do you need all these importunate calls to remind you of your destination, and all these lit-up signs to direct you towards your gate? O man of two shores, cross a bridge and you're there.

In just two and a half hours you'll be settled in your hole, a fate's throw away, and you'll have a grave as cramped as a homeland.

I sat in my seat knowing that beneath me lay the man who had been my twin, seeking refuge in his silence from the insults of the suitcases and trunks among which he'd been cast.

He wasn't the man he used to be, nor the painter he used to be. He was nothing but a box in the cargo hold of an aircraft. But it wasn't the box that set him apart from me. Rather, it was the fact that he'd be staying from now on in the underworld, whereas I was still alternately sitting down and pacing back and forth somewhere above him. I still enjoyed that self-important presence that comes with being alive.

I'd never been in such a strange situation. Here I was escorting a dead body I'd reserved a ticket for so that it could travel with me, or, rather, that I'd reserved myself a ticket for so that I could travel with it.

I recalled the book *Nedjma's Twins*, whose author relates how, by a strange coincidence, he found himself accompanying the bodies of Kateb Yacine and Mustapha Kateb from Marseilles to Algeria, and I found some solace in the thought that he might have suffered double my pain, having had to travel not with one dead body but two.

Then my thoughts led me to newspaper reports from the 1980s of cargo aeroplanes in a certain Arab country that had been converted by necessity into air hearses. For weeks on end the planes had shuttled back and forth, bringing home the remains of thousands of Egyptians who had gone to work in said country for individual reasons, and had come home maimed in wooden boxes that had been closed tight on their modest, and

275

now mutilated, dreams. One dark night, amid celebrations of the return of hero soldiers from their war against their neighbours, it had been officially announced that it was now open season on foreigners, who had been accused of violating women's honour while the country's menfolk were busy defending the honour of the Arab nation.

So this was Arab death, wholesale and retail: death in the singular, the dual and the plural, the death in the face of which you don't know whether it's more painful to travel aboard an aeroplane whose passengers don't know, as they pester the stewardesses with trivial requests, that beneath them lies a dead man, or to be the pilot of an Arab aircraft that has no stewardesses and offers no services, since all its passengers are deceased!

The situation reminds me of a friend of mine who hails from a certain Arab *mamlakah*, or kingdom. One day somebody asked him where he was from, to which he replied wryly, 'From the *mahlakah*' ("the place of peril").' Playing along with the pun, the other said, 'And I'm from *Umm al-Mahalik*' ("the mother of places of peril")!' And the two of them laughed at the joke. Each of them recognised which country the other was from, though they might not have agreed on which of them was the more imperilled!

You're in peril, son. Doomed. And in this airport you'll experience firsthand the extent of the damage the hit-men have done to your green passport.

Your youth is gone, and you're under suspicion wherever you go. Your features and your dark skin give you away as you stand in a line of pushing, jostling humanity surrounded by dogs trained to sniff out people like you.

Ever since some criminals hijacked a French aircraft and murdered some of the people on board, Algerians have been under security quarantine at airports as though they were afflicted with some sort of terrible disease, and you're forced to stand there defenceless before the mighty power of X-ray machines that reveal all, cameras that expose your secret motives, glances that pierce through to your feelings, and tactful insults worded in the form of questions.

So, do you *deserve* what's happened to you?!

From lobby to corridor to airway gang-plank, you're nothing but a number in queues of humiliation. So, now that you've gotten used to being abased, how are you going to demand more respect on board 'your aeroplane'?

You haven't been assigned a seat, so you have to race to get one. You have to push and jostle with the audacity of a VIP. A seat, any seat, is something to be fought for. People have been sent by the thousands to their graves for the sake of winning a seat in Parliament, and you want to get a seat on an aeroplane without having to suffer for it?!

You need a place to put your carry-on, but other people have occupied every space available. Everybody is loaded down with miserable bags stuffed to the gills with precious lifetimes, and they're more concerned about what they have in their hands than they are about themselves. They don't seem to realise that human beings are the only commodity that's quick to go bad.

I can't help but wonder where I would have put that painting if I'd brought it with me. Even if I'd spent half the trip convincing a stewardess of its importance, what more could she have done for me than others had been able to do in similar situations? I remember listening to an Algerian writer who appeared on national television and who related how, when she came back to visit Algeria, she'd had a small bag with her that she never let out of her sight, since it contained her writings and the manuscript of her most recent novel. The aeroplane was arriving from Syria filled with a motley crew of sidewalk merchants who didn't need visas to get into Syria, and they couldn't find any place to put her bag. However, when he learned from some of the other passengers who recognised her that it belonged to a noted author who hadn't been home to Algeria for seven years, one of the stewards volunteered to take care of it for her.

Halfway through the flight, someone came and informed her that her bag had been honoured with a spot in the aeroplane toilet! The steward explained that he personally would take it out when someone needed to go in, and put it back in its place again once the person had left. After all, he said, he'd been instructed to treat it well, and if it weren't for the high esteem in which he held this particular bag and his respect for literature, he wouldn't have put it there for safe keeping. Instead, he would have insisted that it be sent down to the cargo hold with the rest of the luggage, and had done with it!

What do you say to a homeland that insults you with the sincerest intention of honouring you?

A photograph I wish I could have taken was of that writer's bag lying on the floor of the aeroplane toilet while petty smugglers' goods were sitting high and dry in their owners' overhead luggage compartments.

If I took a photo like that, somebody would come along and say I was insulting my homeland in front of strangers and would give me a lesson in good citizenship. After all, the homeland alone reserves the right to insult you, the right to silence you, the right to kill you, and the right to love you in its own perverted ways.

How did this happen?

How did we reach this bizarre state of affairs?

Don't expect anyone here to answer you. You won't find the answer on the aeroplane but, rather, in the place where it first took off.

From now on, and as long as you live, you're going to wonder why you in particular won that prize. Why did you take that photo of that particular little boy and that particular dog? And why did you sell that painting to that particular person as opposed to someone else?

But these are questions that only others have the answers to. Who are you to change the course of history, or the course of a river in which you're nothing but a straw being swept inexorably downstream?

You don't even know what you're doing here, or how you ended up responsible for this corpse when you're already weighed down with responsibilities, weary of intentions guarded by hatchet men.

You wish you were Mohamed Boudiaf, flying joyfully back home to rescue Algeria without a suitcase to your name, your hands stretched forth to greet your well-wishers, gesticulating threateningly against the powerful, fearsome hired guns and thieves. Yet Boudiaf himself came back wearing his shroud, and no sooner had he opened a file than he'd opened his grave with it.

So fasten your seatbelt, man, and pay attention to the stewardess as she explains how to use the oxygen mask and life vest.

I myself chose the elderly lady who would sit next to me. As for the girl who sat down to my left, she'd chosen me. Maybe she thought I looked nicer than the other men there were to choose from.

It's important on a long flight like this not to find yourself stuck next to people who'll make you more worried and distressed than you already are. Otherwise, it's like being in a broken-down elevator with people you don't find the least agreeable.

Once we'd passed through inspection, I offered to help the old lady carry a huge bag she had with her. I couldn't imagine why anybody would have loaded her down with the thing, which she insisted on carrying herself even though she had to stop frequently to rest.

I love our old women. I can't resist the odour of their sweat-drenched cloaks. I can't resist their prayers and their blessings. I can't resist their motherly way of talking that, in just a few words, supplies you with enough tender loving care to last you a lifetime, and then some.

'May God give you long life, son. May the Lord protect you and relieve your worries. May the Lord give you happiness!'

Words like this, and before I knew it I was in a sentimental predicament with this elderly lady. I'd become her porter, her escort, and the one responsible for getting her to Constantine.

Is it my orphan complex? For as long as I can remember, old ladies have taken me hostage and led me off-course.

If I saw an older woman struggling under the weight of a basket she was carrying, before I knew it I'd find myself carrying her burden for her, claiming that she was going in my direction. One time it earned me a slap from my father, who didn't believe my excuse for getting home late from school.

The woman had been on her way to Rahbet Essouf to sell loaves of home-baked bread. I spent an hour walking alongside her, my book bag on one arm, and her basket on the other.

That was the only slap I ever received from my father.

The elderly woman seated next to me was travelling alone for the first time. She'd come to Paris to visit her daughter, who had given birth to her first child, and by the time the plane took off, I knew nearly everything about her life.

Old women have no secrets, and all they lack is a man bound securely to a chair with the patience to listen to the story of their failures and disappointments.

Terrified of the aeroplane, she wanted to understand all the stewardess's instructions on how to use the life vest, the oxygen mask, the seatbelt and the emergency exits. Recovering from her fright, she resigned herself to 'what's written', saying, 'Lifetimes are in God's hands.' Then she went on chattering about her son-in-law, who had bought a butcher's shop in France, and her son, who was trying to get residency in Paris after having come to hate life in Constantine which, having once been the poor man's refuge, was now the city of the poor. The needy had once come to Constantine after hearing about its people's wealth and generosity; now they lived there with thousands of other, equally needy folks who had come from all over and impoverished the city's residents.

'Where are you from, son? Those hungry hordes have gobbled up everything and driven us out of the country. It's such a pity that so-and-so's family and so-and-so's family are gone. All that's left are common folks. By the way, do you know whose daughter I am?'

I wasn't interested in knowing whose daughter this lady was or what line she was descended from. I hadn't come to ask for her hand. But there's nothing you can do to prevent an elderly lady from bragging about her origins, which is all she has left now that she feels she's lost her dignity.

Though illiterate, she was from a well-established family in Constantine. A man of great wealth and prestige, her paternal uncle had been famed for establishing the first tobacco company in Algeria. So I could understand her unwillingness to accept the idea of her daughter marrying a man who'd made his fortune abroad rather than inheriting it from his forebears, or of having to share the aeroplane with plebeians and poor people.

But, as she put it, 'That's the world for you, dear. What are you going to do about it?'

So awed were they by her, the ancients dubbed Constantine 'the blissful city'.

Hence, this old woman's illiteracy had spared her untold anguish. She would never read what had once been said about Constantine. Rather, all she could see was what the city had become in the end.

Behold Constantine the Proud, who doesn't know what to do with a rich past whose streets she tramps down with feet unshod.

Behold Constantine the Virtuous, guarded about by transgressions, ruled by an ever-deepening ennui and the ravings of feverish back streets that reek of long-suppressed cravings concealed beneath the garb of modesty.

She hadn't changed. Her beautiful, miserable women, her delectable, lascivious women, were still gripped by a chronic fear of her goodhearted, spiteful folks' gossip. And here she was seated on either side of me: to my right, a babbling old lady, and to my left, a taciturn girl. My fate, wherever I go, is to get caught in the jaws of her love.

When, some time later, the stewardess came down the aisle passing out newspapers, I heard the girl utter her first word as she requested *al-Watan* (The Nation) and *al-Hurriyah* (Freedom), which left me nothing but *al-Shaab* (The People) and *al-Mujahid* (The Freedom Fighter). So we'd ended up with equal shares of mendacious headlines.

In situations like this I always think of a wry comment Bernard Shaw once made about the Statue of Liberty. He noted that people erect their biggest statues to the things they lack most – which explains why the largest Arab victory arch is located in the country that's suffered the biggest losses and the worst destruction.

So intent are we on magnifying losses that we claim to have been gains, we add what we lack to the names of our countries. Since Algeria came into existence as a 'people's democratic republic', we suppose that we solved the people's problems and the issue of democracy from the day we won our independence, and with regard to freedoms, we proved our superiority from the very start over any European state with a mere one-word name!

We're a nation which celebrates its losses and which, since the days of Andalusia, has passed down the art of whitewashing defeats and crimes by establishing an elegant linguistic coexistence with them. When we assassinate a president, we name an airport after him. When we lose a city, we give its name to a street. When we lose a homeland, we name a hotel after it. And when we stifle the people's voice and steal their power from under their noses, we give their name to a newspaper.

We busied ourselves with browsing newspapers, and didn't exchange a word. The passenger to my left was a mysterious woman, like a house whose windows open towards the inside. I enjoyed sitting next to her unsettling femininity, which stirred up the accumulated residue of emotion inside me.

Then a crazy thought flashed through my mind: What if love were sitting to my left? I'd never been able to resist the allure of a quiet woman, or the beauty of a femininity that surrounds itself with mystery.

When they brought dinner, the old lady exhibited an enthusiasm that suddenly dissipated her fear of death and halted the stream of questions she'd been asking me about the wing of the aeroplane, which she thought she'd seen wobbling when she looked at it out of the window. She even made good use of my loss of appetite by asking me if she could have some of what was on my tray.

Meanwhile, the Constantinian girl to my left was picking at her food as though she were embarrassed to eat with gusto. It made me think of the days when women would go somewhere out of sight to eat as if it weren't proper for them to exhibit any sort of physical craving or pleasure in public.

After dinner the cabin lights were dimmed, and the stewardess began passing out blankets to the elderly and young children. I requested a blanket for the old lady in the hope that sleep might numb her 'chatterbox nerve' and make her stop predicting a disaster every time we hit a bit of air turbulence.

Poor lady – she thought an aeroplane in flight was the most dangerous place a person could be. Little did she know that Death might pull some other prank on you. It might be waiting for you at the bottom of the aeroplane stairs the way it had been for Abdelaziz, a pharmacist who'd been known in the capital for his love of life and for the many services he'd performed for people. The pilot, who'd been an acquaintance of his, had moved him into first class and instructed the stewardesses to ply him with booze. Accordingly, they'd poured him one glass of whiskey after another until, by the end of the two-hour flight from Paris to Algiers, he couldn't stand upright. No sooner had he set foot off the plane than he went rolling to the bottom of the narrow metal staircase, and he died two days later of a brain haemorrhage. Since he'd been flying first class and was the first person to go down the stairs, there hadn't been anybody ahead of him to prevent him from rolling to his death!

Do you suppose the pilot realised that, by upgrading him from economy class to first class, he was pampering him so thoroughly that he'd raised him to the rank of first-class 'martyr'?

On aeroplanes, as in life, you have to respect the law of ranks. You mustn't try to skip a rank on your way up the ladder, since this would-be gain might be your ruin. You have to know from the start whether you belong in first class or second class, and that any skullduggery might land you down in the hold!

You also have to make sure you know where your seat is: to the right of love, or to its left. Tragedy always follows when Fate starts amusing itself scrambling the seat numbers.

I was constantly aware of the girl sitting next to me, of her faint-smelling perfume, and of those unspoken desires that are born in the dark. All it takes is a bit of dim light for the senses to awaken, and for women to become more beautiful than they are.

A little darkness awakens pleasant illusions. As for pitch darkness, it makes us equal to the inhabitants of the underworld.

I couldn't go to sleep. A high-heeled smile greeted me politely from above her womanly aura. And below me – ah, below me – there lay something that kept me from smiling as I sat in that dreadful space where life and death intersect.

Suddenly a stewardess turned the lights back on and began passing out landing cards, while another went up and down the aisles collecting passengers' blankets. I noticed that the elderly lady didn't surrender her blanket to the stewardess. I glimpsed her folding it up and hiding it inside her bag. Her fear of death hadn't stopped her from robbing one of life's trifles.

She was like people who survive an air disaster or a house fire. Despite their brush with death, no sooner do they resume their lives than they go looking for their earthly belongings and bemoan the damage that's been done to them.

She wasn't taking the blanket because she needed it, but just to 'rip off' the airline company. After all, the people who rob the homeland by the millions 'from on top' have given simple folks the right to steal or destroy the little things in retaliation against their would-be protectors.

What use could she possibly have had with that little blanket? The one lying below, in the coldest part of the aeroplane, needed it more than she did.

Would she have lost her appetite if I'd informed her of his presence? Would she have devoted herself to prayers and supplications and stopped stealing blankets if she'd known that nothing separated her from death, and that at any moment she might go to reside 'down there' herself?

Those who sit 'upstairs' generally refuse to think about the fact that wherever they go, there's a 'downstairs' waiting for them.

The old lady asked me, 'When will we get to Constantine, son?'

'We've got twenty minutes to go, mother,' I replied.

I filled out both my landing card and hers. As for him, he had no landing card, perhaps because he enjoyed the luxury of travelling on a ticket that cost several times more than that of any passenger sitting above him.

This has got to be some kind of joke, I thought. He's worth ten times more dead than he was alive. So why is he so cold and sad?

Hadn't he waited his entire life for a rainy day like this when he would come home to Constantine borne on the clouds?

And now he'd arrived at last.

Mama Constantine, I've brought him home to you! Your little boy who's come back from his frigid place of exile trembling like a sparrow – take him into your arms! He spent a lifetime trying to reach your bosom. This aggrieved son of yours belonged to you so completely, he wasn't himself any more. He was Khaled for so long, he stopped being Zayyan. Then he became so completely Zayyan, the only place he could find rest was in his brother's grave.

We're sons of the rock – al-sakhrah. But we don't know any more which of us is Sakhr, and Khansa' isn't with us any more to guide us to our grave with her tears. Everyone on this aeroplane is a 'Sakhr'. But that's all right, Mama. We'll go on enlarging the cemeteries.

Then all of a sudden the girl who had buttressed herself about with silence asked me, 'May I borrow your pen?'

'Certainly,' I replied as I handed a pen to her.

In her voice there were clouds and gentle rain, sadness and a music that seemed to pour from the sky, but I opened my umbrella of silence.

I'd fortified myself against the unexpected winds of desire, and I intended to avoid a meandering road that might lead me to a woman sitting in an adjacent seat. In Constantine with its many twists and turns, there's no such thing as a straight path to your goal. The road is always a zigzag one!

After filling out her form, she gave the pen back to me with a simple, 'Thank you,' and retreated into her silence.

Typically solicitous, our elderly neighbour said to her, 'Since it's dark out, dear, I hope somebody's coming to meet you. If not, you can come along with my son and me, and we'll get you where you need to go. The situation isn't good these days.'

'That's kind of you,' she replied gratefully. 'My brother's coming to meet me,' from which I concluded that she was single and lived with her family.

At that moment a stewardess came by with the duty-free trolley. I asked for a carton of cigarettes, which I was about to pay for when I heard the girl ask her if she had a certain perfume. I sat there, astonished. I felt as though life was trying to get a rise out of me, still trying to play tricks on me.

There was something about it that went beyond the beauty of a coincidental correspondence in choice of perfume to the horror of his coffin's coincidental presence beneath us, especially given the fact that he used to keep an empty bottle of this very perfume hidden among his things.

The question was no longer: where had he gotten that bottle? Which woman had used it? Or, how long had he been keeping it the way an orphan holds onto something whose value he alone knows? Instead there had emerged another question that sent a chill through my body: what if he was the one who had requested that perfume because on this particular day, he needed it more than any of the rest of us?

On the other hand, in the underworld where he was now, he'd been freed by death not only from life but from the ordeal of orphanhood and alienation. So what need would he have now for a perfume to pour into his empty bottle?

Now, at last, he'd become the least orphaned one of us all. He had no more need to be afraid that the sweet fragrance of his joy would run out. He had a fragrance that time could do nothing to diminish – the fragrance of eternity.

Or was it that, isolated now in a corpse, he needed this perfume to restrain an odour that would whet the appetite of maggots and reveal the unsightliness of a man who'd always been keen to preserve the beauty of presence?

Of course, perfume in a bottle is nothing but a fragrance in the making. It only becomes a fragrance in completion when it blends with the chemistry of the body. Consequently, no perfume could have covered up that odour.

Odour is just the apology of a perfume that was so late in arriving that death stepped in to take its place.

When the stewardess came back to collect the girl's money in payment for the perfume, it occurred to me to offer it to her as a gift. The gift would have been in honour of the way the perfume's fragrance mocks the stench of orphanhood.

But then I decided against it for fear that she might think I was making a pass at her, the way miserable men tend to do when they find a woman strapped into an adjoining seat.

Could it be that, on the pretext of perfuming his lifeless body, I was simply trying to lay a hand on her silence?

I was content with the little she'd said, and savoured the delicious awkwardness that had come over me in the face of something resembling love. Taking silence to its limit, I was preparing a hole between us in the depths of ambiguity where I could plant a seedling of raging desire, while my thoughts began weaving the beginnings of stories that might be written about this woman and me.

Beyond the horror of endings, I'd been afflicted with the terror of beginnings, the fear of emotional involvement, its vertigo, its allure. Even if I could find an umbrella to shield me from the drizzle of desire, where would I get a face mask to keep out seduction's pungent perfume?

I caught a fleeting whiff of his odour that, for a moment, blocked my desire for her. However, it couldn't destroy her perfume's power over me.

Love was advancing towards me like wild steeds. However, it was preceded by the dust of the past, because in this woman there was something of the other. I couldn't put my finger on what it was exactly, but I could smell it.

I remembered how, when I saw her for the first time in that café one thirtieth of October at one fifteen in the afternoon, I'd felt the thunderbolt of a passionate, head-on collision between two planets that, so taken were they by each other, were bound to splinter into a million pieces. Fearful of being swept off my feet by something so beautifully destructive, I'd asked her permission to sit down, saying, 'Madame, I thank Planet Earth's circulatory system for not letting us meet before today.'

In the galaxy of love, who is it that directs the course of the planets? Who distances them from one another? Who brings them closer? Who programmes their encounters and their collisions? Who extinguishes one and lights up another in the firmament of our lives?

Does a person have to stumble over a dead body in order to fall in love? In our search for a new love, we always stumble over the dead body of someone we loved before, over the corpses of those we put to death, as though we needed their cadavers as a bridge. In all our emotional stumblings, we fall in the same place, on the same rock, and when we get up, we're covered with scratches that reopen the wounds we suffered from the collision brought about by our first love. So don't waste your time giving lovers advice. There are certain mistakes love is bound to repeat eternally!

Was it possible that I hadn't gotten over her? It was as though she'd seeped into the pores of my memory, of my destiny, and I smelled her perfume wherever I went.

She wasn't Hayat – a woman whose name means 'life'. She was life itself.

How often I'd dreamed of aeroplanes that would take me to her, of new cities we would visit together, of hotel rooms whose doors would close behind us, of morning baths followed by the caresses of her lips in lieu of a towel, of talking far into the night about love, about death, about God, about the military, about dreams betrayed, about double-dealing homelands.

I'd dreamed of seeing her number appear on my telephone screen and having her voice drink my coffee with me, escort me to my office, cross streets with me, board aeroplanes with me and hold me tight like a seatbelt, hover about me with motherly concern, reassure me, check up on me – in short, I'd dreamed of having her voice there to take me by the hand.

But whatever pleasures I enjoyed with this woman had always been under threat. There were always corpses between us, one of which was travelling with me, eavesdropping on me, and guffawing at me from its deathly hiding place.

With a love like this, you don't stumble across a dead body. You stumble across a cemetery.

I was busy reminiscing about her when suddenly I heard the voice of the stewardess saying, 'Passengers are requested to place their seats in an upright position, fasten their seatbelts, and extinguish all cigarettes.'

The old lady to my right began demanding my attention, so I helped her fasten her seatbelt and closed the small blind on the window near us so that, if she had a mind to look out, she wouldn't see Constantine from such a height and panic even more.

'Don't look down, mother,' I told her.

I wanted her to give me a bit of freedom. I wanted to be able to look to my left so that I could forget the underworld. I wanted to steal the final moments of this breathtakingly bizarre rendez-vous to say something to a perfume that had arrived late, and that frightened me as much as the moment of a plane's descent.

The aeroplane touched down at breakneck speed, the way aeroplanes always do. As it hurtled with us down the runway, the high-pitched whizzing of its engines grew so loud that no one could carry on a conversation any more.

My thoughts went to where he was, to his coffin as it jolted at the moment it collided with Constantine's soil.

Here he and I would part. Here the travel fête would end, and all I could do was entrust him to the city. It was night, and not the right time to fling oneself into her arms. Constantine turns in early, and nobody would dare rouse the keeper of the dead, who had donned the nightshirt of heedlessness for fear of the dreaded henchmen.

You have to understand that from now on you'll be under the protection of the maggots, which, while you were away, nested and multiplied both underground and aboveground. Human maggots amassed their fortunes from the tables that were spread thanks to your abstinence from their sumptuous feasts. And now that you've died, they'll incite others against you so that they can gorge themselves on the remains of a body they'd fed in part to the revolution.

We take pride in the maggots' exploits, and in recognition of their insatiable appetite for more martyrs, we offer them our bodies as tokens of our loyalty.

Between your revolution and their fortune, my friend, your lifeblood was poured out. Like your body, it's been dedicated to the homeland's maggots, whose death-dealing breeders prepare the best soil for them the way other countries cultivate pearls and coral in their own special aquariums.

He was resigned to his final slumber. As for me, I was too exhausted to dream any more, and I wondered which of us was the most afraid.

O Madame Constantine, who wakes up only to schedule our deaths – refrain, please, from doing harm to his dream! Pretend to care about him. Wrap him in a bogus embrace and go back to sleep. Don't scrutinise his papers too closely, and don't ask him his name. Wherever he's gone his surname has been al-Qisantani – the Constantinian. So now that he's come to settle here, give his name to a boulder or a tree at the foot of a bridge, since the streets and alleyways have been reserved for martyrs of the past and losses of the future.

The whirring of the aircraft drowned out the clamorous silence I'd shared with him since the journey's start.

What could I do against a fate that had reserved me a seat above a stench and next to a perfume that were travelling on the same aeroplane?

I heard the old lady, who was holding onto my arm for dear life, uttering terrified prayers and supplications.

Meanwhile, a stewardess's voice announced, 'The outside temperature is six degrees Celsius, and the local time is eleven thirty pm. Please keep your seatbelts fastened. The aircraft has landed at Mohamed Boudiaf Airport, Constantine.'

Glossary

17 October 1961: The Paris massacre of 1961 took place during the Algerian War (1954–1962). Under orders from police chief Maurice Papon, the French police attacked a forbidden, but peaceful, demonstration of some 30,000 pro-FLN (Front de Libération Nationale) Algerians. In 1998, after thirty-seven years of denial, the French government at last acknowledged forty deaths, though some estimates place the death toll at over 200.

Bearer of lies: The Arabic phrase, *hammalat al-kidhb* 'bearer of lies' is a play on the Koranic phrase *hammalat al-hatab*, 'bearer of firewood' in Surah 111:4.

Ben Bella, Ahmed: Ahmed Ben Bella (1916–2012) was a socialist soldier and revolutionary who served between 1963 and 1965 as Algeria's first president.

Bey, Salah: Salah Bey (1725–1792) was Bey of the Ottoman Province of Constantine between 1771 and 1792, and one of the province's most famous governors. Salah Bey worked to build up the city of Constantine through the construction of schools and mosques, restored El Kantara Bridge built by the Romans, and developed trade, industry and agriculture in the region. His death was mourned in Constantine long after his passing.

Boumédiène, Houari: Houari Boumédiène (1932–1978) served as chairman of Algeria's Revolutionary Council between 1965 and 1976, and as Algeria's second president from 1976 until his death on 27 December 1978. After a bloodless coup in 1965 in which Ben Bella was deposed, Boumédiène was the country's de facto ruler until, after being treated unsuccessfully in Moscow, he died of a rare blood disease.

Bouzellouf: An Algerian delicacy consisting of sheep's head and feet cooked in a sauce seasoned with garlic, salt, black pepper, red pepper and cumin.

Cheikh Raymond: Raymond Leyris (1912–1961) was a renowned Algerian Jewish lutist and vocalist who specialised in the Andalusian music of Eastern Algeria. Widely admired by both Jews and Muslims, he was later dubbed 'Cheikh' (elder) as a term of respect.

Dishdasha: A long, flowing, sleeved robe.

Donqol, Amal: Amal Donqol (1940–1983) was an Egyptian poet known best for his political poem, 'Don't Reconcile' (*la tusālih*).

Duras, Marguerite: Born Marguerite Donnadieu in present-day Saigon, Vietnam, Duras (1914–1996) was a prolific French writer and film director.

Eid: A word referring to either of two major Muslim holidays: Eid al-Adha, the Feast of Sacrifice, commemorating Abraham's willingness to sacrifice his eldest son in God's honour and God's provision of a ram in his stead, and Eid al-Fitr, the Feast of Fast-breaking, which marks the end of Ramadan, the Muslim month of fasting. It is the custom in Muslim countries to buy new clothes for one's children before each of these two holidays.

'Even the wise die…': Psalms 49:1, Revised Standard Version.

The Fatiha: The opening chapter of the Koran, typically recited in reverence when visiting someone's grave.

Fergani, Mohamed Taher: Mohamed Taher Fergani (1928–) is an Algerian singer, violinist and composer. Nicknamed 'the Nightingale of Constantine', Fergani is known in particular for his interpretations of Andalusian classical music.

'From the lofty, breathtaking mountains': A phrase from the Algerian national anthem.

Gainsbourg, Serge: An important figure in French popular music, Gainsbourg (1928–1991, born Lucien Ginsburg) was renowned for his sometimes provocative, satirical, subversive and scandalous lyrics. His artistic output was exceptionally diverse, including a wide variety of genres.

Haddad, Malek: Malek Haddad (1927–1978) was an Algerian poet and novelist, born in Constantine, who wrote in French.

Hijab: The term *hijab*, meaning 'veil' or 'protective partition', refers traditionally to Islamic attire for a woman, which is understood to mean attire that covers everything but a woman's face and hands. As used in this context, it refers specifically to the stylish headscarves worn by present-day Algerian women in lieu of the more traditional *malaya* (see entry below on *malaya*).

Imam Ali: Ali Ibn Abi Talib, the Prophet Muhammad's cousin and the husband of his daughter Fatimah.

Kamanja: A traditional oriental instrument having one or two strings.

Khansa': Born Tumadhir bint 'Amr ibn al-Harth in 575 CE to a wealthy family in Najd, Arabia, Khansa' came to be widely acclaimed for her poetry, particularly her elegies to her slain brothers, Mu'awiyah and Sakhr.

Malaya: A flowing outer garment, sometimes including a face veil, worn by women in Algeria. It is associated with modesty and with adherence to societal and religious tradition.

'Many an abandonment...': A line of poetry attributed to Sayf al-Dawla al-Hamdani (d. 967 CE).

Miller, Henry: Henry Miller (1891–1980) was an American writer known for developing his own literary style comprised of a mix of autobiography, social criticism, philosophical reflection, sex, surrealist free association and mysticism. He lived in Paris between 1930 and 1939, during which time he wrote his first published novel, *Tropic of Cancer* (1934), which was banned in the USA on grounds of obscenity.

Morice Line: Named after the French Minister of Defence, André Morice, the Morice Line was a defensive line, completed in 1957, whose purpose was to prevent Algerian FLN (*Front de Libération Nationale*, National Liberation Front) guerrillas from entering the French colony of Algeria from Tunisia and Morocco. Along the centre of the line ran a two-and-a-half-metre-high electric fence that carried 5,000 volts and which had barbed wire entanglement on one side. It was flanked on either side by forty-five-metre-wide minefields. The Morice Line was 460 km long along the border with Tunisia and 700 km long along the border with Morocco.

Mu'awiyah Ibn Abi Sufyan: The first Umayyad caliph (602–680).

Nedjma: The title of a novel by Kateb Yacine published in 1956 whose four main characters' life stories are connected by a shared attraction to an Algerian-French woman by the name of Nedjma.

November Revolution: On 1 November 1954, guerrillas from the anti-colonialist National Liberation Front (FLN) began what has come to be known as the Algerian War of Independence, or Algerian Revolution, by launching attacks on military and civilian targets throughout Algeria.

Despite a military victory by French forces, the war ended in 1962 with Algerian independence from France.

Pied-noir: Meaning 'black foot', the term pied-noir refers to a French or other European citizen who lived in French Algeria, and who returned to Europe with the end of French rule in Algeria between 1956 and 1962.

Qalb al-Lawz: A semolina-based sweet, decorated with almonds and served with a sugar syrup.

Qotbi, Mehdi: Born in 1951 in Rabat, Morocco, Mehdi Qotbi studied art in both Morocco and France. A resident of France, many of his works feature Oriental calligraphy and symbolism. In 1991, Qotbi founded the Franco-Moroccan Circle of Friendship, of which he is president.

Sisyphus: In Greek mythology, Sisyphus was a king of Ephyra (now known as Corinth). He was punished for chronic deceitfulness by being forced to roll a huge boulder up a hill, only to see it roll back down again, and to repeat this process eternally.

Tamar, Simone: Simone Tamar (1932–1982) was a well-known Constantinian singer, known as 'the golden voice of Constantine', who specialised in Andalusian music.

'Umar Ibn Abi Rabi'a: An Arab poet from the aristocracy of Mecca, 'Umar Ibn Abi Rabi'ah (644–719) was known especially for his love poetry (ghazal).

Yacine, Kateb: Kateb Yacine (1929–1989) was an Algerian writer known for his novels and plays, some in French and some in the Algerian Arabic dialect, and for his advocacy of the Berber cause.

Zalabia: A sweet made by deep-frying a wheat batter in ball shapes, then dipping them in a sugar syrup.

Zindali: What is termed Zindali music is associated with prison life. Despite their lively, sweet tunes, Zindali songs have been looked down upon for their use of coarse language and their frank references to things such as alcohol and sex. They also describe prisoners' suffering and their longing for freedom. The term 'zindali' is derived from Zindalah, the name of a prison once located in the capital city of Tunisia. The name Zindalah, which reflects Ottoman influence, is derived from the Turkish word *zindan*, meaning prison.

A NOTE ON THE AUTHOR

Algerian novelist and poet Ahlem Mosteghanemi is the bestselling female author in the Arab world. She has more than eight million followers on Facebook and was ranked among the top ten most influential women in the Middle East by Forbes in 2006. The previous books in her trilogy of bestselling novels, *The Bridges of Constantine* and *Chaos of the Senses*, were published by Bloomsbury, and have been translated into several languages.

A NOTE ON THE TRANSLATOR

Nancy Roberts is a prize-winning translator with experience in the areas of modern Arabic literature, current events, Christian–Muslim relations and Islamic thought, history and law.